MOONSHINE
OVER GEORGIA

MOONSHINE OVER GEORGIA

A NOVEL BASED ON ACTUAL EVENTS

CHRIS SKATES

Moonshine Over Georgia
By Chris Skates

Copyright © 2023 by Chris Skates

All rights reserved. No part of this publication may be reproduced or transmitted in any form or by any means electronic or mechanical, including photocopy, recording or any information storage and retrieval system now known or to be invented, without the prior written permission of the author. Exceptions are made for brief excerpts used in published reviews.

ISBN 9798388496430
Independently Published

Cover art by Dylan Nichols

For all the heroes who remained true to the call…

What a chimera then is man! What a novelty, what a monster, what a chaos, what a contradiction, what a prodigy! Judge of all things, feeble earthworm, repository of truth, a sink of uncertainty and error, the glory and shame of the universe.
—Blaise Pascal

AUTHOR'S NOTE

From 1936 to 1952 my grandpa ("Pop") was a state revenue officer in Georgia. Growing up in the '70s, I always spent at least a month with my beloved Pop and Grandma during the summers. Those months were the happiest times of my life. Our daily routine included working in the fields in the morning and then coming inside for a homemade lunch. After our meal, the three of us sat down to watch *The Andy Griffith Show*.

One day during that show, a character came onto the screen named Rafe Hollister, the Mayberry area moonshiner. Suddenly, Pop became agitated. He reached up and abruptly snapped off the television. I looked at him and noticed that his chin had begun to quiver and tears were welling in his eyes. I asked him what was wrong.

"It wasn't like that, son. It wasn't nothing to laugh about," he said gravely. "You've never heard a little child cry, I mean really wail, like I have. I've drug so many men out of some woods somewhere, covered in their own vomit, and carried them home to a shanty. They'd be sick—drunk off liquor that was made out of mash that the day before had been crawling with maggots. I knew what I was going to see at their place before I got them there. Lots of times their children would be out in the yard even though it was late at night, half-dressed most of the time. Folks was poor back then. And here this child's daddy had just spent what little money they had for groceries, on moonshine. The babies likely hadn't eaten that day, and maybe not the day before. And those little children would hold onto my leg and wail. You never get that sound out of your head. And I couldn't stop it all. I couldn't help them all …"

I had never seen Pop cry, but he began to sob loudly. He and Grandma had been married fifty-two years at that time. They bickered constantly, yet that day Grandma came over and quickly pulled up an ottoman as she took Pop's hands in her own. They sat like that for a long time. Nothing more was said. I knew in that moment that I would someday tell Pop's story.

A few days later, Pop began to share things with me that he had never shared before. On many occasions, he took me deep into the Georgia woods and showed me place after place where he had "busted" liquor stills. His eyes would twinkle when he talked of the tracking, the stakeouts, and the footraces as he chased moonshiners through the night woods. I invariably would ask if he ever fought anybody or shot a bad guy. Then Pop's face would grow dark and pensive. He'd say something like, "Buddy, all that's been a long, long time ago," and change the subject.

It was two years later when the narrative nonfiction book entitled *Murder in Coweta County* was released. It purported to tell the story of the infamous Georgia moonshiner, John Wallace, and the murder he committed. That was an investigation in which I knew my Pop had been intimately involved. The book would later be made into a made for TV movie, ironically staring Andy Griffith as Wallace. Again, this version of the story upset my grandpa greatly. Someone gave him a copy of the book, and during the first week of my thirteenth summer, I began to devour it. Pop stopped me from reading one day and took me to a back room. He removed a strongbox from a closet shelf (the same strongbox that I now have on my writing desk) and had me sit down. He opened the box, which was filled with newspaper clippings and papers that looked official, and took out a worn piece of stationary. There was a handwritten note that read as follows:

> *Agent Miller,*
> *It is quite urgent that I speak with you. Meet me at my barn tomorrow night at midnight. Come alone. Do not come early.*
> *Sincerely,*
> *John Wallace*

He went on to tell me how inaccurate the book and movie had been. He told me how the author, Margaret Barnes, had set up an interview with him that she didn't show up for. Sometime in 1995, the year before he passed away, Pop burned much of what the box contained. I have never understood why. However, some papers remain, including a commendation from the Georgia governor in 1946, commending Pop for "rounding up and assisting in the conviction of the Upson County Liquor Gang."

Moonshine Over Georgia is the story of a man and his wife who faced attempts on their life and yet never wavered. During my research in 2013, I had a telephone conversation with an elderly moonshiner (then 93) that Pop arrested in 1948. As I was about to hang up, the man made one last comment. It still rings in my ears. "Son, you need to understand somethin' about your grandpa. He shut down the liquor business in Western Georgia."

Though what you are about to read is a work of fiction, I have included all that Pop taught me, revisited some of the actual still sites in the night woods, and combined archival research and living witness interviews to prepare for the writing. Pop was a man of extreme courage in the face of overwhelming danger and, yes, even evil. Though a man of the Deep South, he had amazingly progressive ideas about race relations, which additionally made him a target of much anger. He made $2,400 a year and encountered moonshiners that could clear that amount in a week. Yet, he rebuffed all bribery attempts.

This is his story.

PROLOGUE

May 5, 1946
Meriwether County, Georgia

Bean Pole Johnson didn't know if he could survive much more of this. Being the target of the Godfrey brothers' wrath, he didn't even know if he would live to see sunset.

The men were gathered in an upstairs room built over Gibbs Junction Country Store. A whirring electric fan in the window pulled the steamy Georgia air into the room, mixing it with stale cigar smoke, spilt moonshine, tobacco juice from an overturned brass spittoon, and the smell of mortal fear emanating from Bean Pole.

"Open his mouth again," Harold Godfrey, the younger of the two brothers, commanded. Daniel Godfrey, the eldest, held Bean Pole's nose pinched tight enough to make it bleed and used the elk antler handle of his Bowie knife to pry Beanie's jaws apart.

Beanie was lying on his back across a poker table, his neck bowed back over the table's edge. His lips and tongue were starting to bleed from the earlier punches and the many times the knife handle had been used. His brain was in an alcohol-induced fog. He'd been drunk before.

Why hell, he'd been drunk nearly every Friday and Saturday night for twenty years. But he'd never swallowed anywhere near this much moonshine. Never been drunk like this.

From within the fog he saw Harold raise the jug again. He braced for the burning white lightnin' that would go up his nose, down his throat, and wash over his face and neck. For a moment he became coherent enough to wonder if this next shot of whiskey would kill him.

Harold began to pour into Beanie's gaping mouth.

"You better swallow it all boy! You want another beatin' like we give you a minute ago?"

Beanie gagged and choked as he tried to swallow. His will to survive was enough that he managed a garbled prayer. He had never prayed before, but now he tried to cry out to the Almighty, promising to never drink another drop of whiskey if God would somehow get him out of this.

"What'd he say?" Harold asked Daniel. "You ain't makin' no sense, Beanie!" Harold kicked the leg of the table. "What a mess. Look at what you done. Look at that good liquor runnin' across my floor."

Beanie began to sob.

Daniel flipped Beanie onto his stomach, not caring that Beanie's nose and mouth banged against the smooth wood of the table, spilling more moonshine across the green felt where it pooled around the leftover poker chips.

"You know what that is, Beanie? That's wasted moonshine," Harold said. "That's what we, in the business world, call a non-return on investment. I don't make no money when moonshine just sits on the floor like that." Harold began to shout now, right into Beanie's ear.

"That's what all them jugs is doin' down there in that storeroom. They's bein' wasted. I got good money that I worked hard for tied up in that liquor and now I ain't getting no return, and you know whose fault that is?"

Beanie blubbered.

"That's right, it's your fault," Daniel added. "Cause you wasn't here when you was supposed to be. You was half drunk off my liquor that you didn't pay for in the first place, and you fell asleep. So since you want to get drunk, we're gonna make sure you're good and drunk."

"That's not all Beanie," Harold shouted again. "When my buyer showed up and you weren't here, he couldn't get in to buy no liquor. So you know what he done? He went over to Stovall, to John Wallace, and he bought *his* liquor. So John Wallace has got money that was meant for me. And now I got John Wallace in business with *my* customer!"

Daniel picked the skinny man up and hauled him to his feet. Beanie's knees buckled. Daniel quickly lost patience and shoved him into a chair. Beanie fell over, landing on the floor in a heap.

"Tell you what we gonna do," Harold spoke slowly, suddenly calm. "We gonna give you another chance. We gonna leave you here till tomorrow and by then you better be sobered up and this place better be cleaned up. I better not hear of any moonshine or nothin' else on the floor or on my good poker table. And, Beanie, the next time we tell you to meet a bootlegger, you better by Jenny be half an hour early, cause if you ain't …"

Harold squatted down close to Beanie's face. Beanie, barely conscious, pulled his forearms up pitifully to try and protect himself. Harold pulled his arms back down and grasped a handful of Beanie's hair, pulling his face close.

"I said, cause if you ain't, this beatin' we give you here tonight gonna look like we was just playin' around. You hear me talking to ya?"

Harold and Daniel took Beanie's slurred words to be a vow to agree. They headed for the door and the outside staircase. As Daniel walked by, he gave Beanie one last kick in the ribs.

"You cost me money, Beanie," he said, as if that point hadn't been made.

The two brothers came down the steps and stopped in the red clay parking area in front of the store. The afternoon sun shone white hot, wilting even the distant pines in a smothering blanket of haze.

"I told you when you built them submarine boilers for John Wallace that it was gonna lead to trouble for us," Harold said.

"I know what you told me," Daniel mumbled.

"I told you if he was wantin' boilers that big, he was getting ready to start up one big-time liquor operation. Missin' out on selling this one batch ain't nothin'. Now we got direct competition for our best customer."

Daniel looked at his brother with disdain. "You think I don't understand that?"

The look stopped Harold before he said any more. Both men stood and stared out at the empty highway in front of them. They heard a crash from the upstairs room. Bean Pole had apparently tried to get up but fell again.

"Think we poured enough in him to kill him?" Harold asked.

Daniel shrugged. "Oh, I dunno. As much moonshine as he had through the years, probably not."

"Well then, maybe I ought to walk back up there and shoot the dumb idiot over what he's cost us," Harold finally said.

"One thing to talk about it. A different thing to do it," Daniel said.

"Ask that revenuer I shot if I know the difference."

"Bean Pole ain't no revenuer. We've known his mama all our lives. But I'll admit, I did study on it for a minute there." He paused. "Let's ride before one of them revenuers comes by and sees us standing at this store in broad daylight. I don't want them to think that we even know where this store is, much less that we own half of it."

The two men slid into the cab of Harold's truck. As the engine fired up, Harold turned to his big brother.

"Instead of going home, we ought to load up our liquor and take it over to John Wallace's place, tell him to give us our money, and then he can have the moonshine."

Daniel squinted at him. "Shootin' revenuers, wantin' to kill Beanie, now you gonna go over to Stovall and tell John Wallace what he's gonna do? Son, you better settle down. You're pretty rough, but you ain't that rough … no sir … chalk this one up to money lost and a lesson learned. You'd best steer clear of John Wallace."

John Wallace rode with an elbow resting on the open window of his old pickup. He could have afforded a new truck anytime he wanted one, but he didn't believe in pretense. John Wallace was nothing if not pragmatic. As he tooled down the straightaway toward the tiny burgh of Stovall, he passed two boys in ragged overalls walking on the dirt road. Waymon "Red" Harrison and his elder brother, Jake, were taking turns kicking a can along the roadside. Both were without shirt or shoes, their feet covered in red Georgia clay.

His meticulously crafted public persona took over as Wallace smiled warmly and pulled the truck over.

"Howdy boys!"

The boys' eyes grew as big as saucers.

Wallace chuckled. "What's the matter, cat got y'all's tongues?"

He opened the door and stepped out, his black Wellington boots gleaming with polish, his khaki work clothes crisply pressed. The boys stepped back as the big man loomed before them like a statue on the town square.

Finally, Red spoke. "Wa … we … we wus jes' playin' a game, with this here can."

"Kick the can? Yeah, I know the game, son." Wallace's smile grew brighter. He liked the boys. They reminded him of a simpler time. "I used to play it too when I was your age. Say, y'all come on around here. I got something I want ya ta have."

The boys' jaws dropped, and they looked at one another, astonished.

Wallace opened a large metal ice chest in the back of the truck, and the boys could feel a rush of cool air from inside. Large blocks of ice, intended for Wallace's icebox, were sitting beside five bags of groceries. The smell of fresh celery and damp brown paper grocery sacks wafted over them and, for a delicious moment, drove the mid-May heat away from their skinny bodies. Wallace took a bag and handed it to Red and another to Jake. This was more store-bought food than they normally saw in a month.

"You boys take them groceries on up to your Mama now, won't ya? Tell her them's a gift from John Wallace."

"GOSH!" Red said. "Thank you, Mr. Wallace."

Wallace beamed at the boy's reaction. "Now hold on just a second before ya go. I got one more thing."

Wallace reached inside the window of the truck and rattled another sack for a moment before emerging with two ice-cold RC Colas, the bottles still covered in flecks of melting ice from the store's cooler. He reached into his pocket and pulled out a Swiss Army knife, opening both bottles. The boys' mouths watered at the crisp sound of the escaping carbonation. "Them's just for you two." He handed over the bottles with a wink.

"Thank you, thank you, Mr. Wallace! Thank you so much!" they said, talking over one another.

"Alright then, y'all get on now before that food spoils," Wallace said. He gave the boys a wave as he got back into the car and drove away. He checked his rearview mirror, seeing the boys trying to balance groceries and sodas, and chuckled to himself.

A few minutes later he turned into his driveway. His home was the closest thing in the county to an actual Southern plantation. His driveway, made of white rock, not red clay, ended in front of a large, white columned house. He parked and Bobby Rodgers immediately began to unload the groceries. Rodgers, his ebony skin radiant in the noonday sun, was dressed in a crisp white shirt, black slacks, and neat black suspenders. He nodded respectfully, careful not to make eye contact with Wallace.

As John Wallace shuffled up the front steps, a car stopped out on the road.

"Oh, Mr. John," a woman's voice called.

He rolled his eyes, but as he turned around, his face creased into a broad smile.

"Why, Mrs. Cravens, how are you this afternoon, dear lady?" he shouted.

"I'm just fine," she hollered back through the passenger window. "I stopped by to tell you again how much we appreciated the invitation to your Fourth of July picnic."

"Yes, ma'am, you sent the note, ya know," he said. *You silly nitwit! Do you think you need to tell me a second time?*

"Oh, I know," she said, her southern drawl particularly apparent. "I just wanted to tell you in person."

"Well, you're quite welcome."

"We shall see you and that lovely wife then." She waved a white-gloved hand and drove away.

"Look forward to it," Wallace answered, shoveling the charm now with a trowel.

He pushed the front door open, locking it once inside the cool house. A man in his position made enemies and could never be too cautious.

"Look, honey!" It was the delighted voice of his wife. She wore a floral print dress that couldn't be purchased anywhere in the state except at Rich's in Atlanta. Her white pumps had a tasteful heel and matched her pearls. A white sweater was precisely placed over her shoulders, the sleeves dangling. To an impartial observer she would have looked as if she just stepped off the silver screen. She was blonde and beautiful, if a little overly made up for the region.

Wallace turned to see a landscape painted onto a stretched canvas. The paint, still damp, glistened in the light from a nearby lamp.

"I painted this for you," his wife said proudly.

Wallace's jaw muscles clenched as he shoved past her. "Not now," he mumbled without giving so much as a glance toward the painting.

His wife, wincing briefly at Wallace's snub, tried again.

"This one is of the spot where we had our picnic that time. You said it was one of your favorite places on the property. I remember …"

Wallace cut her short. "I guess if you're not going to pour me a drink, I'll pour one myself," he said gruffly.

"See I mixed my own paint color for the pines …"

Wallace didn't hear the rest.

"I said, shut up!" Wallace screamed. He punched a huge fist into the center of the canvas. Paint smeared his knuckles as staples ripped from the wooden stretching frame. He snatched the painting from the easel and ripped the canvas the rest of the way from the frame. He wadded it violently and threw it at his wife, staining her sweater and dress with the forest green that a moment before had depicted Georgia pines. She was shocked, but only for a second. For another second she allowed her emotions to feel the hurt. Then her body went limp and her mind numb as she prepared to absorb what she knew she now must. Still, she made a pathetic attempt to ward off the coming storm.

"I'm sorry honey, I thought ..." she began.

She wasn't allowed to finish. Wallace grabbed her by her perfectly coiffed hair and threw her to the floor. "You thought wrong!" He picked up the picture again and began to shove it into her face.

"How many times have I told you to give me time to relax before you start harping on me about some wretched hobby of yours?" He felt the veins bulge in his bald head and neck. His face was beet red, his eyes wild.

She used both hands to try to defend herself. Her teeth cut into her lips. Red lipstick and paint smeared around her mouth and chin.

Wallace dragged her by one arm toward the living room. Dinder-Mae, their maid, ran into the room, knowingly risking her own life.

"Let me take her, Mr. Wallace. Let me tend to her. Mrs. Wallace didn't mean to bother you. She sorry."

Wallace slapped his wife on the side of her head. He went to swing again and Dinder-Mae covered Mrs. Wallace like a mother hen, taking the blow on her behalf. "Get her out of my sight!" Wallace rose to his full height, his chest heaving.

Dinder-Mae whisked his wife from the room. John shouted after her.

"And see to it that you get my supper on the table soon before I fire you, you hear me?"

"Yes suh, Mr. Wallace, I shore will. Will have it for ya in a jiffy."

Wallace stepped over to the glass doors of the curio and removed a decanter of his very own special recipe moonshine. He poured a shot and downed it in one gulp. He poured another, sat the decanter back in the cabinet, and slammed the door shut. He looked in the reflection of the glass and saw several paintings done by his wife hanging from the wall behind him. They were good. Very good. Wallace wasn't sure why that irritated him so. From the room where his wife sat came soft sobbing. Dinder-Mae would be holding his wife like a little girl. They would be rocking back and forth together as they had the time before … and the time before that.

Wallace swallowed another gulp of liquor and sneered. He didn't like the reflection of his face in the mirrored door of the cabinet. And that's what annoyed him most about his wife. She could always lift off his mask, exposing the darkness beneath.

CHAPTER 1
FIRST RUN

Pine boughs brushed my face as I stepped slowly and deliberately toward the still site. I was running late and needed to get hidden before the moonshiners arrived. Suddenly, a match was struck, and I heard the glass globe of a lantern being lifted. In seconds, the forest would be bathed in light. A group of oak barrels stood just to my right, so I dove for cover. Hunkering down between two of them, the all too familiar smell of souring corn mash washing over me, I held my breath for a moment, not sure if I had been spotted. The moonshiners murmured with casual conversation.

I had made it, but I wasn't set up anywhere near where I wanted to be.

Two hours later I was stuck behind the barrels. The still was up and running, and the first turn of liquor, or the "firstlings," was nearly complete. Normally, when I conducted a raid on a moonshine still, I made certain that I got there and got myself hidden at least an hour before the moonshiners arrived. That hadn't been possible on this night. There had been, what you might call, extenuating circumstances. The four moonshiners had walked up at almost the same minute I had, forcing me into this poor excuse for a hiding place.

Wilson Turner, the man I was most interested in, walked around the still site, barking out orders as usual. Suddenly, he turned and walked toward the mash barrel where I was hiding. I pushed myself tighter against the oak slats. Peering carefully between two barrels, I could see him in the lantern light and noticed a .32 pistol shoved into the waistband of his trousers. But that didn't worry me. Still, I would hate to have to pull on men with families to feed. What concerned me more than a shooting was that, if I was spotted, these men would run on me, and I would lose Turner. I didn't want that—I needed to talk to him.

Turner drew close enough that the lanterns from the still cast his shadow across me. I could feel him looking in my direction. I placed my hand slowly and deliberately on the butt of my pistol.

"Y'all, this mash will be perfect tomorrow night. I want to get two runs done then. I'm gonna let y'all go home after we get this proofed, but plan on workin' all night tomorrow. We got orders to fill," Turner said.

Turner stopped speaking abruptly. He was looking over the mash barrel that stood between the two of us. At this distance, I dare not even breath heavy or the raid was going to start, whether I wanted it to or not.

"I'm thinking," he went on, "if we get about ten extra gallons of firstlings off tonight's run, we can mix them with the backins we got left over to make us about forty extra gallons of 'shine to sell." Turner turned and walked back to the still and I let out a long slow breath.

I knew all four of these men on sight. The two black men were Bobby Rodgers and Albert Washington, both experienced moonshiners. I ran Washington four years prior, and he did ninety days for it. Then, of course, there was Wilson Turner and his loud-mouthed brother-in-law, Denton Ellersly. I determined I would let the other three get away if I thought I could get a chance to talk to Turner alone.

As Turner moved around the still, I never looked directly at him. A man can sense that. Instead, I watched him out of the corner of my eyes.

If Turner was smart, I could stand up right now and he would leave with me and cooperate. Then again, if he was smart he wouldn't be working for the biggest and most dangerous moonshiner in the state of Georgia. Turner was in over his head. My reason for being here without any backup was partly so I could help him and his family. But it was mostly so I could send his boss to the state penitentiary. I would consider that a good week's work.

Washington leaned down by the moneypiece, a half-inch copper pipe where the finished moonshine dribbled into a bucket. He moved the bucket out of the way and caught a sample of 'shine in a mason jar. When the jar was about half full, he put the lid on it and smacked the bottom firmly on the heel of his hand. He held the jar up to the lantern light and stared into it.

"Honeycomb, Mister Wilson," Washington said. He was reading the bubbles, a duty reserved for the more experienced moonshiners. A skilled moonshiner could "read the bubbles" to almost the exact proof of the liquor.

"Pull that fire out of there, Rodgers, right now. Hurry up! Don't play around with it, pull it like I tol ya," Turner scolded. "Alright now, y'all fill the jugs, and we'll pour every one of them into this vat here."

Forty minutes later with the jugs filled, Turner went back into foreman mode.

"Now give me that maple stick over there, Washington."

The men poured all their liquor into a crude sheet metal vat they had constructed. I watched as the men filled the vat with the moonshine in jugs and buckets. Ideally, all the different proofs that had been produced that night would combine to a drinking liquor of about 105 proof. From what I had seen, this wasn't going to go anything like ideal.

I wasn't sure I could stay crouched like this much longer. My legs were starting to cramp. I never would have put myself in this position except that I hadn't been able to pull away from a stakeout I had been on in a different county … Upson County … home of what the boys up at the state capitol had nicknamed, "The Upson County Liquor Gang."

The gang was run by two brothers—Daniel, the oldest, and his younger and more hotheaded brother, Harold. The two of them had taken over all the liquor business in Upson, and I was determined to shut them down for good. I had busted a couple of their small stills before but never caught the brothers there. The one I had staked out earlier tonight was no small operation. That raid would have to come later, however. Right now, I planned to make headway against another moonshiner. I suspected John Wallace, the man Turner worked for, was producing more liquor than the entire Upson Gang put together.

"Alright," Turner said. "We got good beads on this liquor. Whoowee boys, we're gonna sell this batch for twenty dollars a gallon!" Turner was excited. "Washington … where the heck did he … Washington! Get over here and get that bucket full of sprang water. I gotta dilute this down."

"Don't fill up no bucket, Mr. Wilson," Bobby Rodgers cautioned. "You don't need no more than a half a mason jar and that'd prolly be too much."

"Who do you think you are?" Turner yanked the cap off Rodgers' head and smacked him across the face with it. "Don't you try to tell me how to proof my own moonshine."

Rodgers and Turner locked eyes. Bobby Rodgers could break Wilson Turner in half like a dry cypress twig in a fair fight, but he was in a no-win situation. Turner was John Wallace's foreman, so Rodgers had to bite his tongue. But Rodgers was right. Turner was about to ruin the entire batch. As far as I was concerned, that was good news.

Albert Washington reluctantly held the bucket of spring water out to Turner, who yanked it out of his grip, sloshing water in the process. He poured about a quarter cup of water into the vat and stirred.

"You boys see how them beads disappear? Do ya?" Turner shouted at them. "It still needs more water."

"Mr. Wilson, Bobby done this a whole bunch. Please listen to him and let me get you a jar."

Turner only bit his bottom lip and scowled. He drew back like he would take a swing at Washington. Instead, he tipped the bucket toward the vat and dumped at least three cups of water in all at once.

I knew what would come next.

As Turner stirred the batch of moonshine with his stick, a look of horror came across his face. He stirred it again, even more vigorously this time. He was using all the strength he had. I could hear what had once been moonshine whirring in the vat. Turner let go of the maple stick and let it fall into the vat of now spoiled moonshine. Leaning over, he gripped the lip of the vat and stared into it for a full minute ... hoping.

"Bead's all gone," he said dejectedly. "I put ... I poured ... y'all wouldn't quit talkin' to me when I was tryin' to ..." Turner's jaw muscles began to work, and his face turned red.

The men were about forty yards from my position. The three men backed up as Turner slowly came toward them.

"Y'all wouldn't shut your big mouths, and you threw me off. The bead's gone!" Turner was almost screaming now. "You got me mixed up, that's what! If you'd a just lef me alone and let me do it ..."

Turner punched Bobby Rodgers in the arm and again in the chest. He then flailed at him and knocked Bobby's cap off for the second time.

"Wilson, don't blame Bobby. Maybe if you would listen ..."

Turner stopped his brother-in-law in mid-sentence by grasping at his .32. Before Turner got his hand on the grip, my Smith had cleared the holster. As bad as I hated to do it, I'd have to put him down from this distance. I couldn't hit him in the hand from this far in the dark, so I decided to shoot him in the thigh. That way, I could stop him from killing the other three men and he would probably live till I got him to a hospital.

"If you weren't Mary's kin I'd put holes in you right here," Turner said, but he shoved the pistol back into his waistband.

"Now instead of standin' here arguin' with me, get your butts over to the other place and get me some beadin' oil, and lots of it!"

The three men stared at him. "Go, I said! Denton, you just come back with it. Bobby, you and Albert go home, jus go home. You ain't helpin' me no more. And don't you pussy foot around, Denton. We got a lot to get done yet before daylight," Turner shouted at the men's backs.

He watched them go over the ridge and then began to pace. He knitted his fingers into his thick black hair so tight that it seemed he would pull it out. I holstered my pistol and stepped from behind the mash barrels. I hadn't anticipated this. Things had taken a good turn for me.

I watched Turner alternately pace, rub his face vigorously, and place his hands alongside his head, as if he needed to keep it from bursting. I almost felt sorry for him ... almost.

As I continued to watch, I rolled a cigarette. Finally, Turner walked over toward me like he was going to look in one of the mash barrels again. He stepped to within three feet of me but was still staring at the ground, distraught. He hadn't seen me, so I got my Zippo lighter out and lit a smoke. Turner jumped, startled. Before he had time to gather himself, I grasped the front of Turner's shirt, pulled him toward me, and relieved him of his pistol. Then I shoved him back. Hard. I wasn't really going for such a big reaction, but Turner stumbled over a root and fell flat on his back. I considered that a bonus.

"You're havin' a lousy night, aren't you Wilson?" I asked, taking a puff.

Turner was shocked. He looked at my face first, then at my badge.

"Bobby Rodgers has made a lot of white liquor in his day. Maybe you ought to let him proof next time." I smiled down at him as I broke his pistol open at the cylinder, dumped the rounds on the forest floor, and tossed the gun up on top of one of the mash barrels behind me. I took another puff.

Turner looked around nervously, contemplating whether to shout out to his buddies or make a run for it.

"Don't bother, Wilson. I'll just be waiting at your house when you get home in the mornin'. You don't want that boy of yours seein' his daddy go away in handcuffs. You act like you got some sense, and maybe I'll let you go in a spell."

Turner squinted up at me in the dark. "You're the one that ran me in three years ago. What was your name? Kid something ... Miller, is that you?"

"*Agent* Miller will do just fine," I said.

"Why you gonna let me go?" Turner got to his feet, wiping leaves from his rump. He frowned and reached in his hip pocket. I drew my pistol. "Easy! I'm just checkin' on my tobacco." He pulled a red Prince Albert can from his pocket. "You done made me ruin my brand new can. It's bent up and half my tobacco has done spilled out."

"And I feel terrible about it too, Turner," I said.

"What you want from me?"

"You know what I want, and it ain't this sideline still here. Course, you might as well leave me that axe over there cause I'm takin' this down tonight before I leave. I want some information."

"I ain't tellin' you nothin'. You think I'm gonna help the man that arrested me? You got any idea how much trouble that caused me? Besides, I don't know nothin' to tell."

"You better think of somethin' to tell John Wallace about all of his liquor you just ruined. I can't believe you think your gonna put beadin' oil in all this mess you made tonight."

"John Wallace ain't got nothin' to do with this still or this moonshine. And by the time anybody figures out it's got beadin' oil in it, I'll be long gone and countin' my money."

"Don't lie to me Turner. I'm tryin' to give you an opportunity here. I can make sure you walk away from this. You can get a legitimate job. The war's over, there's gonna be factories and plants openin' up all around here. I ain't interested in making another case against you right now. I want Wallace. I'll get him without you, but it would go easier with you, easier for both of us."

"He got me out," Turner said. "He brought one of his lawyers up there when you had me locked up. He stood up for me in court. Any man stands up for me, I ain't goin' back on him."

"Don't be stupid, Turner. He stood up for you because you were makin' him money. Sooner or later he is going to be done with you, and that is a spot you don't want to be in. That time might get here real soon, considerin' you just destroyed three thousand dollars' worth of moonshine."

Turner's face flushed, and his fists balled up instinctively. I shoved him to one side and stepped past him.

I walked toward the still and grabbed an axe that was leaning near a pile of firewood. Stepping over to the vat containing the spoiled moonshine, I swung the axe the way I once swung at a high hanging curve ball, power coming from the hips and legs. The axe sank into the sheet metal, easily piercing the thin wall. I wrenched the axe out, and Turner watched helplessly as the spoiled moonshine gushed out onto the forest floor.

"Go home, Turner." I said. "See this for the break that it is. You think about what I said. And when you're ready to talk, you come over to Woodland in Talbot County and find me." I swung again and cut another long slit in the wall of the vat.

Wilson Turner glared at me for a moment, grabbed his empty pistol, and stumbled off into the night woods.

It took me forty-five minutes to destroy the still. As usual, I took special care in chopping up the copper worm and the head pieces. Cutting up metal with an axe will flat take the wind out of a man's sails.

Finally, drenched in sweat, I took a break, walked down to the spring, and took a long drink, using my handkerchief in the cold water to wash my face and neck and ladle water over my head. I looked down at the fluorescent dial on my watch. I could get home in time to get a couple hours of sleep and have breakfast with Judy and Rose.

CHAPTER 2
A SAD HOMECOMING

I was driving home and found myself whistling "To Each His Own" by the Inkspots. And why not? I finally had the youngest Godfrey brother in my sites, and if Turner cooperated, I might have a good source of information on John Wallace. If I could shut down those two, it would cut liquor production in my part of the state in half. Now I had time to go home, sleep a bit before sunrise, and maybe have a few hours to work around the house. The bream were biting, and I might even see if the girls wanted to go fishing.

As I rounded a curve, my headlights shone onto the shoulder of the road, where I saw movement. It only took me a second to realize what it was. Someone was lying in the ditch, most likely drunk, trying to get up. I stopped the car and aimed the lights squarely at the man. He looked up. It was Delbert Mangum.

I got out of the car, pulling my nightstick out of the D-Ring on my belt. Delbert wasn't usually a fighter, but when a man was this loaded, you never know for sure.

"Feelin' a little rough, Delbert?" I asked.

Delbert was on all fours, squinting up at me. There was vomit on his chin and down his shirt front.

"I ain't had much tonight, Agent Miller," he slurred. "Must a been a bad batch. Made me sick after just two or three swallers."

I shined my flashlight around and saw the corked jug I was looking for a few feet away. I picked it up, pulled the cork, smelled it, and shined my light into the neck.

"Nope … nah, Delbert, this 'shine ain't bad. Trouble is, you've done drank half the jug. That's enough to make a mule sick, much less a man your size. This is ridiculous Delbert. Ain't no man got any business drinkin' that much liquor in one night."

"I've had that jug a week or more," Delbert lied.

"Get up," I said, pulling him up by an arm. "Good grief, son, you smell like a pole cat. And look at you—you've done thrown up on yourself and wet your britches. Ain't this a fine way to come home to them babies of yours."

He stumbled and fell twice as I tried to get him to my car. "Come on," I said. "I ought to run you in, but I won't on account of your wife and children. I've got a raincoat I'm going to spread out on this back seat—sit on that. I don't want you stinkin' up my car. And you better not throw up in here either."

I rolled up into the front yard of Delbert's two-room shanty, knowing I wouldn't get home in time to get any shut-eye after all. I just hoped I'd make it in time for breakfast with my girls. I walked around to get Delbert out, shaking my head and mumbling to myself. I wished this was the one and only time I had pulled a fellow out of a ditch or from behind some honky-tonk in this same condition. But it wasn't. I suspect I had done something like this over a hundred times by now.

I was disgusted by Delbert and his kind, but at the same time I couldn't help but feel a bit sorry for them. I rarely arrested any of them, though I did have that authority. They never stayed in jail long enough for it to do much good. Instead, it hurt their families more than it did them.

Then I noticed something. The lights in the house were on, and I could hear a child crying. It was nearly four o'clock in the morning.

Mrs. Mangum came out in her nightgown. She held a threadbare shawl pulled tightly around her shoulders and bunched up at her throat.

I left Delbert hanging onto my car for dear life, still barely able to stand, and walked toward her. Her face was hard and deeply lined for a woman who I figured to be only in her late twenties. Her jaw was set. She looked like someone who had received a lot of heartbreaks and was now braced to take another one.

"He been on another drunk?" she asked. "You takin' him to the jailhouse?"

"No, ma'am, I'm not gonna run him. Just like I didn't run him last time."

"Makes me no never mind if you do. He's of no help to us anyway." She looked out and stared into the darkness of the nearby woods. Despite herself, her lips began to tremble. By the light of a single naked bulb hanging from a cord in the house, I could see the glisten of tears welling in her eyes.

"I don't mean that," she said to no one. "He still works some. Still tries a bit. He wants to do right, but it don't seem like he can for very long."

She wiped her eyes roughly with a corner of the shawl. Then she hollered out toward her husband.

"I'm done cryin' over you … you sorry …"

The front door opened again, stopping her in midsentence. The crying got louder, and two grimy little faces peered out at me. The smallest child struggled to get the door open. His arms, thin as tiny sticks, startled me. Both children were naked, completely naked, and their bellies were distended from hunger.

"I told you to stay in the house!" Mrs. Mangum scolded. She turned back to me, but she didn't make eye contact.

"I guess you think I'm a fine one," she said. "I been lettin' 'em sleep thataway. They barely got clothes to wear durin' the day, much less a nightshirt. I made 'em some out of an old mattress tickin' but they out growed 'em, and I ain't even got a stich of fabric in the house, nor no way to get none either. It don't matter no way. They can't hardly sleep. Their bellies been hurtin' 'em so."

Suddenly the little boy ran toward me. He began to wail and grasped my leg. He didn't know me; he was just frantic. Many have heard a little child cry. But few have heard a child who is hungry, truly hungry, cry. It is a sound that haunts any decent man. It is a cry that's never forgotten. This wasn't the first time I'd hauled a filthy drunk home. It wasn't the first time I had a child cling to my leg and wail like this either. That's when I felt it coming on. I felt it welling up inside me again, and I knew I couldn't control it.

"Mrs. Mangum, why don't you and the children go in the house for a bit? Let me and Delbert talk a minute."

She paused for a moment, then looked at Delbert. It seemed like she was going to argue with me, but her jaw set again. "Yeah, see if you can git through to him," she said, as she whisked the children inside.

As I turned to Delbert, I didn't feel sorry for him anymore. I felt like there was a pot of hot lead somewhere inside me and I was trying to keep it from boiling over.

Before I knew it I had Delbert by the straps of his overalls. He was bigger than me, but I snatched him off his unsteady feet and somehow drug him with ease over to the well and threw him onto his back. I primed the hand pump and quickly filled a beat-up bucket with cold well water. I doused him with the water to at least wash some of the stink and filth off him before his babies saw him. I filled the bucket and rinsed him again and again, as if the water could wash away his sins and make him a new person. A better person. He tried to cover up, but I just kept going. I snatched him to his feet and drug him toward a nearby chestnut tree. It was Delbert who cried out now. I suppose he was afraid, and I was glad for that.

I tried to take a deep breath and get myself under control. I leaned him against the tree and took a step away from him. I rubbed my palm across my mouth and felt the roughness of my whiskers, reminding me how long it had been since I'd shaved, how long it had been since I'd been home.

"Delbert, did you see them children's faces? Did you hear that baby cry? They need …"

"He ain't no baby." Delbert said. The cold well water had apparently sobered him a bit.

"What?"

"He ain't no baby. He'll soon be three year old. He can do for himself some."

The hot lead inside me violently boiled over. I grabbed Delbert's shirt and overalls and shook him as hard as I could. I slapped him. Delbert cried out again and made a half-hearted attempt to flail back at me.

"They're just little children," I screamed as I backhanded him. "They're just innocent little babies, and they're countin' on YOU!" I shook him some more before pulling his face close to mine. His breath reeked.

"You gotta start acting like a man again," I said. "You got to take care of your babies. It's wrong what you're doin'."

I drew back and balled up a fist. At that moment the door creaked open. The light washed over my back and Delbert's face, and I saw myself clearly.

I let Delbert's shirt go. I had had no right, and I knew it. I was ashamed and confused. My Stetson had come off sometime or other, and I walked over and picked it up. I stepped back over to Delbert, my fist balled up again. Instead of swinging at him, I pushed the fist hard against my lips before speaking again.

"You've got to care for them babies, Delbert. You've got to get off the moonshine. Reach down inside yourself and do that. Get in your Bible, get on your knees. Do what you got to do, but you better take care of them. I ain't got time to mess with you Delbert, but I'm gonna make time. I'm gonna be back out here regular. And you better be working and sober when I come by. Next time I catch you drunk, I promise you I am takin' you to jail, you hear me?"

"Yes ... yes, I hear ya," Delbert choked out the words.

"Now you stay out here and sober up a few minutes before you go in and see those babies."

With that I went to my car and reached under the driver's seat to feel for a box I had wired there for emergencies. Ever since the depression, I swore I'd never get caught without a little hard money again. I had twenty silver dollars hidden in the box, and I took out ten, hiding them in my palm before putting the box back. Ten dollars was still a lot of money, and I didn't really have it to be giving away, but I had to. I just had to.

I knocked on the door and called out, "Mrs. Mangum, might I step just inside the door?" I hoped she hadn't seen too much of what had just happened.

She opened the door, and I stepped inside so Delbert couldn't see us. Taking her hand in mine, I pressed the money into her calloused palm.

"Take this as soon as you can and get y'all some groceries. It should be enough to get a bolt of cloth and some sewing effects too."

She didn't say anything, but her mouth fell open wide.

"Don't show it to Delbert," I whispered. "Just get to the store down the road and get what you need." I turned to leave.

"I ain't got no way in the world to pay back this kind of money," she said, still holding tightly to the coins.

"I was blessed enough to have it in the first place. I think I should share it with you."

Before she could say any more, I quickly walked back outside, got into my car, and drove toward home.

CHAPTER 3
THE NOTE

On the way home the dispatcher gave me the message that Agent L. Z. Hitchcock wanted me to wait for him before I conducted my raid later tonight. We had only recently gotten radios in our cars. Now I wished we'd hadn't so I could avoid getting the message.

L. Z. Hitchcock was a revenuer with a big reputation; his name was always in the papers. He made sure of that. Hitchcock was a hard charger and at times a good agent. He was also a self-promoter and a glory hound. I didn't like him for that reason, but I could live with it. What I couldn't live with was the fact that he was dangerous, brutal with suspects and careless with the safety of his fellow agents. I didn't like working with him, and I hoped he wouldn't show tonight. But then, who was I kidding? The Godfrey brothers had some big moonshine operations. Raiding them would go over big with the newspaper.

Hitchcock was the only agent in the state to have killed a man in the line of duty. The shooting had taken place up at Stovall, the tiny burg that I had just left and the hometown of John Wallace. The still where I had talked with Turner was on White Sulfur Springs, only a couple miles outside of Stovall.

I began to fight sleep as I drove toward Talbot County and the tiny town of Woodland where I made my home. I had barely seen my wife and daughter over the past forty-eight hours. When I tried to picture them in my mind, I had to shake my head and rub my eyes to keep from seeing the Mangum children. I rolled down the window to breathe in some fresh air.

I hoped for an uneventful raid tonight. Sometimes we got a still surrounded and nobody ran. Other times we chased moonshiners deep into the woods. I've run moonshiners till I thought my heart would burst. I've run them until I fell down on my hands and knees and threw up. Of course, with the Godfrey brothers, having to chase them was the least of my worries. Those boys were shooters.

I pulled into my driveway at seven in the morning. I sat in the car a few seconds and breathed in deeply. It was good to be home. My house had a fresh coat of paint on the outside, but it needed a lot of work on the inside. It was too cold in the winter and too dad-gummed hot in the summer. All the doors creaked, and some of the windows leaked. But three tar patches on the roof kept us dry, and on chilly nights we huddled close together by the fireplace, laughing and talking. It needed work that I couldn't afford to do right now, but it was home.

Judy was already playing with her dolls on a quilt spread out on the soft grass. I got out of the car and held the door open for a moment, watching her. She was pouring pretend tea. As was our custom, Rose anticipated when I'd be home and had Judy in a dress with her hair combed and curled. I didn't make much of a salary, but I made sure my little girl had nice things. I didn't want to see her with her hair mussed or in dirty clothes, as if she wasn't loved. Rose told me that I was too sensitive about that sort of thing, that I needed to let Judy be a tomboy sometimes. But Rose hadn't seen what I had seen on this job.

"Daddy, you want some tea?"

Judy ran toward me with a little china cup in her hand. I scooped her up, brushed aside her Shirley Temple curls, and kissed her cheek. I carried her back to the quilt and set her down.

"No, honey, Daddy's too tired just now." I turned my back to her and started toward the house.

"Well, Daddy, tea will perk you up!"

I hesitated a moment, then smiled and turned back. I knelt down beside her and saw a little smudge of jam on her downy cheek. I reached up with my thumb and gently wiped it away. Suddenly, in my mind's eye, the child's face I saw didn't belong to Judy and I wasn't wiping away jam. I was wiping away tears from a face covered in filth. I was seeing the face of the Mangum's youngest child while he clung to my leg.

God, how I hated moonshine.

I forced my mind back to the present and stroked Judy's curls. "I'll have some tea with you next time, I promise."

I walked up the wooden steps to the back door and stepped inside. I stopped in the washroom, unpinned my badge from my shirt, pulled my gun belt off, and sat everything on top of the cabinet. This was my method of being completely "off the job" before I stepped into my home.

I opened the door to our den, the smell of bacon and coffee refreshing me. Rose stood at the kitchen window, staring outside. She had her hair up, and the morning sun highlighted the curve of her slender neck and the wisp of hair that had escaped her hair comb. I walked up behind her and wrapped one arm around her waist. Sliding my other hand down to her forearm, I interlaced my fingers with hers and kissed the soft skin behind her ear. She smelled of lilac. For a brief moment I felt her lean into me. She gave my hand a squeeze but pushed herself away suddenly. She walked around the kitchen table to the stove.

"Out all night again? You couldn't take a few more minutes with your daughter out there?" She was annoyed. No, that wasn't strong enough. She was angry again.

"Last night was critical to a couple of cases. I think we are going to crack them both this…"

"Well, it's always critical to the case isn't it, Kid? It's critical to some damned case every night you spend away from us, me sitting here in this rocker, wondering if you're shot and bleeding somewhere."

Rose never cursed, so I knew that she was more scared than angry.

"You know I don't like it when you call me 'Kid.' I hear that enough on the job. I don't want to hear it from you."

"I made biscuits." She wiped her hands on her apron, avoiding eye contact with me. "I'll get your breakfast on the table. There's a pot of coffee on the stove. It's fresh."

She started to walk away, but I reached out and took her arm. She stopped but didn't turn toward me. I held on, hoping.

"I'm not going to get shot doing this job. I told you. I haven't been hurt yet, have I? Rose, I love you and Judy more than anything, but—"

"I'll get your breakfast," she said, pulling away.

Walking over to the stove, I let out a sigh. I poured coffee into a metal cup and felt the warmth run through me as I took the first sip.

"There's a letter on the table for you," Rose said. "When I went out to get the paper this morning, it was sticking in the front door."

"Anything interesting in the paper? They hang those twelve Nazis at Nuremburg yet?" I asked as I turned the envelope over. I didn't hear Rose's answer. The handwriting was precise. Only two words were written on the front of the envelope: "Agent Miller."

I took another sip of coffee, sat down the cup, and tore the envelope open.

Mr. Miller,

We need to talk. It is quite urgent.

Meet me at my barn tomorrow night. Midnight. Come alone. Do not come early.

Sincerely,

John Wallace

CHAPTER 4
THE MOONSHINE BUSINESS

I drove out to my farm to tend my cattle after breakfast. I dreamed of the day when I could farm full time. I owned two hundred acres in an area we locals called, "The Valley." It was a beautiful bit of country. My hope was to establish a successful farm that I could leave to my grandchildren.

I had about thirty head of cattle. They'd usually follow me around like a bunch of lap dogs, always hungry and wanting me to feed them. I watched them eat, then suddenly noticed one of my mama cows looked like she was crying. She had water coming out of the corner of her eye. My heart jumped into my throat, and I felt nauseated. "Oh dear, Lord," I said aloud. "Please don't let it be the pink eye."

I couldn't afford a vet bill right now, but if this was pink eye I'd have to do something or risk the whole herd getting infected. I decided to keep a close watch on her for a while.

I went back to my car, pulling a block of mahogany and my Boker folding knife from my pockets. I hopped up on the fender, set the knife and wood beside me, and made up a cigarette. Once I got it lit, I opened the knife and began. I loved carving and whittling. I liked the smell of the wood and the way it felt in my hands. The sound of the knife shaving through the grain and the feeling of tiny wood slivers falling on my lap relaxed me. Like most of my carvings, this one was destined for a purpose.

Twenty minutes passed before I began to think about the note from Wallace. What did he want? A lot of people, including some lawmen, were scared of John. I didn't see it that way. A face-to-face meeting with him might give me just the tip I needed to find his still. John claimed that he was reformed, that he would never be involved in the liquor business again, but my gut told me different. Wallace was a moonshiner down to his bones. After finishing my smoke, I decided to head home and get some rest.

• • •

When I woke, Rose had supper piping hot and the table set. She worried about me a lot. Sometimes that made her angry, and sometimes she took that anger out on me. But she was a wonderful wife and mother, and one way she showed that was by making sure I was fed or had something to take with me into the field, no matter what time of day or night I had to go.

Now, just as I sat down to eat, a loud rap on the door echoed through the house. That would be my partner, Doc Cook. Before Rose could answer the door he knocked again hard enough to rattle the glass in a nearby window.

"Doc, you trying to knock on that door or break it down? You aren't raiding *this* house are you?" Rose asked with a smile as she let Doc in.

"Sorry, Rose. Don't know my own strength." Without an invitation, Doc stepped into the kitchen and grabbed a biscuit off the platter at the table's center. He moved over to the cupboard knowing exactly where to look for the jar of honey Rose kept. Before he could go for the icebox and the butter, Rose intervened.

"Sit down and let me fetch you a plate and a knife to go with that biscuit," she said, smiling. "You may as well let me pour you a glass of iced tea to wash that down with."

"Well if you insist." Doc pulled up a chair, looking hard at me.

"What are you starin' at?" I asked. "Have I broke out in polka dots or something?"

"I'm contemplatin, Kid. You see, I'm a thinkin man, not like you. You're more of what intelligent folks call a brute. You just go at a problem like a bull in a china shop. I think things through."

"Oh, I see." I figured where this was going.

Rose, who was never idle, set everything Doc needed in front of him and whisked off to another room.

"I'm thinking about man-hours, Kid. Man-hours and motivation. You've put in a lot of overtime trampin' through the woods looking for this Godfrey still we're going to tonight. That's not to mention how long you've nearly lived in the woods around Stovall the past three months looking for the Wallace still. You're never gonna get approved for all the overtime you're putting in on these boys, you know that, dontcha?"

"I'll worry about my own pay, thanks. I don't need you to worry about it for me."

Doc raised his voice a bit. "I *am* worried about it, 'cause you're makin me look bad."

I smiled slightly, shook my head, and scooped up a fork full of mashed potatoes.

"What's eatin' you, Kid? I've been on the job for eight years now, ridin' with you that whole time. It seems to me that every year you push harder and work longer. Do you really love this job that much?"

"Leave me alone and let me eat my supper," I said, my mouth half full.

"Maybe it's the taxes. Maybe it eats you up to see the state of Georgia miss out on some tax money, and you want to make it right."

"Just eat your biscuit and stop yakking. You know good and well I could care less about the state collecting more taxes."

"I'm poking you a little, Kid. But you ought to think about easing up a little bit. A lot of these moonshiners are just trying to get by. Just trying to make a living."

With that, I tossed my fork onto my plate with a clang. "Are you going to start that again? Do you have any idea how many times you have told me that?"

"You don't have to get sore."

"I am sore, Doc. I've let it go every time you've brought that up before, but you know what I think? I think that's a pile of baloney."

Doc rolled his eyes and dipped his biscuit in honey before taking a bite. "See, now I'm sorry I brought it up. I should have known you'd get all worked up."

"You been on this job eight years? I've been on it nearly twice that. I've seen things that maybe you haven't seen, or at least I've seen a lot more of it. And by the way, do you know what I did for a living before I took this job? Do you know what I did to feed my family during the depression? I was trying to survive with a wife and three children on a dollar-a-day job picking peaches. I painted houses when I could, though few could afford to hire a painter. We lived on grits, an occasional chicken from our hen house, and what small game I could hunt, and what vegetables I could grow in the garden. Times were tough as hell, but I tell you one thing, I never even thought about making moonshine."

Doc waved his hand at me, but I wasn't done.

"As a boy, I saw things folks did when they were on the moonshine that I didn't like one bit, things I never forgot. So when I found out that the state of Georgia would pay me twenty-four hundred dollars a year to chase moonshiners and bootleggers, you best believe I jumped at the chance. So no, I don't much care about the state missing out on tax revenue. But I do care a great deal about hungry children whose daddy is a drunk. I care about ladies we've both seen on this job with black eyes or bruises. And I care about people who are looking for hope in a brown jug where it won't ever be found."

"Why don't ya preach a sermon while you're at it," Doc muttered under his breath.

I knew I was overdoing it, but I couldn't stop myself. "The moonshiners can justify what they are doing by saying they have to 'get by.' I see it different. I reject the notion of the harmless 'good ol' boy' moonshiner, and I stand against any man who claims otherwise. I've seen too many hungry kids and had too many nights like I just had at Delbert Mangum's house to have any sympathy for moonshiners. I got by through the Depression all right. I worked like a dog to feed my kids, but I never pedaled 'shine, and I have no sympathy for any man that does."

"Good googly moogly man," Doc exclaimed. "If I wanted to hear a sermon, I'd go to the church house. Just 'scuse me for bringin' it up. 'Scuse me all to pieces!"

We didn't talk for a bit, and I finished the rest of my meal, which was now cold.

Finally, Doc said, "Kid, you can get riled up more than any man I've ever been around in my life. You're a brute, I tell ya. Not sure how a thinkin' man like me can put up with ya."

I laughed slightly, then balled up the gingham napkin from my lap and threw it at him. The napkin hit him in the face before it slid to the floor. Rose walked in holding Judy, so I stood up, kissed both my girls on their foreheads, and walked into the laundry room to strap on my gear.

Rose looked at Doc sympathetically. "Set in his way's aint he?"

"Stubborn as a mule," Doc said. He stepped outside, closing the door behind him.

Rose came alongside me. "Cullen," she said, calling me by my real name, the one I preferred. "Be extra careful tonight. Please. I know you're going after Harry Godfrey. He's got a bad temper. I've heard from several of the ladies at church that he was the one that shot that agent. I just know—"

"I'll be careful. I'm always careful."

I put my hands on her shoulders, and she let me pull her close. It felt good to hold her tight for a moment before I followed Doc to the car.

CHAPTER 5
MY NAME IS MARK

The sun had set and tree frogs sang along with the cicadas as the men stood around me. We were deep in the wilds of Upson County, gathered about a quarter mile past the end of Thunder Road. The road meandered along the backs of ridges overlooking the dozens of streams and small creek branches that crisscrossed the valley below. The valley, known by moonshiners and revenuers alike as "Over the Top" was bordered on one side by the mountains and on the other by the Flint River.

"Alright fellas, it's just beginning to get dark, so we probably have about two hours till Godfrey and his boys show up to start runnin' the still. Let's be especially careful on this one. We all know that one of our agents was shot in this same area and Harry Godfrey was probably the shooter. I didn't let that agent come tonight, even though he's recovered. I don't want vendettas. We are here to—"

"Miller, if you're so sweet on the Godfrey brothers, maybe you should stay back with the cars. Let the rest of us deal out the punishment."

The voice belonged to L. Z. Hitchcock. I could feel the blood rushing to my face.

"This is my raid, L. Z., so if I need you to say something I'll let you know." I looked directly at him as he glared back at me. Even though I didn't want him here, I probably needed him. I expected at least six or seven men to be working this still. We would need all the manpower we could get to catch them once they ran. And they almost always ran.

I turned away from Hitchcock and faced the others. "If we do our jobs correctly, there shouldn't be any shooting. Once they flush, y'all call out who you're going after. When you catch your man, meet back at the still and we'll walk all of them out together. That's it then. I'll take the lead. Like always, walk quiet and don't leave sign. We are too close to a conviction to tip them off now."

There was nothing else to say. It was time.

• • •

We arrived at the still's perimeter and settled in. I sat well hidden in the midst of a wild blueberry hedge. The night air was thick with humidity. I mopped my forehead one last time. I hurried to put my handkerchief away before the wary moonshiners saw it like a beacon in the light of the crescent moon. When you spend half your life hunting for food in the swamps of north Florida and the other half stalking moonshiners in Georgia, you reach a point where you stop thinking about the heat. It simply … is.

I'd been looking for one of the Godfrey brother's larger stills for so long I couldn't help but be anxious for the raid to begin. If I could arrest Harry, it would send a message to moonshiners all over the region.

I found this still a few days ago when I noticed a faint trail that started just off the shoulder of Thunder Road. By this point in my career, I could spot a moonshiner's trail from fifty yards away. Doc often said I could track a kitty cat down a paved road. That was a bit of an exaggeration … but I wasn't half bad.

I had staked this place out for several nights, taking names of the workers who appeared there. The law stated that a revenue agent had to witness suspects in the act of making liquor in order to make a case against them. I hadn't seen Harry at the still yet, which was exactly why I thought he would be here tonight. This was a good sized operation that

Harry hadn't checked on in a few days, and I imagine he'd be itching to get down here.

Sitting on the ground astride a chestnut tree root, I dare not move, even with the prickly chestnut pods leftover from last fall sticking me through my pant legs. The sweet smell of a distant crepe myrtle, the last living symbol of what had likely been an old civil war era home site, hung in the thick night air. As I waited, I began to think of the letter from John Wallace. What did he want? Had he gotten wind of my talk with Turner? The snap of a twig suddenly interrupted my thoughts.

"Pick up your danged feet," a voice said.

"You're makin' more noise than I am by hollerin at me," a second man spoke in the blackness.

Suddenly, a flashlight nearly blinded me. The beam swept the area but we were hidden so well that the two moonshiners didn't see us.

"You better hope Harry ain't here already," one of the moonshiners said. "If he thinks we're bein' too loud, he's apt to beat the hell outta both of us."

The first man lit a match and held it to the wick of a lantern that was hanging from a tree limb. In the glow, I recognized his face. He was from up at Thomaston. I had run him a couple of years before for drunk and disorderly, just so I could pump him for information. I think he did thirty days. I forgot his name. I didn't recognize the other fella.

They lit a fire, and soon flames began to lick the bottom of a large turnip shaped boiler. The firelight illuminated the men's faces in an orange glow.

A few minutes later, a black man approached the still from a different direction. He worked silently, efficiently, while ignoring the crude barbs the other two began to throw at him. The other men would have been wise to keep their mouths shut, for as this man began to split more wood, his strength became apparent. He removed his shirt and wore his overalls without so much as an undershirt. Muscles rippled on his back and biceps as the logs flew apart in just a few swings from his axe.

The first two moonshiners watched with fascination for a moment. "Boy, what's Harold payin' you to work here?" one of them asked.

The black man stopped and looked at him.

"Mark."

"What?" the first man said puzzled.

"Mark," the black man replied. "My name is Mark. You know, like in the Bible. Matthew, Mark, Luke … my name isn't Boy."

The hard look in Mark's eyes let his fellow moonshiner know that it was more than a correction he was issuing. Mark spoke differently than most of the people around here. He sounded educated.

"What the heck do I care what your name is? I asked you a question … *Boy*."

Mark tossed the axe over to one side and took a step toward him.

"What business is it of yours, what my arrangement is with Mark?" a voice called from the darkness. "Harry" Godfrey, owner of the still and the land it was built on, and two other men stepped into the firelight from the far side of the still. One man wore a convict's shirt that was nearly worn through. Several wraps of twine held the soles on his shoes. I smiled, wishing I could chase that one, might slow him down a bit.

"You stickin' your nose in my business?" Harold asked the man from Thomaston as he stepped in close, their faces only inches apart.

"Now, Harry, you know I didn't mean it like that," fear was in the man's voice now. All eyes, including those of my fellow agents, fell on Harold Godfrey.

"You'd best get back to work," Harold said in an even tone. "Maybe do a lot less talkin' and more workin'."

"Yes … yes sir," the man answered. His head drooped a bit, but as he walked away, he glared at Mark who continued splitting wood. Mark's jaw muscles flexed as he watched Godfrey walk over to the boiler where the mash was starting to cook.

I decided to wait another ten minutes before giving the signal. There were a couple of workers on my list who weren't here yet.

Footsteps approached. Someone was walking clumsily in the woods, shuffling his feet among the dried oak and sweetgum leaves that covered the ground.

"Harry ... Harry, it's me."

I knew it was Delbert Mangum without even seeing his face. I gritted my teeth at the thought of him coming here after our talk last night.

"Delbert, what in the hell are you doin' coming down here? You probably got every revenuer in West Georgia followin' you!"

"I was careful, Harry, real careful. Don't be mad. And Harry, I got money this time. I need some good 'shine real bad."

"I've told you before, don't come down here to the still wantin' to buy. You want some of my liquor, then you can buy it at the store." Harold shook his head. "But since you're here, what kinda money you got, Delbert?"

Mangum pulled out ten silver dollars and let them clank from one palm to the other. My temper flared, but I had to remain under control.

Harold Godfrey took the money I had intended for Delbert's wife and children and gave that drunk a half-gallon brown jug. Delbert pulled the cork, held the jug by the small finger hole, rested it in the crook of his elbow, and poured clear moonshine into his stupid, selfish mouth.

I'd seen enough. I stood up, my hand on the butt of my Smith &Wesson, and spoke nice and loud like a Sunday morning preacher.

"Who has bloodshot eyes? Those who linger over wine, who sample bowls of mixed wine. In the end wine bites like a snake—" Before I could finish reciting the Proverb, one of the moonshiners yelled, "It's Miller! Every man for himself!"

The chase was on. Out of the corner of my eye I saw Delbert Mangum stumble and fall, then watch in horror as his precious liquor ran out on the ground. One of the other agents shoved a knee in his back and put cuffs on him a moment later. The black man, Mark, turned from his work and ran right into Doc Cook and another agent. I zeroed in on Harold Godfrey, shouting to the others that he was mine.

Godfrey took off like a deer. Why did I always have to draw the fastest one? I was pushing forty years old. Still, I didn't hesitate. I was determined to take Harold this time.

He ran through the woods, weaving between trees and trying to lose me by jumping logs. I knew he could run all right and had outrun faster agents than me. I nearly lost sight of him in the dark, but I stopped and listened for a second to pick him up again. He broke into a small open meadow, and for the first time I knew I would catch him. Harry was running drunk. He had probably been sampling his own brew before he got to the still. I gained on him across the open ground. He zigzagged a bit and then busted through some thick brush on the far side of the meadow. Limbs whipped at my arms and face as I ran through the opening he had just made.

Suddenly, Harold misjudged a cut. His left shoulder smacked hard into a six-inch sweet gum tree. He spun away from it, caught his heel on a fat Virginia Creeper vine, and went down on his backside. He pushed himself up to a sitting position, but I was on him, slamming into his chest with everything my 155 pounds could deliver. Air rushed from his lungs, but he rolled away from me as he fell, and I ended up astride the small of his back. I reached for his right wrist to cuff him as he put up quite a fight. His left hand was beneath him and probing around the waistband of his trousers. I had about a second to make a decision, and I made it.

I drew my pistol.

I pushed the barrel firmly into the soft tissue of Harold's skull, just behind his ear.

"Want to find out how big a hole this ol' cannon will make in your head Harry?" I asked, cocking the hammer while my chest heaved.

The movement stopped.

"Now, you pull your hand out of that pocket, and if it comes out with a pistol, I'm gonna give you a headache you won't never recover from. That's nice ... good ... good ... nice and easy. Now put that hand back in the small of your back next to this other one." With my left hand I snapped a cuff around his left wrist, then holding his right forearm down with my knee, I holstered my pistol and cuffed the other hand. I stood up and pulled him to his feet. Then I reached around and pulled a Smith like mine out of a holster that had slipped around to rest next to Harry's belt buckle.

"You got good taste in pistols, Harry, I'll give you that." Harry cussed me, but I shoved him back toward the still site.

Harry Godfrey outweighed me by a good eighty pounds. I couldn't rely on physical intimidation very often. Instead, a genuine air of confidence, an intense manner born from competence, and the authority that rested in the badge I proudly wore, kept me respected and alive. Of course, the ability to shoot the eye out of a squirrel at thirty paces didn't hurt either.

By the time I marched Harry back to the still, the other agents were starting to arrive with their suspects as well. I should have been pleased. But when I approached the circle of light given off by the lanterns and mash fire, my satisfaction over a successful raid suddenly evaporated.

CHAPTER 6
FREEDOM OF THE WOLF

As I approached the still, I saw L. Z. Hitchcock, holding his drawn revolver against his thigh and leaning over the black man who was handcuffed and sitting on a stump.

"Boy, do you see this pistol?" Hitchcock asked as he waved the pistol under Mark's nose.

"Yes, sir, I see it."

"You don't think I'll put holes through you with this pistol, boy?" Hitchcock said.

"Yes, sir," Mark answered. "I am certain that you will."

"You hear that?" Hitchcock raised his voice so the other agents could hear him. He tried to mimic the Mark's baritone voice.

"He is certain that I will. Where'd you learn to talk like that, boy? Somebody give you some book learnin'? Let me show you what this pistol will do to you. You're about to tell me everything I want to know." Hitchcock holstered the pistol momentarily and then drew.

BLAM, BLAM, BLAM, BLAM.

Hitchcock fired four rapid shots toward some five-gallon milk cans that were about fifty paces away. The large cans had likely been used to transport mash. There was only one problem. He had missed every can.

Normally, Hitchcock was a decent shot, but he had been too busy quick drawing like a cowboy and had made us all look foolish.

"Hitchcock," I yelled.

BLAM, BLAM.

"HITCHCOCK!"

"Boy, you see what I can do with this pistol?" Hitchcock asked. "Now you gonna tell me what I wanna know, ain't ya?" he said, ignoring me.

"Sir, I will talk to you, and I might tell you any number of things, but you have not asked me a question yet."

I ushered the handcuffed Harry Godfrey over to the custody of Doc Cook and walked up to L. Z. I grabbed a handful of his shirt sleeve and spun him toward me, knowing his revolver was now empty.

"Hitchcock, you holster that weapon right now before you do something we'll all regret."

L. Z. Hitchcock had dark brown, almost black eyes, snake eyes, cold and unfeeling. He stared at me. I realized I had made a mistake. I had forced a showdown and now I had to win it.

We stood there for what seemed like a long time. Hitchcock sneered at me, lifting one corner of his mouth. We were locked in a stare for what seemed like a full minute but likely wasn't that long. Suddenly, he looked down at the ground, clicked open the cylinder on his revolver, ejected the empty shell casings, and methodically reloaded. I could feel the eyes of every agent and handcuffed moonshiner on my back. Hitchcock closed the cylinder by snapping the gun to one side, the way they do it in the movies. He held the pistol an extra second before speaking.

"Well, hell Miller, no need to get all worked up. I was just gettin' the suspect's attention." He laughed awkwardly. No one at the site laughed along. Hitchcock holstered his weapon, snapped the flap closed over the butt end of the gun, and walked over toward the moonshine holding tank.

I let out a deep breath. The best thing to do now was to put everybody to work.

"Doc, you want to get that copper worm out of there and cut it up? Spence, help L. Z. bust up that worm box. Some of you men start hauling the gear out of here."

I turned back to Mark who had his head hung low. He was in big trouble, and he knew it. He would likely get the maximum for moonshining. As a black man in Georgia with a criminal record, he might never get back on his feet after he got out. But I had a feeling this man was different. He would make the most of a second chance.

"Now, if I take those cuffs off you, are you gonna make me chase you? If you do, I might not stop Hitchcock next time," I said.

"I'm not going to run, sir," he said politely.

"Good, then I'm going to ask you to help me a minute." I unlocked the cuffs, and he rubbed his wrists.

"What's your name? All I've heard anyone call you so far is Mark."

"Mark Anthony," the man said.

I turned abruptly. If he was going to get smart with me, I was going to put the cuffs back on him. When I looked at him, I realized he was completely serious. I couldn't help but smile at the name, but he didn't offer further explanation.

"Step over there and help me lift the lid off this mash pit. We're gonna scatter this stuff for the birds," I said.

During liquor making, mash would be shoveled from this pit into the boiler of the still and heated. As soon as I lifted the lid off this mash pit, I realized that it was like many others I had seen. It stunk, and the whole wretched mess was working with maggots. I gagged momentarily, then looked up at Mark, who appeared to be ashamed.

"No need to scatter this mash. We'll can just leave the lid off and let the maggots take care of it."

"L. Z. was right about one thing. You sound like an educated man," I said. "How in the heck did you end up here?"

"Agent ... uh ..."

"Miller," I said. "Name's Miller."

"Well, Agent Miller, that is a very long and very tragic story indeed."

"You know I have to take you to jail now, don't you?"

"I know that, sir. I understand."

"I've got the feeling you didn't really want to be here. I'll try to put in a good word for you with the judge. Maybe you can help me with a couple pieces of information sometime."

"I would appreciate that, sir," Anthony said.

"How well do you know Delbert Mangum?" I asked.

"I know of him. I don't know him. He has come to the still before and purchased moonshine. One time Mr. Harry slapped him and told him not to come back. I was surprised he let him buy tonight. I guess the sound of those silver dollars swayed him."

I didn't say anymore to Mark Anthony about Delbert, but I surmised that those children of his never got their new clothes.

I grit my teeth for a second, then bent over, picked up a rock and threw it hard at the still, causing a clang to echo through the surrounding woods. I looked over at Mark Anthony who only hung his head.

"You know," I continued. "I don't have a formal education; I went to a one-room schoolhouse to the eighth grade. But my Papa used to read to us kids, my sisters and me. He read everything he could find, from the Bible, to the dictionary, to books by great men of history. He read us a quote one time. 'Somewhere, there must be a control on will and appetite, and the less of it there is within, the more of it there must be without.'"

"That was Edmund Burke," Mark said.

I was surprised and impressed that he would know that, but I said nothing about it.

"Then he read us a book by John Adams. That man loved freedom and liberty as much as anyone who ever lived, but he feared complete freedom. Papa read to us that Adams warned future generations about giving men so much freedom that they felt free from the rule of law. Adams called it the "freedom of the wolf."

For some reason, I kept talking. "That's the way I see my job, Mark. My job is to protect my little girl, and innocent children like Delbert's children, from wolves like the Godfrey brothers. Wolves that will take a mama's grocery money for a gallon of moonshine and then claim they was just doin' what they had to do to get by."

My anger gave way to embarrassment that I had said such things to a stranger. I felt my face flush and turned away.

Mark Anthony didn't seem to notice. He stood silently. "Mr. Adams was a man of great wisdom," he finally said.

I tilted my head toward the stream nearby. "Let's take a little walk," I said.

Though this was a still site, it was a pretty spot where the stream gurgled over smooth stones. We walked downstream, and it didn't take me long to find what I was looking for. The smell hit us first. I reached onto my belt and unclipped my flashlight. The beam revealed a dead doe. A bit further downstream was a dead opossum. I shined the light across the stream, and there was a swollen rabbit carcass trapped in the roots of a tree on the far bank. The first type of alcohol produced from a still is methanol, which is poison. Harry would have instructed his people to throw that portion away. Their operation was big enough that there was enough waste methanol to poison the stream. Like the maggot-infested mash, this site was not uncommon.

"I sense something in you, Mark Anthony. I'll stand up for you in court but once you get out, you need to do whatever it takes to find a new line of work," I said without looking up from the rabbit.

"I would like that very much, Agent Miller," Anthony said.

CHAPTER 7
THE MEETING

By the time I got Mark Anthony in a jail cell and did all my paperwork, it was morning again. I went home, did a few chores, and got some sleep. As soon as I woke, John Wallace was on my mind.

We were to meet on his farm, on his turf. I suppose I should have been dreading it but I wanted Wallace locked up so bad that was the last thing on my mind. Still, I couldn't rush up there without thinking things through.

I went to the bathroom and washed up. Just as I finished shaving, Rose walked into the bathroom.

"Kid, I've never questioned you on how you did your job, even though sometimes I wish you weren't doing it. But I am asking you tonight, please don't go up there and meet this man in the pitch black night!" my wife pleaded.

"Rose, people blow things out of proportion. Wallace isn't gonna raise a hand to a lawman. He's got better sense than that. Besides, if he tried, I'm not gonna just sit there and let him do it. I can handle Wallace if it comes to that."

"He's twice your size," Rose cried. Judy was sitting on the floor with a book of paper dolls, but she wasn't playing. She was watching us.

"He's not *twice* my size. Will you just calm down? You're upsetting Judy."

"What's upsetting Judy is that her Daddy is about to go off into the dark of night and meet with a man who once threw his wife through a screen door! Now if he will do that to his own wife, a kind, decent woman if there ever was one, what will he do to you?"

"My Aunt Sienna shouldn't talk about John Henry's Sheriff-business down at the beauty parlor" I said. John Henry was Sheriff of Talbot County not Meriwether where Wallace lived. Wallace fell under the purview of Sheriff Hardy Collier. But I guess Sheriffs gossip to one another because John Henry had gotten that little tidbit about Wallace from somewhere. He had told his wife, my Aunt Sienna, and Sienna had told Rose, or at least that's where I suspected Rose heard it.

I stepped into the laundry room and put on my gun belt and badge. I reached into a wooden cabinet over the washing machine and retrieved my nightstick, sliding it through the ring opposite my holster. I didn't always carry it, but tonight it seemed like a good idea. I also reached back on a shelf and got my sap, a weapon that was easy to conceal in a pocket. The sap was made of black leather and shaped like a beaver's tail. The leather encased ball bearings on one end. Spring steel ran inside its length giving the user the ability to whip it toward a combative suspect. In some particularly bad situations in the past, I'd been able to stop a good sized man with one good slap alongside the head. I might need such a capability with a man like Wallace.

"You're still going?" Rose was nearly screaming at me now. She ran across the room and grabbed my arm. "Cullen! Please, I am begging you; don't go out to his place. What will we do without you?"

Tears were rolling down her cheeks. I paused. She had to be overreacting, didn't she?

I didn't want my wife to be afraid, but at the same time I just had to know what Wallace was up to.

I looked at Rose and then at Judy, whose little chin was starting to quiver. She was too young to understand, but she sensed the fear and tension in her mama. I reached up and stroked Rose's face. She leaned against the warmth of my hand for a moment. Then suddenly, closed her eyes tight and shook her head as the reality set in that I *was* going to go. She slapped my hand away and turned toward Judy, scooping up our little girl and storming toward the back bedroom.

I knew it wasn't fair. I got to go and participate in what happened. I got to have a say so. All Rose could do was wait, with no idea of what was going on out in the darkest corners of Meriwether County.

• • •

It was every bit of twenty five miles from my house to John Wallace's place. All along the way I passed one location after another where I had busted a still during the past ten years. Still, I had a hunch that somewhere John Wallace had a liquor operation that would produce more moonshine than almost all of those added together. Sadly, I couldn't make a case on a hunch. And so far, nobody around Stovall was willing to talk.

When I busted Wallace in '38, his operation was unlike any I had ever seen. It was a serious production facility. Wallace was the kind of fella, that when he decided to make liquor, he went all the way. I was certain that I could stop more moonshine by busting him again than I could by busting four or five versions of the Godfrey brothers. Other revenuers and folks in the area kept trying to tell me that Wallace was done with liquor makin'. That he'd been reformed. But I just knew he was up and running again.

Wallace owned 2,000 acres and leased another 1,200, much of it heavily wooded. Some of it included deep swamps. There were lots of springs and branches and lots of places he could hide a big still. But Doc and I had searched for nearly a year without finding it.

Oddly, we had also had yet to find a single person that would admit to buying any of John Wallace's moonshine, which was why this meeting could be important. All I needed was one slip from Wallace to point me in the right direction.

My green Ford Sedan bounced over the rail road tracks as the pavement turned to dirt road once again. I would be at Wallace's farm in about ten more minutes. The sweet unmistakable smell of peach orchards overwhelmed my senses and made my mouth water. Harvest time would be here soon and I thought back to the days of itching with peach fuzz, sweating gallons back during the depression when I picked the fruit by hand for a dollar a week, all while painting houses on the weekends.

A few minutes later, I crossed another railroad junction at Stovall, passing by the old depot. Another mile down the road, I turned into the white rock road of John Wallace's farm.

As his note had instructed, I headed to the barn, not the house. Once there, I shut off the engine and let my eyes adjust to the dark. Then, taking a deep breath, I reached for the door handle. Before I could pull the latch, my passenger door flew open.

John Wallace slid into the seat right beside me. The springs of the Ford creaked with his bulk. By the dome light, I could see that he wore pressed dungarees and a light denim work shirt. He was a big man with particularly big hands. I thought about what my Aunt Siena had told Rose about Mrs. Wallace and shuddered at how damaging those hands could be to a petite woman like her.

Rumor had it that Wallace been exposed to chemicals in World War I. Whatever the cause, he had absolutely no hair on his body other than eyelashes. He had no eyebrows and was completely bald. Wallace shut the door and the interior of the car went dark again.

"Agent Miller," he said as he closed the door. I could barely make out his outstretched hand in the darkness, but I managed to reach out and shake it firmly. Though I had no animosity towards some of the moonshiners I went after, I didn't like Wallace. Any man that would hit his wife was just stomp down mean as far as I was concerned. I had no respect for him. Of course, I also didn't like the business he had chosen. I found it odd however, that Wallace seemed to genuinely like me.

"Mr. Wallace, it's late and my wife is worried, so what say we get to the point of this meeting right away?"

"Certainly, Miller," Wallace said. "I agree, let's get to the point. I asked you to come here tonight, because I want you to run Wilson Turner out of the state of Georgia."

CHAPTER 8
WALLACE ON FIRE

John Wallace's words hit me like a sledgehammer. I gripped the steering wheel tighter with my left hand, but I dared not allow him to notice. I had to keep my cool until I could determine where Wallace was going with this. Did he know of my meeting with Turner? Or did he only suspect something and he was now fishing for information. Maybe he was trying to read my reaction at this very second. At first I wasn't sure how to respond.

Then as the reality of what he was saying and how he said it sank in I began to get mad. Wallace had grown used to the local Sheriff, Hardy Collier, doing what he was told. I wasn't Hardy Collier.

"Well, Mr. Wallace, I am not really in the business of running people out of the state. I'm more in the business of arresting them when I catch them making moonshine."

"Well, do that then." Wallace was already starting to raise his voice. "Arrest him, because I can tell you, he is making liquor on my land. I can show you where. I will take you and show you his operation. I told him to stop it. I told him I already spent time in The Tower up in Atlanta for making liquor, and I ain't goin' back for a crime he is committing."

I could feel the hostility coming from Wallace. He wasn't just fishing for information. There was something more here, something that ran deep. I should have explored that, but right now I was angry because Wallace assumed I would do his bidding.

"What is it you think I do for a living, John?" I asked. "I knew Turner was making liquor before I ever got your note. But I don't arrest people on your orders. I arrest them when I can make a liquor case against them."

In the darkness I heard Wallace take in a deep, rapid, breath. His huge fist balled up tight in the seat next to me and he raised it a few inches. I could feel him shaking as he struggled to bring his own temper under control.

"I'm tellin ya, I want something done with him!" he shouted, his voice thick with rage. "I want him off my land, and I want him out of the state."

Wallace may have been trying to get a lid on *his* temper, but it was already too late for me. I wheeled in the seat to face him.

"Wallace, I would rather you not get me all the way up here to Stovall at midnight to tell me lies. I don't believe your story," I said. "Turner is making moonshine alright, and he is making it under your direction. I am not interested in seeing some two-bit still he has on the side. I am interested in finding the large still that I believe he is working on your behalf. When I find that still, you won't have to worry about Turner being on your land anymore 'cause he'll be at the state penitentiary in Reidsville instead. And you'll be bunking right next door to him."

The car went silent. I'd pushed too hard and I knew it, but the arrogance of Wallace was more than I could take. I turned back to look out the windshield. I carefully placed my right hand across my lap and onto the handle of the sap. Wallace stared out the passenger window for a long moment, then another. Finally he turned to me again, his countenance had changed.

His jaw set firm and I could tell he was gritting his teeth. He fidgeted in his seat.

"Well, if you don't get him out of here, then I can promise you, I will kill him," Wallace said.

Though we had spoken many times I had never heard his voice sound as it did in that moment. He sounded the way I imagined the serpent might have sounded in the garden when he spoke to Eve.

"You do realize that you are talking to an officer of the law, don't you John?" I asked.

Wallace didn't seem to hear. He was fixated. He went on.

"I saw him last week, fishing in my lake."

Turner was a sharecropper on Wallace's farm. That's how he came to be hired to work Wallace's still.

"I watched him for a while from up at my barn. Finally I decided to put my pistol in my pocket and drive my truck down there. By the time I pulled in I had determined I would just shoot him in the head and be done with it. Wasn't gonna say nothing or get into any argument about it. I was just gonna step up to him and shoot him in the head."

A chill went up my spine.

"But when I got down there and got out of the truck, I saw he had his little boy with him there. He was holdin a little homemade cane pole, the little boy was. I already had my hand in my pocket and was about to cock the hammer but I just opened my hand and let that pistol slide back down into my pocket. I didn't want to do it in front of the boy like that. Just didn't have the heart."

I sat there for a minute sort of stunned. I had heard stories. I had heard that Wallace had already killed other men. But to hear him describe his earlier attempt on Turner so matter-of-factly was shocking to say the least. Then again, I knew Wallace was a bad one. That was the reason I was so hot on finding his still. That was the reasons I went to Turner's still alone the other night. Wallace had to be stopped.

I could feel Wallace's staring at me as I looked straight ahead. Finally, I turned toward him and held his stare, unsure of what to say next. Suddenly, I noticed that Wallace's right hand, the one opposite me, was in his pocket. I sensed that he was gripping that same pistol he had just described to me. I couldn't possibly draw my Smith in these tight quarters, so I gripped the handle of the sap tighter, ready to swing it in an arc onto the bridge of Wallace's nose in a split-second if need be. Eventually Wallace looked back out the side window. He took in a deep, ragged breath, then let it out slowly.

"You're a good man, Miller and I believe you to be a fine officer. I hope you take care of Turner soon."

Without another word, he jerked the door open, slammed it shut, and walked off into the darkness.

CHAPTER 9
WHERE IS WILSON?

"Dispatch, have you got that patch ready yet?" This was the fourth time I had asked the question. I was trying to get through to the Meriwether Sheriff's office. Radio communications between agencies still had a long way to go. For now, I had to be satisfied with talking to my own dispatch sergeant, who in turn relayed communications by phone to Sheriff Hardy Collier's office by phone.

"I could probably get everything working quicker if you would stop bellering at me through the radio," the dispatcher said. "Stand by. Here, I just got one of the deputies to answer. Hang on…Sheriff Collier is asleep… you'll have to give your information to the Deputy."

I relayed the message about the threat Wallace had made against Turner. The dispatcher asked me to wait a few seconds after every sentence as he took the information down. When we finished, I signed off and stomped the accelerator.

My Ford was a fairly new car but it was a post-war model. The factories were trying to switch back over from making tanks and planes to making automobiles once again. The car companies had put very little thought into the design and my car was a big disappointment. Compared to the cars the bootleggers had it was slow, and besides, it drove like a buckboard wagon. Despite that I was pushing it to the limit.

I wanted to get to Turner as fast as possible. I hated to wake up his family at nearly one o'clock in the morning, but I had to. I didn't believe Wallace suspected that I had been working to make Turner an informant. I suspected that if Wallace had found out about that, Turner would already be dead. Turner had put himself in a very dangerous position by working in the liquor business with Wallace. Still, I couldn't be one hundred percent certain that I hadn't helped put the kid in even more danger. I felt obligated to warn him for the sake of his wife and boy.

I had never been to Turner's shack but I knew where Wallace's other sharecroppers lived. I had walked all over these acres when I made the liquor case against Turner in '43, and Wallace in '38. The shacks were far from Wallace's house and this late at night he wouldn't know I had gone there.

I pulled into the dirt yard without killing my headlights. This time, I wanted those inside the house to know I was here. I didn't want any surprises. If Turner already felt threatened by Wallace, he might be paranoid enough to come out shooting if I rolled up in the dark. Once I stepped out of the car, it only took me a second to realize that some things weren't right.

The lights were on in the house, even at this late hour. There was a sparkling new tricycle in the meager yard and a new catcher's mitt and bat lying beside it. Nice toys for the child of a sharecropper. The screen door was closed and latched. I could hear someone pacing inside the kitchen as I approached.

"Wilson Turner," I called out. "This is Revenue Agent C. E. Miller. I need to talk to you. I'm afraid it's urgent."

I heard someone running through the house. Suddenly, a small slip of a woman crashed against the screen door, her eyes wide, her hair disheveled.

"You know where Wilson is?" she asked.

"No, Ma'am," I answered. "I came here looking for him myself. I need to talk to him."

"I know he's in some kind of bad trouble," she said, opening the door and standing to one side.

"Mrs. Turner, if Wilson is not home, it wouldn't be fitting for me to come inside at this hour," I cautioned.

"I ain't talkin to ya out here. Somebody is libel to drive by and shoot a hole right through me. You wanna talk to me, you come in or you be on your way."

She was scared, really scared.

"Very well then," I said. "I suppose I could step just inside the door."

I took time for my eyes to adjust to the yellow light of a buzzing fluorescent fixture in the center of the room. New electric wire was crudely run up the wall to the light. I took one step back outside and glanced at the brand new service pole on the side of the house.

Back inside I saw a shiny chrome electric blender and toaster. Two new coloring books sat on the kitchen table with a new box of crayons. Colored pictures, clearly done by a toddler, adorned almost every square inch of one wall. There was a nice new radio sitting on an overturned apple crate. This was too much new stuff for a sharecropper and a small time moonshiner. Now I suspected why Wallace was so mad at Turner. The boy was spending his liquor earnings too fast. That kind of carelessness could raise the suspicions of a guy like me.

"I knowed this couldn't last. I knowed somethin' wasn't right," she said. "Every couple of days Wilson shows up with some new do-dad for either me or the baby. You probably know he's driving a new truck."

I didn't know that actually, but I wasn't going to stop her in the middle of a confession.

"Agent Miller, what's my husband done gotten into? I ain't seen him in two days and two nights."

There were butterflies in my stomach at the question. What *had* Turner gotten into? She hadn't seen him since he left me at his still. How did I tell his wife that she might lose her husband?

"Well," I answered. "I know he has been making liquor, I've seen him at it. But I also suspect he is working a much bigger still for John Wallace."

Mrs. Turner placed a palm on her stomach as though it ached, rubbed her temple with her other hand, and began to tear up.

"I told him…his Daddy told him two or three times too. We tried to tell him to get clear of Mr. Wallace. Agent Miller, that man will kill me and my baby for sure."

"I don't believe you are in any danger Mrs. Turner, but Wilson is. Can you think of any place he might go to lay low?"

"He's stole," was her only response.

"What do you mean?" I asked.

"He stole from Wallace. He got mad about some money he said Wallace owed to him, and just the other night he stole some cows."

"You mean he stole cows from John?"

"Yeah, high priced, registered cows. Mr. Miller, he ain't hisself. Ever since he hooked up with Wallace, he's acted different. Oh, Mr. Miller when he couldn't get one of them cows to load the other night he gone and cut its throat and left it lay there. Cut it from ear to ear," she cried. "This ain't like him."

This was getting worse by the minute. Now I knew the source of some of Wallace's rage toward Turner.

"I've called the Sheriff already, Mrs. Turner. I let him know that Wilson might be in danger. They are going to try and watch out for him. Beyond that, I really don't know what else to do. Obviously I will keep an eye out for him and I'll tell the other agents to as well. If nothing else, we can bring him in to protective custody."

Mrs. Turner looked at me but her eyes were far away. She looked toward the end of the room where her boy was sleeping, perspiration soaking his hair into little curls. Then, she seemed to come back to herself and looked me in the eye.

"I shore hope you find him first Agent Miller, cause I got a bad feeling way down in my soul."

CHAPTER 10
CHRYSLER IMPERIAL

I stayed out till three A. M. looking for Turner. I even walked back down to Turner's still site, but there was no sign he or anyone else had been there. I had no idea where else to look. I had done all I could for him. It is hard to help a man who doesn't want to be helped.

The next morning I slept in a bit till about nine o'clock. Today I had farm business to conduct. I had decided to sell a few head of my cattle. I was careful to choose some whose eyes were nice and clear. My cousin Richard "Dick" Alsobrook had a much larger cattle operation than mine, which meant he also had a cattle truck. Today he was going to haul a few head for me to the sale barn along with some of his.

After breakfast, Dick picked me up and we headed out into the valley. My place was in a pretty spot, and I always enjoyed the ride out there. It would break my heart to lose this farm. I had nearly lost it during the depression. Even now I was barely bringing in enough income to make the payments. After loading my cattle, we headed up toward Columbus to the sale. We talked and visited some to pass the time but the cattle truck was a bit loud for long conversation.

I took out one of my carvings and went to work. Dick sure didn't care if shavings got mixed with the mud and cow manure on his floorboard. This carving was starting to take shape and working on it relaxed me once again. As I rode I had time to roll things over in my mind. What did I know?

Though I had no proof, I was certain that John Wallace, formerly the state's most prolific moonshiner, was back in business. I knew Wilson Turner was working for Wallace. I knew Wallace, at this same sale barn I was headed to, had bought some high priced registered cattle. I also suspected that his dairy wasn't doing *that* good, so I figured liquor money paid for the cattle. I knew Turner had crossed Wallace, and that Turner had stolen some of Wallace's prized cows. I knew Wallace wanted Turner dead, and I knew Turner was missing.

As I rolled these things over in my mind, I came back to the same conclusion that I always came to. The best thing I could do for Turner, my peace of mind, and folks all over this community, was to find John Wallace's still. I was a revenuer. I wasn't a police officer. The best contribution I could make, the best way I could protect Turner's wife and baby boy from the wolves, was to do what I did best and make a liquor case against Wallace.

Even if Turner went to jail along with Wallace, his family would be better off with him out in a couple of years, than for him to be dead. And there was no doubt in my mind that was where Wilson Turner was headed.

What I couldn't figure out was, where was all of Wallace's moonshine? None of my informants, not even the unintentional ones like Delbert Mangum, reported purchasing any Wallace liquor. Everybody I had encountered was buying Godfrey moonshine or 'shine from one of the hundreds of small family stills in the area.

I was lost in that thought when a car passed Dick's truck. The driver cut back in so quick that he nearly ran us into a ditch.

"Whew wee, Kid! Did you see the way that fella went around us?" Dick asked, pushing his hat back on his head.

"Yeah…yeah I did," I replied. But I wasn't thinking about the man's reckless driving. I was looking at his car.

"That was a Chrysler Imperial," Dick continued. "They say that's one of the finest cars ever made. You don't see many of those around here."

"No, no you surely don't. Say Dick, ease up just a bit. That fella is about to turn into that little store up the road. Let's hang back so I can watch him a minute."

As I watched, the driver of the car got out. He wore a suit but the jacket was slung over one arm. He seemed relaxed as he walked over and began to ascend an outside staircase that led to a door above the store. As our truck passed by, I watched the driver knock on that door.

"Kid…Kid, what are you thinkin? I don't like the look you're gettin'."

Dick knew me well enough to know when my mind was in the game, and he was right this time. That big Chrysler was riding mighty low. There was some kind of load in the trunk of that car. And I intended to find out what it was.

I reached under the seat and pulled out my pistol and holster. My badge was hanging over the outside of the gun belt. I pinned it to my shirt. Dick's eyes got as big as saucers.

"Now Kid, what are you about to do?" he asked.

"Don't worry about a thing Dick. You just pull over up here on this shoulder past the store and wait in the truck for me. We've got plenty of time to get to the sale barn. Let me take care of this little piece of business and I'll fill your truck up with gas and buy your lunch."

"You're gonna buy my supper too, puttin me to all this trouble. I don't have no interest in this kind of an affair. This is your line of work, Kid."

He continued to complain non-stop but he was pulling the big truck over at the same time. We were well over a quarter mile past the store when I got out. I didn't want the folks inside to get too interested in the cattle noises, or in me. I wanted them completely caught up in their own business.

I jogged toward the Chrysler, slowing down when I got about ten feet away. Tiny pieces of white rock that made up the parking lot crunched under my feet. I crouched down, keeping one eye on the outside staircase and occasionally glancing at the front door as well. I didn't want anybody stepping outside and hollering a warning to the driver. I squatted down beside the driver's door of the Chrysler and took a quick glance into the store window. Somebody was sliding the door closed on a chest cooler, having removed a cold soda from the chiller. They never looked up toward the parking lot.

I stood up slowly, all my movements methodical. Quick movement always draws people's attention. As I rose even with the car window, I peered in. There was no backseat. My instincts had been right. This was a bootlegger's car. The rear seat had been removed. In its place was a carpeted false floor. I reached into a pouch on my gun belt and retrieved my lock pick. I was in the car in a couple of minutes. I opened the back door slowly and lifted the carpeted plywood sheet.

There was every bit of a hundred gallons of moonshine neatly stacked in jugs. No wonder the car had been riding low. I noticed some initials branded into each cork, C.L.C. I made a mental note of those initials, I would write them down in my notebook later. Right now it was time to go visit the upper room.

CHAPTER 11
FOUR OF A KIND

I eased around the back of the car and walked as if strolling through the park toward the outside stairs. I stepped up each step carefully and quietly until I was standing beside the door, the upper half of which was a four paneled window. The window was covered inside by a shade, which hung crooked, providing me a half- inch crack to look through.

There were four men sitting around a table covered in poker chips, playing cards. Poker was illegal in Georgia anywhere outside a licensed establishment. I would now be able to make at least four arrests, since I was certain this was no such place.

Smoke rose from cigars resting in ashtrays or clenched in the corners of the players' mouths. A mason jar of moonshine sat in front of each player, some drained, some half full. An open jug of moonshine sat on a nearby side table. I leaned in so I could look into the corner nearest the door. No one was there standing guard. What I did see was a craps table shoved far in the corner with a stained felt cover. A stain near the center was dark brown. I wondered momentarily if it was a blood stain, perhaps the result of a fight…or worse. Leaning against the table were the pieces of a broken chair.

The windows were open with ceiling fans whirling. The men sat in shirt sleeves, perspiration beading on their faces. The man at the far side of the table had a .45 automatic in a shoulder holster draped across the back of his high-backed wooden chair. That wasn't a problem. He'd never get to it in time.

The man with his back to me, who wore a suit vest and no jacket, had a pea shooter nestled in his belt at the small of his back. It looked like a .25 caliber. I would need to keep an eye on him. Even from the door I could see most of his cards. It looked like he was working four aces. I couldn't see the fifth card. Boy, was I about to ruin his morning. Against a far wall, near the man on the right, there rested a double barreled, sawed-off shotgun. The man on the left appeared unarmed.

Most folks probably think this is where I would kick in the door. That's all well and good for the picture show, but this was real-life. Busting in a door leads to mass confusion, guys diving behind cover and grabbing guns, which is not a manageable situation. My methods tended to be a bit more subtle. I was excited when I slowly turned the door knob, confirming that it was unlocked. I was about to make the biggest bust of my career.

I opened the door slowly and stepped inside like I was an invited guest, my hand resting on the butt of my Smith and Wesson.

"Do not drink wine nor strong drink, thou, nor thy sons with thee, when ye go into the tabernacle of the congregation…" I quoted part of the verse. "That's from Leviticus boys, but I'm sure y'all already knew that."

The man on the right cut his eyes towards his shotgun. At the same time the man opposite me lay his cards down. He was thinking about reaching for that .45.

"Now Mister, you ain't gonna be in the joint long for running an illegal game. Surely that ain't worth dying for. And you," I nodded toward the man on the right. "I'll put two in your ear hole before your hand gets halfway to that shotgun. Now let's all just be friends, can't we?"

Ten minutes later I had the four of them sitting in the dirt parking lot, their hands tied snugly behind their backs by my cousin. Dick had messed with cattle his whole life, so he tied as fine a knot as any man around. Right now he looked a little funny holding the sawed off shotgun in the crook of his right arm, the .25 in his pocket, and the .45

uncomfortably between his thumb and forefinger. I made sure that the store clerk joined our little gathering as well. The bridge of his nose was swollen purple and his lips were still puffy from a recent beating. I wondered if that was his blood up there on the felt.

"Kid, I want you to know that was one of my best ropes you made me cut up to tie these boys with. And if I don't hurry up and get out of here, I'm gonna miss the sale."

I reached in my pocket and took out ten dollars. I walked over and stuffed it into Dick's shirt pocket. I made a mental note to turn that ten in on my expense report. "I promised I would buy your lunch. That'll cover the rope, your lunch and your gas money. Head on to the sale and sell them three heifers for me and I'll split that with you for your trouble. You may as well go. The Meriwether County deputies will be here any minute. I called them from the upper room yonder." I turned to the store clerk and shouted, "Say, I never did thank you for the use of your phone up there. Much obliged."

The clerk mumbled something obscene instead of "you're welcome." I turned back to Dick and said, "Me and the boys here are just gonna sit around and fellowship a bit.

"I'll show you fellowship if I get out of these ropes," the tall man said.

"Now don't be like that pardner," I said. "I was beginning to think we were gonna hit it off."

About that time a little boy, pulling a smaller girl in an old timey wagon, came walking up. The girl wore a faded dress. I guessed she was his little sister.

"Sorry, kids," I said. "Store's closed for the rest of the day."

Their faces fell.

"But Mister, we saved up," the boy said. "We got money for a soda pop and a bag of peanuts." He held a grimy fist up containing the money.

I felt bad for them. "Well, in that case, go on in there and lay your money on the counter. Only thing is, that looks like enough money for two pops and two bags of peanuts, so get your sister one too."

The children's faces lit up and they started inside.

"You lousy son of a…" the store clerk began.

"HEY!" I said. "You watch your mouth in front of them kids before I give you a kick."

The clerk practically spat his words. "Do you know who I work for? Do you know who holds interest in this store? The Godfrey brothers themselves own half of this store. I've heard them talk about you. Your name's Miller, ain't it?"

I didn't answer so he kept talking.

"You have messed in their affairs for the last time, Miller. I heard Daniel Godfrey say that one of these days he was gonna kill you. He'll do it for sure now. You might not live till you get that cattle money."

"Why if it ain't Bean Pole Johnson" I said. "Beanie its been so long I almost didn't recognize you. So Godfrey is in on this store? I appreciate you tellin me that. I likely never would have made the connection without your help. I hauled Daniel's sorry brother to the calaboose the other night. Maybe they can be roommates now. I know their Mama's proud though, what with them being in the mercantile business and all." I had no case against Bean Pole and I knew it. He would be released in a couple of hours. My hope was he would take my comments back to the Godfrey's, give them a little something to worry about.

The driver of the Chrysler spoke up next. "The Godfrey brothers are the least of your worries, cow-tipper."

I could tell from his accent he wasn't from Georgia that was for sure. I was glad he was in a talking mood. Now we were about to get somewhere.

I reached down and grabbed him by the collar of the shirt, dragging him toward the stairway. I surprised him so we were almost to the steps before he got his feet under him and tried to stand up. He was plenty mad. I had him kind of sized up as not being the running type, but more of a scrapper, so I knew if he got onto his feet, he would try and wrench away from me. If he did, he would likely jump me, tied hands and all. For that reason I let him get mostly upright before I kicked him hard at the back of his knees. He buckled onto the second step in a heap. I took two steps back and grabbed a stick of firewood from a stack beside the store.

"I know you want to fight me pretty bad right now, but you need to know I don't fight fair," I said. "A better idea would be for me and you to get along. You see, I don't really care about those boys over there." As I spoke I could hear a faint siren in the distance. I only had minutes.

"No," I said, "you're the one that's got my attention, you and that Chrysler with all that moonshine in the back."

"You dumb Cracker! That ain't moonshine in that car. That's pancake syrup. My granny makes it before she goes to church. I was going to sell it to this store and they invited me to play cards, that's all."

Now I laid my Southern twang on thick. "Well gah-lee, that there is an ironclad story if I ever heerd one. Do I ever have egg on my face, causing you all this trouble over your dear grandma's syrup?" I dropped the heavy accent. "Say, whose initials are C.L.C?" I asked.

"How should I know? Probably the guy granny buys kegs from?"

He had cooled off a bit. I put one boot up on the bottom step, rested my firewood on my shoulder like a baseball bat, and leaned in closer.

"Look, I've got you for running liquor. Bootleggin is a serious offense in this state. Those boys are just goin to county but you'll end up in the penn, bud. And you're going for a long time. Now I can help you with that, but I want to know who made that liquor and where it was headed."

"The men I work for will get me out a long time before you will," the man smiled. "I don't know nothing and I ain't sayin' nothing."

The sirens were a loud wail now. I stood up, checked on the others to make sure they weren't going to try to run before the deputies arrived and smiled my best smile.

"You know what I believe I'll do? After they send you up, I believe I'll borrow that fine, fine, Chrysler of yours from the impound lot and drive it up to Atlanta. Maybe let my old flea-bitten bird dog ride in the passenger seat and hang his head out the window. I believe I'll drive by the prison and wave real big at you while you stare through those bars."

The driver tried to spit on me but missed, and instead dribbled spittle on his own shoe. In a few more moments the deputies' cars pulled into the dirt lot, skidding to a stop in a cloud of dust. One large deputy who I had seen around but whose name I didn't know, walked heavily toward the two of us. I had time to ask the driver one more question.

"You got a name?" I asked.

The driver just sat there and stared at me defiantly.

"I'm gonna find out from the Upson Sheriff anyway," I reminded him.

He shook his head real big from side to side. "I can't believe I got pinched by a bumpkin like you," he said as the deputy reached him, grasping the driver's bicep and pulling him to his feet.

"You're under arrest," was the deputy's only comment as he began to lead the driver away. Finally the driver pulled up short, looked around, and shouted at me over his shoulder, "Dantonio," he said. "The name's Dantonio."

CHAPTER 12
DANIEL GODFREY COMES TO CHURCH

I made the arrests at the store on Friday. That night I made a drive through Meriwether County to check with several informants. None of them had seen or heard from Wilson Turner. I took Saturday off and Rose and I worked in the garden. Judy played the whole time in the shade of a pecan tree, all dolled up in a white bonnet. My older daughter Billie, who was eighteen and living in Columbus while she went to secretarial school, was home for the weekend and she kept her baby sister entertained. It was a fine day. It had been a hot summer but today the humidity had dropped quite a bit and there was a breeze.

We sat at our picnic table in the back yard and ate a late lunch of fresh pulled corn, tomatoes, butter beans and a bit of thick sliced bacon I had carved off a hog hanging in our smokehouse. Rose and I grew up that way. Our families had always been self-sustaining, and we continued that tradition. It had helped us survive the depression. It was our way of life.

The following day was Sunday, and as was our sacred tradition, we went to the Woodland United Methodist Church for services. We very rarely missed church services. My Papa moved back here from Florida when Rose and I first got married, and he helped establish the Methodist church in town. He built much of it with his own hands. Rose worked with the children's church program. To say that Rose loved children would have been an understatement. She was called to nurture them. All the little ones at church seemed drawn to her.

We'd had a nice service, and as I stepped out into the bright sunlight after shaking the Reverend's hand, I felt renewed. It had been great to spend time with my family for a couple of days. Then I saw Daniel Godfrey leaning against my Ford. Rose stepped out from behind me holding Judy by the hand. I looked back at them. Rose wore a brilliant deep blue dress and matching pillbox hat. Judy's dress was a light pink satin with matching bonnet, and her little white patent leather shoes were gleaming. Neither of them had looked towards the car yet. Rose turned to talk with some of the other ladies exiting the sanctuary, so I decided that was a good time for me to conduct my business.

I slipped out of my suit jacket and folded it over my arm as I stepped across the street towards Godfrey. He smiled like a Cheshire cat. He had one elbow resting on the roof of my car and had a foot up on the back tire. He wore his Sunday best as well.

"I lean Presbyterian when I attend services," he said, as he continued to smile. "But I decided to make an exception today. Do a little visitin'."

"Well then, you must have come in late," I said. "I didn't see you during the visitor greeting time." I smiled ever so slightly. But I wasn't in a smiling mood. I walked up close to Godfrey. If he wanted trouble with me, I decided I would just as soon get it over with now. I opened the front door and tossed in my coat, never taking my eyes off him. He stared at me and his face got hard.

He leaned closer as well. Even now I smelled 'shine on him. He'd had a nip before coming here.

"Miller, you think I'm gonna let you off free and easy after you locked up my baby brother? You got plenty to keep you busy bustin' up these little fifty gallon stills around here. Let me recommend that you stick to those. Revenuers who mess around with me and my brother don't tend to fair too well."

"Well, gosh Godfrey," I said, keeping my face close to his. "I took double that fifty gallons you're talkin' about out of the trunk of that Chrysler at your store. That's not countin' the seventy-five more the deputies poured out from your back room. Of course I also busted up Harold's still, and now I've got your sorry brother locked up in a ten by ten foot room up at the county pokey. I'd say I'm fairing just mighty fine."

Godfrey's face reddened and his cheek began to shake visibly. He took his foot off my tire and stepped back, looking towards the church. Rose was still laughing and talking. I wanted to end this before she became aware of it.

"You are going to be disappointed, Miller, when you find out that there ain't no paper to connect me with that store, or the liquor you claim is mine that you found there. And you got nothing connecting me to those stills you mentioned. Why, my brother Harry wasn't doing nothing more than making a little family recipe, cause it helps his rheumatism. As for the liquor in that car, what you just said about it was the first time I ever heard of it. But uhh…I will tell you this. I sure would be careful out there in the woods. Somebody might mistake you for a varmint. You might get yourself shot."

I knew I needed to keep my own lid on, but I didn't like the way he was looking at my family. "You threatening a state officer?" I asked, my jaw starting to clench. Godfrey wanted to say it. He wanted me to know that he was going to try to kill me.

"You better believe I am, Miller." He took a step toward me but I met him halfway. Our noses were nearly touching now. "I'm gonna kill you Miller. You better watch over your shoulder every minute, cause I got a .44 slug coming right for your heart."

I wished for my sap but I didn't pack such a thing to church. And I couldn't fist fight Daniel out here in front of my little girl. I narrowed my eyes and the voice I heard come out of me didn't sound like my own.

"Get out of the liquor business Godfrey. Get out of it this afternoon 'cause if you don't, I just know something real bad's gonna happen to you."

He stepped back, and tipped his hat toward the Reverend, who was looking over at us with suspicion. Daniel Godfrey said loud enough for anyone close to hear, "You enjoy your afternoon, Agent Miller."

He turned to walk towards his car then stopped. "You know," he said, quietly. "That's a pretty little cemetery over there. It'd be a nice place to spend eternity, don't ya think?"

CHAPTER 13
MARK ANTHONY GOES FREE

Monday morning my partner, Doc Cook, and I had a court date, so I dressed up a bit. I wore khaki pants and a white dress shirt with a pair of tan boots that I kept polished up. I traded my straw Stetson for the felt one. I didn't splurge on myself much, but three nice items I did own were my Smith and Wesson, my winter Stetson, and my summer Stetson.

The courtroom smelled of old leather and varnish with just a touch of body odor mixed in. The gallery was nearly half full. The oak floorboards creaked as I headed for my spot behind the prosecutor's table.

I had been told that the Judge on both Harry and Mark Anthony's cases was Edward English. There was a time when I was convinced that, had we still conducted hangings in Georgia, English would have been a hanging judge. In the last few years however, Judge English had changed.

He had gone off for some additional schooling in California. There he met some pretty famous people. He let it slip once that some of his old college friends were now in the movie business. Since then the Judge had views on things that I just couldn't agree with. Today would be one of those times.

Court was called to order. Harry Godfrey was to be arraigned first. Daniel Godfrey walked in just after I sat down on one of the pew-like benches in the gallery. I was sitting two rows back from the prosecutor's table. I sat on the end of the row, and when Daniel walked by me he stopped. I handed my Stetson over to Doc and decided I would stand up and give Godfrey a good opportunity, if he had something he wanted to say. Our eyes locked for a second but he just moved on and sat behind his brother.

"What was that all about?" Doc whispered.

"Nothing," I said. I felt Doc's eyes on me. He leaned up and looked at Godfrey before relaxing against his seat back.

I got quite a jolt when Harry plead guilty and laid himself on the mercy of the court. His attorney said that Harry had just strayed off the path a bit, and since this was his first offense, could the judge go easy on him. I knew that was a lie. This was at least Harry's tenth offense, and he had about four others going at that very moment. I just hadn't found those yet. The only first involving Harry was that this was the first time he'd been caught.

Still, the Judge seemed appreciative for not having to go to trial and he went easy on Harry, who got two years at the county work farm and a two-thousand dollar fine. I was disappointed. Harry had that much liquor money in his billfold on most days.

Next came the other workers at the still, who each got six months at County. Finally, at the very end of the proceedings came Mark Anthony. After the charges were read and the formalities were out of the way, the Judge asked the prosecution if they had anything to add.

"Your honor," I said. "I request permission to speak on this man's behalf."

I should have talked to the district attorney prior to this, but I just hadn't had the chance. Now he wheeled around and gave me a "what the heck" look.

Judge English was surprised too. He looked over his glasses at me.

"Why Agent Miller, weren't you the lead officer in this case?"

"I was your honor."

"Well, would you mind telling the court why you sat here in silence through the lead defendant and several other workers of the still, all white men I might add, but now you choose to stand up and speak for this defendant? Mr. Miller, this is highly unusual. I have had your cases in my courtroom many times and have never known you to engage in this kind of outburst before."

I ignored his silly comment about an outburst and stayed on track. "Your Honor, I only spoke up now because it is my professional opinion that the other men were working the still because they wanted to. I believed that night, and have since verified, that this man was working the still under duress. Not only did he not want to be there, your honor, he tried to avoid being there."

I had done some follow up after Mark Anthony was taken to jail. I didn't know his whole story yet, but I believed he deserved the benefit of the doubt. Meanwhile, I could feel Doc's eyes on me. I hadn't told him I was going to do this either.

Judge English sat back in his chair and placed his left hand on the armrest. "Well, this is positively heartwarming to watch unfold. Agent Miller here is going to the mat for this boy," he said sarcastically.

"You know what you need son?" The judge spoke directly to Mark Anthony now. "You need a program." All eyes were on Judge English. No one was sure what he was going to say.

"What I see about to happen here, is Agent Miller is going to make himself feel all warm and fuzzy inside cause he helped this boy out. And then," English pulled back his robe and looked at his watch. "Oh, I would say by about…nine thirty tonight, this boy here is going to be right back making moonshine and laughing at all of us."

The judge continued, "You see, Agent Miller expects this boy to just up and take responsibility for himself, and the tragedy is, the boy has absolutely no capability to do that. He's got no training, he's got no education and he's got no skills. Now if there was a program, if the state of Georgia, or maybe even the Federal government was to create a program where we could rehabilitate a boy like this…well…then he might have a chance. We could give him a decent bed to sleep in, we could feed him, and most importantly, we could educate him in the way that we wanted our citizenry to be. Now that would be a real solution."

"But then, there is no such program because none of the illustrious leaders of our state have seen fit to even attempt to create one. Therefore, since Agent Miller has a good reputation as an officer, and since he has not made such a request of the court in my recent memory, I am going to grant his request. And then the court is going to wait and fully expect to see Mr. Anthony right back here just a few short days from now. And at that time, I am going to do all in my power to send you up for the whole live long day, Mr. Anthony."

Judge English looked sternly at me. "Agent Miller, are you prepared to assume custody of Mr. Anthony here, until such time as he can be transported to whatever hovel he subsists in? And keep in mind Agent Miller, the court expects you to be responsible for him until such time that you deem him…uh… in your professional opinion…to be prepared to make a go of some lawful form of existence?"

I hadn't wanted it to go this way, but now I was determined to prove English wrong. "Yes, your honor. I will assume that responsibility."

"Then under the aforementioned conditions, I hereby declare Mr. Mark Anthony a free man. I now declare a forty minute recess for lunch."

The gavel banged and everyone went their separate ways. Harry was taken away to jail and Daniel Godfrey stepped out ahead of me. Mark Anthony nodded once toward me and turned to let the bailiff remove his shackles.

Doc stood up beside me and placed a hand on my shoulder.

"Kid," he said. "What in the sam hill are you doing? You don't know that boy. Now you gonna be responsible for him?"

"I know his *type*," I said firmly. "He's gonna do fine. He won't *need* me to be responsible for him. He will be responsible for himself!"

"Kid, you've lost your mind or something. You can cow-tow to him if you want to. I ain't riding in your car all over the county with some moonshinin' black boy."

Doc and I had ridden together a long time. I had heard this kind of talk before and Doc knew I didn't like it. Doc truly wasn't a bad guy but he was ignorant.

"Well Doc, if it's gonna bother you that bad, then I guess you'd best get in your own car and just ride on out of here. Why don't you go check out that section of Big Lazar Creek where we suspected there might be a still? Go find something else to do where me and my new friend won't offend you so bad, because as you just heard, I've got an assignment from the judge."

Doc stared at me another minute, then snatched his own hat up from the back of his chair and stormed out of the courtroom.

CHAPTER 14

WHITE SULFUR SPRINGS

When we got to my car, Mark rode in the back seat as if he were still in custody. We both realized that it would be better for me and him that way. We would be less prone to raise a stir.

I stopped by Helen's diner on the way and ordered two of her outstanding chicken dinners, which she put in a basket and covered tightly with a red gingham cloth. She knew I would bring the basket and cloth back my next time through. I walked out with the lunch and two cold RC colas, and we headed on down the road.

Anthony had a cousin in Durand, a little community about five miles east of Stovall, and he asked me to take him there. We talked a bit on the way and he thanked me several times. As we passed through Warm Springs, where President Roosevelt had had his Little White House, I turned down a dirt road. The town got its name from actual springs and I knew a pleasant spot along the bank of one of them to eat our picnic lunch.

I pulled the car off the shoulder and we walked a short distance to a little sandy area in the bend of White Sulfur Springs. We were about a mile upstream from where I had talked with Wilson Turner at his still, and less than eight miles from the John Wallace's barn. I sat the basket on a big red oak stump that was the perfect height for a makeshift table, and we sat on a log beside it.

"I'll thank the Lord for this good lunch if you don't mind, Mark." I said.

"Not at all Agent Miller, please do." Mark's voice had a rich baritone quality to it.

After I said grace, Mark started in on a biscuit while I grabbed a piece of chicken.

"Mighty fine," Mark said. "Mighty fine."

"Yeah, you can't beat this chicken anywhere around here." I said. "That is unless you come to my house and eat my wife's cooking." Both of us smiled, and then Mark changed the subject.

"So you know about my troubles then," he said.

"I know you had trouble. I don't know the details. Don't want to know."

"Well, I got in some debt to the Godfreys. I was stupid, really. My cousin offered to let me farm his little piece of ground with him, where you're taking me now, but I thought I could do better."

"I got up there to Upson County and borrowed money to get started from the Godfreys, and next thing I knew I was overextended. I couldn't pay when they came to collect. I owed them and they weren't willing to wait until I could raise the money. They wanted me to work off the debt by helping at their stills. They told me that they would drive over here and burn out my cousin and his family if I gave them any trouble. I don't know how much longer they would have held me to that commitment if you hadn't come along that night, but likely a long time."

"Well, you need to pay them every penny you owe them in any case," I said between bites. "That's only right, no matter whether they were making liquor or not."

"I intend to, Agent Miller. It may just take me a while seeing as how my income will be limited to half a crop for now."

"You might be surprised," I told him. "You'll have to work hard but you don't seem shy about that. You can make a summer and fall crop and bring home more than you might think. I know, because I grew up vegetable farming with my Papa."

We didn't talk for a while as we finished eating. I lit a cigarette and finished my RC. Over in a sunny spot there was a pretty nice blackberry vine covered in ripe berries. I stepped over and shook out a clean handkerchief, and in just a few minutes I had a double hand full picked and cupped in the kerchief.

"This'll have to do us for dessert," I said, laying the handkerchief flat on the oak stump.

Mark took four or five and tossed them into his mouth. The rain had been good early this year, and these were nearly as big as my thumb. Sweet juice exploded onto my tongue as I bit down.

I got out one of my little carvings and worked on it as we sat quietly. Mark watched with more than a passing interest and finally broke the silence.

"I'm not what the Judge said I am," Mark said suddenly.

"I know you're not," I said.

"I have a home. My cousin has always told me that his home was my home. It is a nice home and his wife keeps it that way. They might be poor, but they take pride in what they've been blessed with."

I only nodded, not sure why this man felt he needed to justify himself to me.

"It's not a hovel. I have a nice bed with nice crisp sheets and a quilt. I don't need the Judge's government bed. It wasn't that I didn't have a home; it's that I made a poor choice to leave it. I got greedy."

"I understand," I said.

We sat quietly for a bit longer.

"Maybe it is more important what you do with the opportunity now," I finally said. "We should go, I need to get moving."

Mark Anthony stood. He was nearly a half foot taller than my six feet.

"Mr. Miller, why did you stand up for me? The last man to do that was my father…and of course, my cousin Charlie."

"I just felt like it was the right thing to do."

"But why, sir? The judge said it in court. With all the people you have arrested, you never did anything like this before. Why do it for me, who you barely knew?"

"Well first of all, I have done it before, many times. The judge doesn't know all my cases. Also, I sense something in you, Anthony. I sense honor."

We didn't talk anymore as we gathered our things and walked back up to the car. As we started to get in, Mark rested his forearms on the roof and looked across at me.

"You know Agent Miller," he said smling. "I sense that you're a man of honor too."

I smiled back and then looked at the ground. We got in the car and I drove Mark Anthony home.

CHAPTER 15

REVELATION

We rode along quietly for a time. We had to pass right by John Wallace's farm to get to Mark Anthony's cousin Charlie's house. I saw Wallace as I drove by. He was walking around the corner of one of his dairy barns leading a Guernsey cow.

"Pretty things, those Guernseys," I said. "But they cost about twice as much as a Holstein."

"I once heard Mr. Wallace say he planned to revolutionize the dairy business by building up a herd of them and selling a higher quality milk, cream and butter than most dairies around Georgia," Anthony replied.

"You know Wallace?"

"Agent Miller, everyone in the vicinity of Stovall or Durand knows Mr. John Wallace. And very little happens in these little communities that he doesn't know about."

"Then you know that he's buying those cattle with liquor money?" I was fishing but I hoped Anthony didn't realize that.

"It wouldn't surprise me, but I haven't heard that directly," Anthony said.

I tried to read his expression, but he was staring out the passenger window as we went past Wallace's place. It looked like Wallace would be busy for a spell with his dairy, so I made a mental note to check on Julia Turner while I was out this way.

We pulled into Charlie's front yard right behind his old Dodge pickup. Mark sat there, still staring out the window. Movement caught my eye and I looked up to see a pleasant looking black woman step out the front door and over to a window box full of Posies. She carried a pitcher of water and smiled over at us as she watered them. I threw the car into Park and decided to try and soothe Mark Anthony a bit.

"I'll be keeping the Godfrey brothers busy with their own troubles for a good while. They aren't likely to drive across two counties looking for you. You've got some time to get your life together, make a crop and start paying back that money you owe them."

We had enjoyed a pleasant lunch, some fellowship, and I felt good that I was about to leave Mark in what seemed to be an almost ideal setting. Suddenly, Mark Anthony set a bomb off in my car.

"He killed my friend," Anthony said, still staring out the window.

"What?"

"My friend and I went to a black folk's honky tonk up the road towards Greenville."

"They serve 'Shine there," I said. "I know of it."

"We both drank too much that night but he had more than me. He started mouthing with the bartender, punches were thrown and my friend, his name was Will, acted out. He threw a chair through the window. Somebody called the law. A fat deputy showed up and Will was still out of control. He hit the deputy, bloodied his nose, and knocked him to the ground. He got away from all of us. He ran into the darkness and I lost sight of him. But he didn't really get away because he worked for John Wallace."

Anthony's voice was so low it was as if he wasn't sure he wanted to tell me this.

"Mr. Wallace sent somebody for him early the next morning. Told him to come up to the house, that Wallace wanted to find out what happened. They tell me when my friend knocked on Wallace's front door, Wallace shouted from inside for him to come around to the back."

I turned in my seat to face Mark Anthony.

"As he rounded the corner the back door flew open. Wallace didn't say a word. He just shot him down like a dog. He unloaded that big .44 into my friend's chest. Then Mr. John Wallace called one of his other black workers and told him to 'get this trash out of my yard'."

I breathed in deeply; I had heard rumors before but now I had confirmation. My thoughts went back to Wallace's words to me in this same car the other night. *'I wasn't going to say nothing to Turner. I was just going to step up to him and shoot him in the head.'* That detail made me certain that what Mark Anthony was telling was true.

"Did you tell the Sheriff?"

Mark turned on me. There was anger in his expression.

"A black man, try to turn in a white man the likes of John Wallace? You want me to end up like my friend? You want my cousins hung from a tree somewhere in these swamps?"

"I know," I said with a grimace. "I know how things are."

"I had to tell somebody," Anthony said. He looked into my eyes for a moment before saying, "I believe you are the kind of man I can trust." Then he opened the door and stepped out of my car.

CHAPTER 16
TIME TO THINK

With Mark Anthony's words still echoing in my mind, I thought of Wilson Turner again and decided to see if I could get lucky and find him. I drove by his house to find Julia Turner still scared and still wondering where Wilson was. She hadn't seen or heard from her husband, and it had now been four days.

I had several small cases pending, but my main focus right now was on the two that were potentially the most dangerous. I had wanted to use Turner to help me close in on John Wallace. My motive had been to take a whole bunch of moonshine out of circulation. Now I had another motive. With Wallace threatening Turner, and Turner having disappeared, a liquor conviction against Wallace could be a very good thing for Julia Turner and that little boy. It might help keep Wilson out of danger.

Then there was Daniel Godfrey. I had known I would kick the hornet's nest when I busted his brother Harold, and I was right. On top of that, I had a court date tomorrow regarding the Chrysler bootlegging car and the poker game I had busted up. All this took place at a store which, according to Bean Pole Johnson, Daniel Godfrey had some interest in. Now, Godfrey had threatened me just yards away from my wife and little girl.

I was plenty motivated to close these two cases even before all the recent trouble started. Now, I wanted to lock these fellas up all the more. But as things currently stood, I didn't know where to go next with either case.

As I left Stovall, I decided to make a little round through Meriwether County, maybe drive back through Manchester. I wanted some time to think.

CHAPTER 17
THE BASEMENT

Once in Manchester, I cut through town and drove down Eighth Street. There were still a few genuine antebellum houses that, for whatever reason, Sherman had spared as he burned his way to the sea. Suddenly, for the second time in the past four days, a case just fell right into my lap, only this one didn't involve burly men playing illegal poker.

I was tooling along slowly, my window down and my elbow resting on the top of the door, when I saw her. A pretty blonde woman in a white sundress with big yellow flowers printed on it was walking from her house toward her garage. Her house was a nice brick two-story with a detached, white-framed garage. If she had looked like most of the elderly ladies who owned these grand old houses, I probably wouldn't have noticed her, but I have to admit, I hadn't seen very many women like her. I continued to watch in my rearview mirror as I coasted past her place.

I slowed down, careful not to tap the brakes and trigger the taillights, while I kept an eye on her. I suppose, as a married man, I was looking at her a little longer than I should have. Then, I became more interested in her behavior than her looks. She stepped toward the side-by-side garage doors and closed them abruptly, as if she hadn't intended for them to be open even a crack. She began locking several padlocks mounted up and down the doors. Finally, she walked back toward her house. And did she ever have a walk. She moved with the confidence of a woman who owned the whole world, not just that big two-story house.

I wondered to myself why a nicely dressed woman in this fine neighborhood would need so many locks on her garage. I decided to find out.

I drove around the block and parked my car in front of the empty house right behind hers. I got out of my car and walked up the driveway, straight into the backyard, as if I lived there. There was a high, white wooden privacy fence separating the two lots. I drug a metal lawn chair over to stand in, peeked to make sure the woman wasn't still standing by the garage, and vaulted myself over.

I landed quietly in her back yard and walked over to the side window of the garage. The panes were painted white, and I couldn't see through. Now I was really suspicious. I eased around the front of the garage and tried to look in the crack between the doors. The doors were mounted tightly together and the seam between them was small, with the exception of an inch long section about three feet from the ground. I knelt down and peered through. Just as I suspected, the floor of the building was covered with wooden crates. One had the lid off and I could see the tops of mason jars likely filled with moonshine. She may have looked like a movie star, but when it came right down to it, she was just another criminal.

I crouched down and moved toward her house. It wouldn't be right for me to go into a woman's home alone to arrest her, but I wanted to get a better look before I left. I would bring Doc back with me later. I couldn't enter any of the structures, the house or the garage, without a warrant. But I could take a look from outside.

I eased toward the house and got down on one knee to look into a basement window protected by decorative bars. A wooden shutter inside the window was closed, but it wasn't latched completely. I peaked in closer. That's when I saw the still. This lady had her own operation going right there in her basement. Suddenly, a ladies white pump, attached to one of the nicest legs I had ever seen, blocked my view.

"See anything you like Mister..." she asked.

Despite myself, I followed the leg up to the knee, then, catching myself, jerked back so that I fell from one knee to flat on my rump. I stood up, flustered. I had chased a lot of moonshiners, but never one who looked like this.

"It's Miller," I said. "Agent C. E. Miller, Georgia Department of Revenue."

"Well, my, my Agent Miller. It looks like we find ourselves in a very awkward situation here, don't we?" She smiled, and she had quite a smile.

I didn't answer for a long moment. She had eyes that were so brown, a man could sink into them and never find his way back home. Her blonde hair was curled and up on her head like Betty Grable's. She stood there with her hands on her hips and her chin thrust forward as if she were issuing a challenge. When I didn't answer her, she spoke again.

"It appears to me that we are going to have to come up with a compromise. Perhaps there is something I can do for you and in return, you can do something for me...like forget what you have seen here and just move on to some other still."

She smiled again and took two slow, deliberate steps toward me. I knew that I had a decision to make. In my time as an agent I had run across men who were willing to fight me. I had tackled men who, like Delbert Mangum, smelled worse than any pole cat. And I even encountered men like Harold Godfrey who were willing to shoot me. But I had never encountered a challenge like this.

I knew that I could go inside the house with her, and most likely, no one would ever know. The neighbors weren't home, and no one else could see us back here. I thought about Rose for a second. Instead of thinking about all the wonderful things about her, I allowed myself to dwell on recent times when she was angry with me. This lady sure wasn't mad at me.

She took another step closer, and for the first time I could smell her hair and perfume. She smelled like flowers. She looked up into my eyes.

Her skin was perfect, her lips painted a sultry red. Finally, I focused on those brown eyes and found myself in even more trouble. She took my hand. I was surprised by how soft and petite her hands were.

"Now, Agent Miller," she cooed. "Surely you realize that a lonesome lady has to do whatever she can to get by in times like these."

I have heard folks talk about how, in extremely intense situations, their lives flash before their eyes. That happened to me in that moment. I thought about the Judge that morning, and how he had trusted me because he respected me. I thought about what Mark Anthony said, and how he sensed faith and honor in me. I even had a mental image of myself standing behind a lectern a couple of weeks prior, teaching Sunday School. Finally, I saw Rose's face on the night she clung to me, begging me not to go see Wallace.

I knew that it was time to decide what kind of man I truly was. Everything honorable, anything good, I had done prior to this moment would mean nothing if I decided wrongly.

I held her hand more tightly in mine and she smiled knowingly. I sensed that she was thinking, "Yes, just as I suspected. This one is just like all the others." That is, until I pulled her hand part way towards my lips and slapped a handcuff on her wrist.

CHAPTER 18
TOWN SQUARE

The following day I had a court appearance for the arrests I made at the store. I thought I would be called to testify, but instead the DA, Reed Allen, pulled me to one side before the judge came in.

"Agent Miller, I need to talk to you before the judge calls us to order."

"Glad to, sir," I said as we stepped into an anteroom.

"Miller, the state is not going to press charges against the store owner, and we are going to accept a plea bargain on the poker players. We're going to come down pretty hard on the driver though. So, you are still entitled to some portion of the confiscated goods, and I won't stand in the way of you getting what's coming to you."

"What?" I said. "What do you mean you're not pressing charges…"

"You are wasting your time arguing with me, Agent Miller. This decision came from up top. It came all the way from the Georgia Attorney General's office."

"This is stupid! I have reason to suspect that that store is connected to…"

"You'd best not worry about who may or may not be connected with the store. The store is no longer your concern. Now, you may be called to talk about what led you to the arrest of the driver and the confiscation of the moonshine and the car, but you are not to bring up the store or any details about it in court, is that clear?"

"No, it's not clear worth anything," I said.

"Then perhaps the best thing for you to do is to follow the orders of the Attorney General and not try to figure out why he gave them. That should give you clarity."

I said nothing.

"Good," District Attorney Allen said. "See that you do just that and this will go smoothly."

I was furious throughout the court proceedings that day. I did get called to the stand and Allen made sure to question me in a way that would minimize my answers. Finally, the driver of the Chrysler, who still refused to give anything more than his last name, Dantonio, was sentenced to 36 months for bootlegging. As the bailiff took him away, he turned to find me in the gallery. Our eyes locked as he glared at me. I held his gaze and fully expected him to have something to say to me, but he never spoke up.

Finally, Judge English said, "Agent Miller, by law you are now entitled to some compensation. You and District Attorney Allen see me in chambers."

We stepped inside the judge's chambers and the smell of old leather-bound books and stale cigar smoke hit me. He told us to have a seat.

"The law gives the court latitude in this case to award the arresting officer all or part of the materials confiscated in the arrest. District Attorney Allen," the judge began as he pulled his wire rimmed spectacles on and stared down at the papers, "the car was purchased in cash by Mr. Dantonio for the price of two thousand, one hundred and forty-three dollars. Shockingly, Mr. Dantonio did hold clear title to the car. It is my inclination, unless Allen here has any objections, for the court to sign the title over to Agent Miller in full."

My heart leapt in my chest. I didn't really expect to get the entire car, just some portion of the sale price. I didn't need the car, but the money I could make from selling it certainly would help my family. I waited for Reed Allen's response.

"My office certainly has no objections, your Honor. We would like to extend our appreciation to Agent Miller for a job well done." Allen stuck out his hand and I shook it. I would be lying if I didn't admit that it was a pretty good moment for me, and I temporarily forgot my outrage over the way the case was being handled.

"Very well then," Judge English said as he signed the documents.

The Judge went on to award me two hundred dollars from the confiscated poker pot.

I suppose my excitement got the best of me, because it didn't really occur to me until I was leaving the now empty courtroom, that perhaps my silence on the illegal gambling charges had just been rewarded. Had I allowed myself to be bought? Then again, I'd had no choice. I didn't know what the Attorney General's office might be planning. Perhaps they were working a larger case.

The president of the Greenville Savings and Loan approached me in the hallway. "Mr. Miller, I just discovered that you confiscated a fine Chrysler automobile during a recent liquor case you made."

I watched the DA disappear out the front door of the courthouse. I would have to catch up to him later.

"Yes, I did." I said a bit suspiciously.

"Well then," he said in a halting, high pitched voice. "Would you mind terribly if I asked what you plan to do with the car? I mean, surely a man in your line of work doesn't intend to drive a luxury automobile."

I scowled at him and started to demand what he meant by his snotty remark, but he held the note on my cattle herd and land and I didn't want to be on his bad side.

"No, I don't intend to drive it," I said. "I intend to sell it."

"Well," he said. "That being the case, I would like to make you an offer on the car. I have been over to look at it and it only has a few thousand miles on it, and I have even located a matching rear seat that I could have restored into the car. My wife would just be delighted to drive such a lovely automobile. Of course, we will not share the history of the car with her. I could make you a very fair offer."

I asked him his offer and he was real close to the price that Dantonio had paid for the car new. The bank president could take care of everything to do with the deal at his office, so we shook on it.

• • •

A few minutes later, I was sitting behind the wooden fence that separated the officer's desks from the teller area in the Savings and Loan building. Just as we were concluding our business with the car, the front door opened, and none other than John Wallace stepped inside.

"Why Mr. Miller," Wallace said as he saw me, the heels of his boots clicking across the marble floor of the entrance. He opened the little gate in the fence near the bank president's desk and stepped through. He thrust out a hand as though we were best friends, so I stood up and shook it. He began to make small talk like he might have with a close buddy. I was a bit surprised at first, but then decided to just jump right in and keep him talking. I wanted to see where this was going.

As we were talking about the state of the alfalfa hay crop this year, another man entered the bank. I didn't know the man well, but I knew his name was Herring Sivell, and I knew that he was a buddy of Wallace's, but something was wrong. When Wallace turned and saw Sivell come in, I saw some color drain from his bald head and face. For a second, he seemed to stumble over his words and forget what he was talking about.

A few seconds later, Sivell looked up and saw the three of us, but his eyes clearly focused on Wallace. He turned nervously toward the table in the lobby. He fumbled to pull the chained pen from its holder and took a deposit slip from one of the slots in the table. Without writing anything he returned the pen, wadded the deposit slip and dashed back out of the bank. All of this, from Wallace stepping through the gate to speak to me, to Sivell nervously leaving the bank, took maybe a minute. I glanced over at the banker, and it was clear that he hadn't noticed anything out of the ordinary.

Wallace seemed to come back to our conversation, but his entire countenance had changed. He clearly was no longer interested in talking about the hay crop, and after saying something like, "Yes…um…well… as I was saying…we need another rain on this hay before it gets cut… uh…listen…nice talking with you Miller, but I have to go."

Without another word Wallace turned on his heel, walked back through the gate, and headed out of the bank.

The banker still didn't have a clue anything unusual had happened.

"Well, then, I think we have one more paper to sign and I can write you a check. I can go ahead and have Ava deposit it into your account if you would like," the bank president said. "I think you have a cattle payment coming up; this certainly will make that easier."

"Yes," I said. "Yes, it will. Sir, if we could wrap this business up, I should be getting on as well."

"Yes, of course," he said. "I'll be right back."

Ten minutes later I was pushing my Stetson down on my head as I stood in the hot mid-morning sun. By now there was no sign of Wallace or Sivell, but as I looked back up toward the courthouse, I did see another man who I wanted to talk to. Meriwether Sheriff Hardy Collier was sitting atop a three-foot rock wall that surrounded the courthouse, drinking a bottle of RC Cola and smoking a cigarette. I crossed the street and walked the block towards him.

Collier was in his sixties. I felt he had gotten a bit lazy now, but a few years ago he helped me a bit with some liquor cases that didn't involve John Wallace. Still, I disliked the man. Either because of our age difference or because he was Rose's cousin, Collier felt like it was okay to treat me as if I were still wet behind the ears.

"Howdy, Kid," Collier said. As I stepped up to him, he took another swig from his RC and tapped his ashes into the green grass of the courthouse yard. "What are you up to this fine morning?"

"Sheriff, I just saw something that struck me as odd. You might want to look into it."

"Well now," Collier began, already adopting a condescending tone. "Anything strikes you as odd, I sure better rush right out and check on it, huh Dick Tracy. What exactly did you see, son?"

I felt the blood rush to my face, and I started to tell Collier what I thought about his name calling. But I needed him on this and future cases, so I bit my tongue. I told him about seeing Wallace and Sivell and how they had done everything they could to avoid one another in the bank. I told him how uncomfortable they had looked, as if they hadn't intended for anyone to see them together today.

"Well, that sho is an ironclad clue there Kid, thanks for stoppin by. I may call for Federal help on this one," Collier said.

I no longer cared if I offended him. I took a step closer. "Hardy, why don't you give me a break on your cheesy commentary and just look into it? I am telling you right now those men are up to no good."

Hardy Collier was a bit surprised by my reaction and he looked me in the eye for the first time.

"Alright Kid," he said as he stood. "Alright…I've got my squad car around yonder; I'll ride around till I see one of them and maybe talk to em a spell. If something turns up, I'll let ya know. But you be sure and watch the way you talk to me son. Family or no family, I won't put up with no attitude in my own county seat," Collier said.

"Fine," I said. "I would appreciate it if you would look into it." With that I turned and walked down the side street where my Ford was parked.

As I got to the car, I opened the door and stood with one arm resting on the roof. I pulled the microphone out of the holder and held it in my hand, watching Collier. If he didn't do something right away, I was going to try to get patched into the State Police. I saw the Sheriff's squad car cruise slowly onto the square on the opposite corner from where I was parked.

"Miller!"

I heard a loud, hoarse whisper.

"Agent Miller!"

It was coming from the little alley beside the post office. I walked over and stepped into the alley. All I saw was a wooden fenced in area around a garbage bin stuffed with packing paper.

"Agent Miller, over here."

Finally, I walked over behind the fence and came face to face with Mark Anthony.

"Mark," I said, "what are you doing back here? Everything okay with your cousin?"

"Yes, Sir Mr. Miller, we are getting along fine, just fine. But I don't have much time. I don't need to be seen talking to you. It wouldn't be safe for me or my cousin."

"I understand," I said.

"Listen," he went on. "Godfrey…Godfrey has put the word out on you. He is gonna kill you Mr. Miller, and I don't want to see that happen."

"Mark, you better not still be hooked up with those Godfrey boys…"

"No, no sir, I promise I am not. But I still know men who are, and I hear things."

"Well, I plan on seeing Godfrey locked up. Sooner or later, I am going to catch him at his still."

"I knew that's what you would want to do Mr. Miller. That's why when I saw your car from the drugstore, I knew I had to make my way over here. You see, I can help you with that still. I don't know where it is, but I know somebody that does."

"Who is that?" I asked.

"You know Punkin Woodley?"

"Oh yeah. I've come across Punkin before."

"He's workin at that still, Mr. Miller. Follow Punkin and you'll find the still."

"Mark, I appreciate this very much. As far as I am concerned, we are even from here on out."

"No sir, I don't see it that way. You gave me a second chance. I owe you more than this little bit."

I stepped out towards the street again and looked across the square. Hardy Collier was tooling around the square slowly in his patrol car. I had done all I could do. The thing with Wallace was Collier's ballgame now. I thanked Anthony again, got into my car, and headed for the far side of Meriwether County.

CHAPTER 19

PUNKIN'

I had no idea what Sivell and Wallace were up to, but all the way back toward the ridge that Punkin Woodley called home what I witnessed on the Square in Greenville nagged at me. Was I getting too concerned with Wallace? Was I just imagining wrongdoing where there was none? So, Wallace hadn't spoken to Sivell and looked uncomfortable, was that really grounds for me to talk to Sheriff Collier?

By now it had been nearly forty-five minutes since I had left the Sheriff. I had yet to hear anything from him on the radio. Had Collier found nothing wrong and figured the situation didn't merit a call back? Probably. Or maybe he just never saw Wallace or Sivell again. Perhaps they knew I spotted them, and they had given up on whatever scheme they were running. There was also the possibility that Collier didn't try very hard to find them.

There were rumors about Collier. Some said he was for hire, and that Wallace had hired him long ago. I knew the sheriff to be lazy and a bit of a coward, but I didn't believe he was *that* crooked. Rose was probably more suspicious of her Sherriff cousin than I was. He wasn't much of a Sheriff, but I didn't think he was a criminal. I had to assume that no news was good news.

For now, I had to get my mind clear. I was in a sparsely populated section of Meriwether County that included some beautiful and deeply wooded areas. An old grist mill sat in a section so pretty that it looked like a painting. Unfortunately, there were also lots of deep "hollers" and heavily wooded creek bottoms, so the whole area was full of moonshine stills.

I passed by the mountain that the locals called "Turkey Knob", crossed Blue Creek, and drove until the road turned from blacktop, to gravel, to red Georgia clay. This dirt road ran for miles into a remote area. I didn't know specifically what house Punkin lived in, but I planned to look until I found him. Normally I wouldn't have gone out this far without Doc. I was getting into an area where a man needed someone to watch his back. Still, I didn't want anyone else to have to get involved in something I considered personal. I was going to get Daniel Godfrey before he got me.

I slowed my car over one deep rut after another, hoping I wasn't about to break an axle or get stuck. Finally, I came to the section of shanties that I had been heading for since I left Greenville. I feared that I would have to knock on lots of doors until I found someone who would tell me where I could find Woodley. Instead, the man I was looking for was right there in the front yard of the first house I came to.

The front porch of Woodley's shack was falling in on one side. Rusty tin was pulled up on the opposite side of the roof by a long-ago windstorm. There was no glass in the windows and almost every screen was torn. Mosquitoes must surely have infested the place. There was a broken bicycle lying on its side in the yard, a chair with three legs balanced on a cinder block next to that, and an old sofa, with dingy cotton spilling out of the cushions, on the front porch.

Punkin was surprised to see me.

"Mister Miller, mawnin to you suh." he said, glaring at me through narrowed eyes. The heavy accent was largely an act. Punkin always did like his sarcasm. He also didn't mean good morning. He really wanted to tell me to go to hell and get out of his yard. Punkin hated me as much as he hated any other law officer.

Woodley had some kind of skin condition, leaving his pale white skin covered in freckles and tiny moles. From a distance it gave him a speckled appearance, like a pumpkin seed. I assumed that's where he got his nickname. Then again, if he had another real name, I'd never heard it.

"Punkin." I touched the brim of my Stetson to acknowledge his greeting.

"An what done brang you all da way out heyah ta Punkin's ol place? You ain't got Mister Doc wid ya?"

As he asked about Doc, he looked past me and into my car.

"Nope, just me," I said. "I'm all by myself today. I thought we could talk straight with each other that way. And since we're talking straight, I'm sure you know why I am here."

"I don know nothing gonna hep you."

He knew I was alone, so he turned up the attitude. It was what I had expected. I was leaning back on the front grill of the Ford, but now I hoisted myself fully upright and stepped steadily toward him. In the past, he might have stonewalled a bit and I would have left, maybe come back and tried again later when he was too drunk to shut up. This time was going to be different. This time, before I left here, Punkin was going to tell me what I needed to know.

"I know you wouldn't lie to me, now would ya, Punkin?" I asked as I stepped into his space. There was a well-worn butcher knife, probably used for cutting off corn or cleaning fish, sticking in a stump to his left, but I had noticed once before that Punkin was right-handed. It was the kind of thing I like to make a mental note of. A man never knows when information like that might come in handy. I had noticed the knife before I got out of the car, but I didn't figure Punkin' would go for it when it was on his opposite side.

I pulled up short about a foot from him. The strong stench of body odor stopped me as much as anything. He was shorter than me, and much more powerful and compact. I had to hope that I was quicker. But then, I didn't intend for this to come to blows.

"Naaawww suuuhhhh," Punkin said, purposely dragging out his words and ramping up his ignorant act. "I wouldn't never lie to you. Why we just a little ol white trash family tryin to scratch out a livin up on this ridge. We don't want no trouble with big law like you."

I ignored the insult.

"You're workin a still for Daniel Godfrey, Punkin. I know you are. Now, before I leave here, I want you to tell me where that still is." Just as I said that, the entire situation changed.

"Daddy!" a little voice called.

I looked past Woodley and saw a little red-haired girl coming out of the shack. She wore a worn and dirty party dress; likely someone else's throw away. The skirt was supposed to be puffed out with a petticoat, which the little girl didn't have. One sleeve was torn off the dress. The little girl's hair was tangled and unkempt. She was only three or four. When I saw her, I took a step back from her father. I didn't want to frighten her.

"Youngun, you get back in dat house and watch dat pot, like I tol ya!"

"But Daddy, I…"

"Get back in dat HOUSE! Fo I do you like I done yo brother."

Involuntarily, the little girl covered her face with her skinny little forearms. She was very afraid of her Daddy. I didn't want to think about what her life with him was like. I wondered where the brother was.

"Didn't know you were a father, Punkin," I said. Now I was the one playing up a sarcastic tone.

He didn't answer. He only looked at me with quiet contempt.

"Looks like you've got stuff to do here Punkin. Why not tell me what I need to know and I'll let you get back to it. Where's Godfrey's still, Punkin? I already got Harold's. I'll eventually find Daniel's too."

He continued to stare in silence.

Now Punkin stepped forward and leaned in so close that the tips of our noses nearly touched.

"What's the matter Miller, Mister Godfrey done made you wet yo pants? You 'fraid to die?" he hissed.

He knew what Godfrey had told me. Hearing Punkin repeat it infuriated me, but I don't think that alone would have made me do what I did next. At least that's what I want to believe. I'll never know for sure, because at that very moment, the door of an old, abandoned chicken coop tied closed with rope began to rattle, then the rope falling to the ground, it flew open. A boy, not a day older than six or seven, came out of the coop. He was weaving as he walked and he fell down twice in his first few steps. I had seen it many times and I could see it in his eyes now. He was drunk.

He got up onto his knees and stared at his hands in disbelief. It was only when he turned his hands over that I saw the flesh hanging from his palms. The little girl ran out to meet him. She was carrying a dirty rag or handkerchief, as if she were going to try to doctor him. Somehow, I just knew what had happened. Punkin Woodley had held that little boy's hands up against the stove. Then he filled him full of moonshine to make him numb and get him to stop crying. I knew it because he had mentioned that the girl needed to watch a pot before he 'done her like he done her brother'. For some reason all of that came together in my mind like pieces of a jigsaw puzzle snapping into place.

I didn't think about my next move. I only reacted. Woodley was looking back at the boy so I stepped on his left foot, leaned back so I could extend my arms and backhanded him as hard as I could across the face.

I caught him off guard and he fell against the stump that held the butcher knife. I heard ribs crack. He grunted but quickly recovered his wits and wrenched the knife out with his right hand. Before it could clear the stump, I kicked him hard in the wrist, breaking his grip and sending the knife flying.

He bull rushed me, coming in low, but I side stepped and brought up a knee into his lips, splitting them both. He went down on his back, rolled and crawled quickly for the knife. I tried to beat him to it, but he got there first. He turned to face me, still on one knee and clutching that rusty butcher knife. There was murder in his eyes as he started to launch himself toward me.

Before he came fully upright, my revolver cleared the holster and I aimed at the bridge of his nose. "That'll be the last step you ever take," I said.

I cocked my pistol and, thinking of what he had done to that boy, I began to squeeze the trigger. Then the little girl ran over to him and she put her arm around his neck. She took that little rag she had and dabbed it at his bloody lips. Punkin pushed her away and she fell on her bottom in the dirt. For the first time I realized something. Punkin was a brute, but he was the only daddy she had ever known. I knew then that if I shot him with them watching, I would hurt those babies more than they had already been hurt.

Punkin sensed my intentions because, when I threw him my keys, had him open my trunk, and made him cuff himself to the spare tire, he didn't protest. Once I had him secured in the trunk of my car, I scooped up those children and put them in the car with me. I found what I could in the house and I drew some water out of what passed for their well. It was the coolest thing I could find to wrap the boy's hands in.

I took them to the hospital over at Warm Springs as fast as that Ford would go, my siren blaring. They had burn treatment facilities there. They also had a foundation where they both could get a hot bath and maybe some long-term care. They would both get a new suit of clothes and hot meals until the foundation could find someone to care for them. On the way, I talked as gently as I could to the children and they confirmed my suspicions about what had happened. The little boy was partly in shock, but even so, he tried to defend Punkin. The little fella had probably been beaten down so often that he felt he deserved what his daddy had done to him.

I walked the two children into the white tiled hallway of the hospital building. There was a fully equipped hospital as well as dormitories for those needing long term care, along with the swimming pools and exercise areas for polio victims that were fed by the natural warm springs in the area. This was where President Roosevelt had sought treatment for his polio, and it was the reason he had the Little White House built here. I decided that I wouldn't mention to the hospital administration that I had a man handcuffed in the sweltering hot trunk of my car.

A clerk walked up to me. She didn't look pleased to see two dirt poor children walking into her hospital.

"Excuse me sir, may I help…"

"It's Miller," I pointed to my badge. "State Agent C. E. Miller and no you can't help me, but you can help these children."

I held the little boy's forearm gently and showed the lady his palms.

"Oh my Lord!" she exclaimed. "That does look very serious, but… umm…well we don't normally see them here," she said.

"By them do you mean poor white trash?" I asked.

"I will thank you Agent Miller to lower your voice. Now I am certain that they can be taken to the clinic over at LaGrange. They do charity work there."

"The problem with that is," I said. "I didn't take them to LaGrange for help. I brought them here." Rather than keeping my voice down, I was getting louder.

"What is going on here?" A man was walking hurriedly up to me in a white coat. He had a stethoscope around his neck. A black nametag with white lettering read, "Dr. Carrington".

"And who might you be?" I asked.

"I am Dr. Leonard Carrington, Chief of Medicine here. Am I to understand that you have brought these children here for treatment? This is not the way we conduct our business here at..."

Before he could finish, I grabbed his upper arm hard and whisked him into the nearest exam room. There was a nurse in the room putting some gauze bandages on a shelf inside a white metal cabinet with glass fronted doors.

"Excuse us a moment, please ma'am," I said. "Dr. Carrington and I have an important law enforcement matter to discuss." I held out the front of my shirt to accentuate my badge. The nurse left the room without asking questions.

"Now see here..." Carrington began.

"No, no sir, you see here. Those children have been through hell. The boy needs emergency burn treatment and they both need a bath, new clothes and a few hot meals until you can get them placed. I work for the state, Doctor. I know you have funding to cover this sort of thing. Now I am personally going to be following up on the welfare of these two children and I just know that when I do, I am going to find out that you have given them nothing less than the best care you can provide here. And if that proves not to be the case, then I am going to consider that a personal matter between me and you."

Whatever he saw in my eyes as I spoke encouraged him to issue no further protest.

"We'll see to it that they are cared for. I can assure you we have nothing but the welfare of all of our patients as our top priority, no matter the circumstances. It was just that you, since you are not the next of kin, bringing them here, that is what made this an irregular circumstance."

"It's settled then," I said.

I jerked the door open and walked back out into the hallway. The nurse that I had run out of the room now had the boy on a gurney and was gently wiping his face with a white washcloth.

"Doctor," she said, "This child has been given some kind of alcohol."

"Yeah," I said. "That was somebody's idea of providing treatment. That's the part of all this I will handle." I knelt down and picked the little girl up.

"Now honey, I know you don't know me and you don't know any of these people. But these nice ladies are going to take good care of you." I reached out and stroked her brother's face. I didn't know which was worse, the site of his hands, or of his red, bloodshot eyes. "I'll be back when I can to check on you."

I handed the girl off to another nurse who had walked up. As I headed back to the front doors, I could hear the Doctor beginning to bark out medical orders.

CHAPTER 20
PULLING THE TRIGGER

I drove Punkin Woodley to the same spot where, just two days before, I had enjoyed a peaceful lunch with Mark Anthony. I had never killed a man. I had never seriously considered it. But I was going to kill Punkin Woodley. I parked in a remote spot and opened the trunk. Punkin was drenched in sweat.

"Hot ain't it Punkin," I quipped though my voice was thick with rage. "Well, it'll be a hell of a lot hotter where you're goin in about 5 minutes."

I stepped over the lip of the trunk and put a boot on the side of his head pushing down hard while I unlocked the handcuffs from my spare tire.

As I marched him down to the creek, a black, dark, anger was rising up in me like I had never known before. "Stop right there, Punkin'" I said. "Kneel down and don't turn to face me or I will gut shoot you and leave you to lie out here clawin' the ground till you bleed out."

I made Punkin kneel down at the bank of White Sulfur Spring. I was unaware that I had drawn my pistol until I heard the hammer cock. The click of the cylinder spinning almost jolted me to my senses, but not quite. I aimed at the base of Punkin's skull, and I started to squeeze the trigger, but for some reason I hesitated.

I shook my head violently to clear it and began to take up the slack on my trigger. And then I thought I heard a voice. It wasn't an audible voice but a voice in my head. It said, "Cullen, I didn't call you to this so that you could be *like* them."

That was it. No burning bush, no angel appearing. The voice was brief, but I knew all that it meant. I couldn't do this thing I was about to do. If I did, I wouldn't be any better than Punkin, or the Godfrey's or John Wallace. I would *be* them. I took my finger off the trigger and let the hammer down on my Smith. Punkin heard that, and for the first time in a while, he spoke up.

"Give me another chance, Agent Miller," he said.

The sarcasm was all gone.

"Don't kill me out here," he pleaded. "I'm gonna live right if you'll let me go."

He was lying and I knew it. I also realized that he was genuinely scared, maybe for the first time in his life.

I flopped down near that same stump where Mark Anthony and I had eaten. I suddenly felt washed out. I took a deep breath and did something I didn't want to do at that moment. I prayed. And when I finished, I knew Punkin would live after all.

"The way you are feeling right now," I said. "That's how your little boy felt before you burned him like you did."

I saw Punkin's shoulders start to shake. I sensed he was sobbing for himself, not for his son.

I tilted my Stetson back on my head and realized how dry my mouth was. I walked over to the spring and scooped water into my cupped hand, gulping it down. Then I splashed some on my face and neck. Punkin was still kneeling with his back to me.

"If you ever want to come out of this bottom," I told him, my face still dripping. "You'll tell me where Daniel Godfrey's still is and you'll do it in the next thirty seconds." With that I stood, placed my hat back on straight and listened as Punkin' Woodley told me everything I wanted to know.

I put him back in my car and headed up the road to the Greenville jail. I would do everything in my power to make sure that he went from there to the penitentiary.

CHAPTER 21
DRAMA AT THE JAILHOUSE

I drove back across the same square where I had seen Wallace and Sivell just hours earlier. I pulled up to the curb at the Greenville jail and parked. The old jail had been built in the 1880's. It included an indoor tower where they held hangings until the 1920's. Though I had been here many times, the place still made the hair stand up on the back of my neck. I walked around the car and got Punkin out. I had let him ride in the back seat after we left the springs.

I marched into the front door of the jail and saw that there was no deputy on duty to check in my prisoner. I called out and heard shuffling in the back room where there was a coffee pot and a small lunch table. I led Punkin by the elbow and stuck my head in the back room door. Jake, the jailer, was in the room by himself. One of his eyes was swollen nearly shut.

"Jake," I said. "What happened to you, and where's the deputy on duty?"

"I done the best I knowed how," Jake said. He was twisting a handkerchief around and around his forefinger nervously.

"What are you talking about Jake? I have a prisoner here."

Jake didn't answer but instead waved his hand at a ring of keys on the table across from him.

"I done my best. I tried to do like da Sheriff said."

I frowned. Jake had always been a bit simple minded but this wasn't just muttering. He was trying to tell me something.

I stepped over and got the keys. "I am going to lock this man up, and then I'll be back and we'll talk," I said.

Jake shuffled nervously in his chair. He stood up, holding onto one corner of the table. Then he sat back down again.

"Okay," he said. "Alright den."

I found an empty cell and pushed Punkin in, slamming the door behind him.

"Turn your back to the bars and push your wrists over here."

As he did so, I took the cuffs off. Punkin looked up at me and I saw a glimmer of that old hate and bitterness in his face. His remorse was short lived, as I suspected it would be. He started to speak, but instead went over and flopped down on the crude cot suspended from the red brick wall with two heavy angled chains.

I walked over to the log book and logged him in. Then, something made me glance at the name above his. I felt a knot deep in the pit of my stomach and my throat began to tighten. There, one line up, was the name Wilson Turner. He had been logged in last night…then someone had started to log him out but stopped writing. There were only the numerals "12" in the column for hours. That would have been today, sometime after noon. I had seen Wallace and Sivell this morning at 11:30. I looked at my watch. It was fifteen after three now.

"Jake, was Wilson Turner in here today? What was he in…"

I stepped into the back room again. Jake was gone.

My mind was racing. What was going on here? I ran outside and headed for my car. Suddenly I heard the unique sound of a state trooper's siren. Then I heard the trooper's car speeding along the highway, coming towards the square. I jogged to the corner in time to see a Georgia State Patrol car heading my way with the blue light flashing. It was J. C. Otwell. I flagged him down.

"J.C., what's going on around here? Jake was in there with a black eye and…"

"No time now, Miller, I am headed to Coweta county," Otwell said. "Looks like we have an assault up there. Sheriff Potts is already on the scene. He says they found a new pickup truck abandoned in the parking lot where the assault took place. Registration says it belongs to a boy named Turner."

Otwell spun the tires of his patrol car as he sped away, leaving me standing with my mouth agape.

• • •

I had the accelerator to the floor as I headed toward Coweta County, my siren blaring. I had tried to get through to Otwell or the Coweta Sheriff, Lamar Potts, on my radio, but I could barely make out what the dispatcher was saying. My signal was too weak. I tried to put the microphone back but missed the hook and the mic tumbled to the floor. I was rattled…bad.

Had I gotten Wilson Turner beat up? And where was he now? What was happening to him? My mind was racing so fast that it took me a minute to remember my midnight meeting with John Wallace. "If you don't run Turner out of the state, I am going to kill him," Wallace had promised. I knew something wasn't right about Wallace when I saw him earlier this morning. Had he gone to the jail and grabbed Turner somehow? Is that what Jake was afraid to tell me? Is that why Jake had a black eye? And why didn't Sheriff Collier do something like I asked him? What's more, I had warned his deputy about Wallace's threats on the night he made them.

The Ford began to shudder, and when I looked down at the speedometer I was doing over 100 miles an hour. I had never driven it that fast. I lifted my foot off the gas a bit. I couldn't help Turner if I wrapped my car around a tree.

I didn't know where I was going. All Otwell said was that the assault was in Coweta County. I pulled a big breath in, and then let it out slowly as I drove. I thought back over what I knew. All that I knew for certain was that Turner had been missing for days. I had just seen where he had been logged into the Greenville jail yesterday and that someone stopped before logging him out. This morning I saw Wallace and his best friend Sivell acting suspicious in the bank. Now Otwell had just told me Turner's truck was in Coweta at the site of an assault.

Then I realized something else. At the same time I was telling Sheriff Hardy Collier to watch Wallace and Sivell, Turner was sitting in Collier's jail only a half hour from being released. Had something happened to Turner right after he had been released from jail?

My car came up out of a dip and I saw lights flashing far ahead. If those lights were in Coweta County, then they were just barely across the line.

I turned off the siren and let it wind down as I slowed the car. As I crossed the county line I coasted to a stop behind the Coweta Sheriff's cruiser, which was parked at the Sunset Truck Stop. Trooper Otwell's car and one other one were parked to one side. I knew the place a bit. I had eaten in the diner here a few times. As I stepped out of my car, I saw a new pickup and recalled what Turner's wife had said about Wilson acting pretentious for having a new vehicle. My heart was in my throat at the site of it. The driver's door was still open and there were skid marks from the pavement and across the dirt leading right to it. Turner had raced the truck to within ten yards of the front door of the diner.

I jumped out of my car and into the hot sun. It was then that I realized who the third car belonged to.

"Miller, you just head back to Talbot County where you belong. We got this investigation under control." The voice belonged to L. Z Hitchcock.

"Get out of my way, L. Z. I've got an interest in this case."

"What interest do you have?" he asked. I pushed past him and walked toward J. C, whose uniform shirt was soaked through with perspiration around the throat, chest and underarms. I figured I probably looked about the same.

"Miller, what did you come all the way out on this one for?" Otwell asked.

Before I could answer, Lamar Potts stepped out of the restaurant, followed by the owner and cook Steve Smith, who was still wearing his white kitchen apron. The two of them were followed by a man with a red gingham napkin still stuffed into his shirt collar. Potts was writing some notes in a tablet.

My jurisdiction on liquor cases stretched all over the state. I had worked two or three cases through Sheriff Potts' office and had always found him to be a solid sheriff and a decent man. He was a no-nonsense type. I guess we had that in common.

He looked up at me. "Agent Miller," he nodded. "We have a lot going on here. What brings you to my crime scene?"

"I knew Turner," I said. I didn't want to say much in front of L. Z. because, quite frankly, I didn't trust him.

"The same Turner who owned that truck?"

"Yes," I said, taking note that he used the past tense.

"I have some information that may be helpful," I continued.

Potts looked up at me from underneath the brim of his hat, which he wore low in the front, as I did mine. When I said no more, he sensed that I wanted to talk away from the others.

"Let's step over to my car," he said. "L.Z., I sure would appreciate it if you would head towards Meriwether and see what you can find out from your contacts."

L. Z. eyed me suspiciously. He was jealous and he desperately wanted to know what I was about to tell Potts. But he wanted to please the Sheriff more.

"I'll see if anybody knows anything. I'll call you later at your office."

"I appreciate your help."

I remained poker faced. Hitchcock wouldn't find out anything. Nobody around Stovall was going to talk to him after Hitchcock had shot one of their own. They especially weren't going to tell him anything about John Wallace.

"There goes the best tracker in the state of Georgia," Potts said admiringly. I knew right then that I couldn't trust Potts with impunity. If he didn't have any better judgment than to buy what L. Z. Hitchcock was selling, then he might not be quite as savvy as I thought. I said nothing about my opinion of Hitchcock.

Instead, I told Potts what I had seen in the bank between Wallace and Sivell. I even told him about my meeting with Wallace. Finally, I told him about my negotiations with Turner back when I caught him at his own still.

"I am mighty afraid that I pushed the kid too hard. Sheriff, I may have gotten that boy beaten, maybe killed."

Potts stared at me intently for a long time, then said, "I don't know much about this case yet, but something tells me that isn't what led to this. It sure as heck isn't all that led to it. No, there was something more going on here, Miller." Potts turned and looked at the torn screen door of the restaurant, the signs of an intense struggle in the sandy parking lot, and the sand and gravel that had been thrown from the getaway car.

"Right now, the victim is missing. The assailants are missing, and I've got a diner full of witnesses who all say they saw a man beaten nearly to death in this parking lot. Something dark happened here Miller, something that was fueled by hate."

CHAPTER 22
IT RATTLES A MAN

I should have done more. That thought kept rolling around over and over in my head as I stood in the dusty parking lot of the Sunset Truck Stop. I had seen Wallace and Sivell outside the Courthouse some twenty miles from here and I had trusted that Sheriff Collier *would* question them and find out what was going on. My priority at that time had to be following up on the lead Mark Anthony had given me. Chasing around after Wallace within Greenville city limits hadn't been my job or jurisdiction.

None of that mattered however, as I stood here now, looking down at a combination of clay, sand, and what I suspected was Wilson Turner's blood. The spot was right next to the tire tracks of the assailant's car. This had to be the work of Wallace. It just had to be. I had offered as much to Potts, but he wasn't ready to name suspects just yet. This investigation was still new to him. I had been pursuing John Wallace for years. I had heard him threaten to kill Turner. I knew Wallace had done this.

Potts and his brother, who was also his deputy, had questioned all the witnesses, including an elderly man from across the highway, and a woman who lived two lots over from the diner, and gone back to their office. They were going to call the state crime lab to come and dust the truck for prints. They also asked Trooper Otwell if he would head back to Meriwether County. There were already reports coming in that the assailants had chased Turner through a construction site, even firing shots from the car. The commotion caused some of the men working on the road to focus in on the man hanging out the window shooting at Turner. A positive ID was possible.

As for me, I walked over to an outdoor cooler, lifted a bottle of RC cola out, and popped the top in the installed opener. I would go in and pay before I left. I stepped over to an outdoor bench alongside the door of the diner and plopped down like a sack of flour. In one day, I had appeared in court and been awarded an automobile, which I sold for nearly half a year's salary. I had an adrenaline rush from the Wallace/Sivell sighting, talked to Collier, gotten an explosive tip, driven into the boonies to end up in a fight with Punkin Woodley, rushed two children to the foundation for treatment, contemplated murder, heard from God, realized that the missing Turner had been right under my nose at the Greenville jail, and then raced across the county line to discover that he had been beaten.

At the very least I needed an RC and a minute or two to gather my wits. I pushed my Stetson back on my head, mopped my forehead with my handkerchief and took a long draw off the cold bottle. Just then Steve Smith, the owner of the diner and truck stop, let the screen door slap closed behind him. I reached in my pocket and flipped him a dime for the RC. He caught the coin in midair.

He sat down on the bench beside me. "Well, this situation has killed my bidness for the rest of the day, that's for sure." He looked at me and tried to manage a chuckle, but neither of us was in a laughing mood. "You're name's Miller, ain't it? Revenuer from over at Talbot County? I believe you've been in here to eat before."

"I have," I answered. Then holding the pop in my left hand I leaned over and shook his with my right.

"You kind of look like you're done in," he said. "You know anything about all this?"

"More than I care to," I said.

I said no more and he realized I wasn't going to share any information.

"What do you think of Potts?" he asked.

"I only worked with him a couple of times. He seems like a good lawman."

"Yeah," Smith said. "Most folks around here think a lot of him."

I drank some more RC. I was going to do something about Turner and Wallace. I just wasn't sure what. At the same time, I had the best tip I had ever had on the location of Daniel Godfrey's still. We were quiet for a long time. Then Smith, staring blankly into the distance, spoke up.

"It rattles a man," he said. "Man like you might get numb to it. Man in your bidness might get used to seeing things like what I saw today. I never have seen nothing like it I can tell you. Wish I hadn't seen it still."

"I've seen some things," I said. "But I ain't used to it. I hope to the Lord I never get used to it."

Steve shook his head for a long time. He was doing what good people do in these situations. He was replaying it in his head. It would replay for a long time. It would never fully go away.

"It was an awful thing they done to that boy," he said. "He fought. I tell you he fought like a wild animal, but he wasn't no size. I wish now I had done more, but I was so stunned I couldn't think."

"Yeah, I know what you mean," I said, "about wishing you had done more."

He didn't seem to notice what I had said.

"That bald fella, the one who claimed he was a guard from the Greenville jail, he was in a rage man, a rage like I ain't never seen before. He whaled on that boy, first with a pistol then...." Steve Smith, with his big thick wrists and massive forearms resting on his apron, began to cry. He gathered himself again.

"Then he took a sawed-off shotgun that other white haired man was holding,"

"A big bald headed man and a man with white hair," I thought. "That's Wallace and Sivell alright."

Smith went on with the story that I didn't want to hear, but that I had to hear.

"He took that shotgun and he came overhanded like he was going to chop wood with it, and he brought them double barrels down on that boys head….the boy was holding onto the sides of the opening of the car door and he was screaming…man, I mean he was screaming… 'Somebody help me! Help me! They're gonna kill me!' he says."

Smith's voice broke again and he wiped vigorously at his eyes with a corner of his white apron.

"He had his feet up on the edge of the floorboard and was holding on with his hands on either side of the door and they both couldn't get him in that car, but when he hit him with that shotgun, it went off and, Agent Miller, that boy went limp as a dishrag."

I felt my throat start to burn and I grit my teeth. I suddenly saw Mrs. Turner all frantic in that kitchen of hers. She was still living in Wallace's sharecropper shack. Somebody would have to tell her what happened to her husband. Somebody might have to protect her.

Steve was bent over, elbows resting on his knees. His head kept shaking from side to side slowly, trying to get his mind around what he had witnessed. I put my hand on his shoulder and squeezed.

"It will be hard for you for a long time. You just have to go on with your daily work. Keep living your life. Stay busy. The busier you are, the less time you will have to replay what's going through your head right now."

He looked over at me for a few seconds with what seemed to be relief, and maybe appreciation in his eyes.

"I've got to go," I said. "I am not on this case but I'm on another one that's related. I can work mine and maybe help find this boy, if he is alive somewhere."

I stood up, put my Stetson on firmly and took a few steps towards my car. I heard Smith speak up again. I didn't turn to face him this time. His voice suddenly sounded like a lost child's.

"Agent Miller," he said weakly. "That bald man, he jumped in the back seat on top of that boy. I didn't tell the Sheriff this and I don't know why, maybe I was ashamed. But he jumped in on top of that boy, and the boy was in the floor all limp. The other man, the white-haired man, he ran around and drove out of here screeching tires and all. And I looked up into that back window as they headed back to Meriwether County, and Agent Miller, that bald man had that boy pulled up by the hair of his head and he just wouldn't stop beating him with that pistol. I never saw such rage in a man. I never saw such hate. He whaled on that poor limp boy all the way up the road till I couldn't see them no more."

He took a deep but ragged breath. He was trying not to sob. "Something like that Agent Miller, it rattles a man."

I looked down the highway and toward the Meriwether County line. All this trouble had moved back there, across that imaginary line that bisected the pavement. It was a line I knew I had to cross and trouble that I knew I would get in the middle of. It was late afternoon, and the heat waves were shimmering off the pavement, the sun still white hot.

"Yeah," I said. "I know what you mean."

CHAPTER 23
DEEP IN THE SWAMP

I went back to the Greenville jail. Hardy Collier still wasn't there, so I gassed up my car. I had done quite a bit of driving today. Then I pulled over at the Courthouse and got the clerk to let me use the phone to call Rose. I told her that an urgent case had come up and that a man's life was in danger. I told her I would be very late getting home. After her usual cautions, I assured her that I would be careful and started to hang up the phone. Then I stopped.

"Rose, honey, I love you very much," I said. "I have heard of and seen some things today that just made me want to tell you that. I don't tell you often enough."

Rose was taken aback. She shouldn't have been. She should have been used to hearing that I loved her.

"I…I love you too, Kid…Cullen," she said quietly. I sat the receiver down gently in the cradle and noticed that the female clerk smiled up at me sympathetically.

I got into my car and tried to reach Doc on the radio to see if he wanted to meet me at John Wallace's place. I usually had good reception in Greenville. The elevation was a little higher than surrounding areas. Still, I couldn't raise him and I wasn't willing to wait.

I drove past the jail again and this time I took a longer look at the old building. There was such an eerie air about the place. I looked up at the barred windows and imagined Wilson Turner peering out, probably calling down to passersby for help. I turned on my siren and hurried toward John Wallace's farm.

Wallace had 2,000 acres, much of it covered in heavy woods and swamp. There was no telling where he had taken Turner. He could be beating him right now, or lynching him for all I knew. I figured Sherriff Potts would be here soon, but I had seen no sign of him as I drove by Wallace's house, turning my siren off a full mile before I got even with his driveway. There were no cars at the house either, which led me to wonder if Wallace was still about some awful task.

I drove past his house and went straight to Mrs. Turners place. There was a black Ford pickup, looked to be about a '40 model, with stake bed sides, backed up to the front door. I stopped well away, got out of my car, and stood behind the open door. I rested my hand on the butt of my gun and kept my thumb ready on the hammer.

About that time an old man in overalls with a white dress shirt, buttoned all the way up, even in this heat, stepped out of the house. He sat an apple crate brimming over with stuff into the back of the pickup. He startled noticeably when I called out to him.

"I'm Agent C. E. Miller, Georgia Department of Revenue," I said.

"You liked to scared me into a coronary, officer," the man said. He looked drawn and haggard. He was jumpy.

"I apologize. I thought you heard me pull up. I'm here to talk to Mrs. Turner. Can you tell me where I might find her? There is something she needs to know."

"You mean about that fool husband of hers. I told her about that boy. He don't have no judgement. I told him over a year ago that if he kept messin' around with John Wallace, he was going to end up dead. I told him that over a year ago."

I felt myself relax a little. Even with all I had heard from everyone I talked to about the history of bad blood between Turner and Wallace, I was still carrying the weight that my trying to turn Turner into an informant had caused this. But if Turner's father-in-law had warned him over a year ago, then it proved that the boy was in danger long before I raided his still.

"So Mrs. Turner already knows…"

"I came out here and told her about it. She aint got no phone. He had all his fancy liquor money to buy trucks but he didn't get my daughter no phone. I went in to Greenville this morning and the whole town was talking about a car chase. Said some black haired boy, sounded just like Wilson the way they described him, had been released from jail and gone tearing through town in a pickup with John Wallace and another man chasin' him in a car. Next thing I knew folks was already talkin about some deal up in Coweta County. Somethin's done happened. Somethin awful, I just know it. I told that boy. I told him and told him. I've done got my daughter and that baby out of here. I got em far away from Wallace and his kind."

The man sat down heavy on his tailgate and wiped his eyes with his handkerchief. I tried to think of something comforting to say.

"Sir, we don't know…"

"He was cocky….Wilson was. Cocky and didn't know his place in this world. I told him, a man like Wallace ain't gonna be crossed up by the likes of you. I told him he better give him that money back. He wouldn't listen. Then he went and took those high priced Guernsey cows. That's what done it. I just know that's what got him killed."

"He may still be alive, sir," I said.

For the first time the man looked me straight in the eye.

"You really believe that?"

I wanted to say that I did, but I hesitated, and Turner's father-in-law looked back down at the ground.

"I didn't like him sometimes, but I loved him. He was good to my girl most times."

"I'm gonna go now sir," I said. "I'm going to look for Wilson."

He only nodded and looked at the ground once more. Before I could get my door closed, he called out to me again. I stood halfway up and looked through the seam between the door and the windshield.

"God Bless ya, son!" The old man called out. "I'll pray for ya to find him."

• • •

I drove the Ford around as much of the perimeter of Wallace's place as I could get to. I was looking for anything that might tip me as to where they had taken Turner. I wondered if Wallace would take the risk of hiding a body on his own property. I knew Wallace owned multiple small farms, in addition to his main property. Turner could be on any one of them. Wallace would want to regain control of this situation. He certainly hadn't controlled it earlier. After all, look at all that had gone wrong. I had spotted him just before the chase began and then Turner had made it into Coweta County where Wallace had no pull. Things weren't going as they'd been planned, I was sure of that.

As I looked for signs of Wallace, Sivell, or Turner, I also kept looking for anything that might lead me to the still. If I could lock Wallace up for moonshine, he couldn't come after Turner anymore, assuming Turner wasn't already dead. I was trying to be hopeful, but after talking to Turner's father-in-law, I wasn't very confident.

Finally, I turned into a rutted road that had once been used when Wallace cut timber off the back of his place. It was thick back there. It would be rough walking. That's where I would go if I was trying to hide something…or someone. I stopped when the road got so rough that I couldn't drive anymore. I got out and started looking around on foot. I opened my trunk and changed into some Chippewa high topped boots. I had a canteen as well that I put around my neck. I kept such items in my car all the time. A man in my line of work never knew when a walk in deep woods might be called for.

I started searching toward the west. Because timber had been cut here recently, there was no tree canopy, and bright sunlight could reach all the way to the ground. That sunlight had caused the weeds and blackberry briars to thrive. I was having a devil of a time getting through the thicket. I was looking down and watching my step closely, when I saw it. I couldn't believe I even noticed it. There, laying on top of a sweetgum leaf from last fall, was a button. It was a light green button, similar to what might have come from a man's shirt. I looked around closely, squinting my eyes so as not to miss any clue. Then I saw something else. There was light green thread caught on one of the briars. I put both the thread and the button in my shirt pocket and kept looking.

I thought back to that night I had talked to Wilson Turner at the still. It had been dark with only lanterns for light. Yet, I was pretty certain that Turner had been wearing a green shirt. I continued to search through the thicket and on into where mature oak bottoms began. I pushed deep into the forest as daylight turned to dusk and then into the black of night, but I didn't find any more clues. I looked for more thread, I looked for footprints, I looked for scuff marks that a man might leave if he was being dragged. I found nothing.

I listened for voices, hoping to hear Wallace cursing Turner...anything to point me in a direction. I used my flashlight as much as I dared. I didn't want to spook anyone away if they were still nearby. After hours of searching and with my canteen having been empty for some time, I was starting to stumble. I hadn't eaten since breakfast of the previous day and I had put my body through a lot in the past sixteen hours. Even if I headed back now, I still had a long, difficult walk to my car.

I finally admitted to myself that I wasn't going to find Wilson Turner tonight. As I made my way back to the car, my flashlight off, and with the sound of tree frogs all around, I came to a gigantic cypress stump, the left over remnant of some ancient logging operation. I sat down heavily using the smooth side of the stump as a passable backrest. I was exhausted, probably dehydrated, and all out of adrenaline. I wondered if it was too late. I had come to a place where the trees were tall and the forest canopy was thick. I looked up through the tree limbs to see a bright full moon. I wondered if Turner was seeing it. I wondered if he could.

CHAPTER 24

DAYBREAK STROLL

As I shuffled back to my car, I had time to think. Turner's father in law had said the trouble between him and Wallace had gone back a year. He also confirmed that there had been a cattle theft. The loss of the cows would not have interrupted Wallace's primary income stream, which I believed was liquor. But registered cattle were expensive. What's more, Wallace was proud of them. He was the only man for three counties that had any like them. He liked to talk about them at the sale barn.

If Turner was spoiling batches of moonshine, as I had witnessed, possibly skimming off Wallace's liquor proceeds, and stealing cattle, and if Wallace then found one of those cows with its throat cut…Wallace would never take that from anyone. Maybe if Wallace found out that Turner talked to me, that was the last straw, but not likely. Wallace losing those cattle was the last straw.

I got back to the car and was so tired that I nearly fell asleep when I sat down in the seat. I needed to get home and get some food and rest. I started the Ford and got turned around. I eased down the logging trail but once I got out onto the dirt road, I was driving fast. I had had enough. I wanted to get far away from Stovall, at least for a while.

I was going too fast for the road. The car lost traction around one curve, then another. Still, I didn't slow down much. The car bounced hard as I crossed a wooden bridge. For some reason, everything hit me at once and I was ready to get home and see Rose and Judy. The car topped the next hill after the little bridge and I slammed on the brakes hard. The road was suddenly filled with dogs…and one old lady.

The car skidded across the packed clay and gravel. I pulled the wheel hard to the right, deciding to put it into the ditch if I had to, rather than plow through the lady and her dogs. I turned back to the center slightly, fighting to keep the car on the road. I finally came to a stop with my front tire not more than two inches from the ditch. I felt my knees go watery.

I sat in the car for a few seconds to collect myself. I really didn't need this today. I opened the door and got out. I looked around for the old lady. She startled me again by walking silently right up behind me. I wheeled around.

"Lady, what the heck are you doing walking down the middle of the road in the dark? Are you trying to get killed?"

"What the hell are you doing racing up and down this road in the dark?" she shot back, one hand on her hip and her jaw set. "You trying to run somebody over?"

I was taken aback, partly by her response and partly by her appearance. The woman was very tall, close to six feet. She wore a long skirt made out of flour sacks, and men's brogans on her feet. An army cap, maybe something like MacArthur would wear, rested slightly crooked on her head. And staring back at me, with the dome light from my car reflecting off it, was a glass eye.

"Ma'am, I am not trying to be disrespectful, but you and those dogs were hard to see in the dark. You really gave me a scare. I thought I was going to hit you."

She leaned back and squinted at me, clearly rolling my words over in her mind. After another long pause she spoke again.

"I don't care for walks in the heat of the day, and we don't have all this traffic where I come from. I am down here staying with kin, me and my elderly sister. It ain't safe for ladies at my home right now. I been robbed twice this year."

The lady had to be in her seventies, and I found myself wondering how old that would make her sister.

"I'm sorry to hear about you being robbed," I said, not really believing that I was having this talk, with this woman, at this hour of the night, in the middle of nowhere, after spending hours looking for a victim of assault, and probably murder.

"You should at least walk well over to one side of the road," I cautioned. "I can't think of a house near here. Where are you walking *to* exactly?"

She didn't answer, but she leaned in toward me. I almost thought she was going to kiss me, but instead she peered deeply into my eyes. She pulled back abruptly and cocked her head, squinting at me once again out of the corner of her one good eye.

"All these years and I finally meet one face to face."

"What are you talking about Ma'am?" I was too tired for this and my tone reflected how annoyed I was getting. "Lady, I've been out all night…"

"Kind of man Diogenes was lookin for. You got a problem though. Think it's up to you to right all the wrongs. The Book might call that pride."

I didn't answer. I just stood there looking confused.

"Some does it because they think a badge makes em someone they ain't, but not you." She chuckled to some joke I wasn't privy to. "No sir, you do your job for different reasons. Some of which you don't understand yourself I'd imagine." She laughed out loud and doodled in the dust of the road with the end of a walking stick I hadn't noticed before.

"I don't think I follow," I began.

Suddenly her head jerked back. She began to moan. She looked back at me and her one good eye had rolled back into her head. Despite myself, I recoiled for a second. Then I began to wonder if she was having a heart attack or something.

"Ma'am are you…"

"I see walls," she said in a voice that suddenly sounded very different. "Rock walls are all around. They're pressing in on him. It's like a tunnel, and he's trapped inside it. There's water in the tunnel. He can't see because he's in the water and closed in by all that dark and all that cold."

Was she still talking to the dogs? "Walls pressing in on whom? On me?" I asked. "What tunnel? Lady I don't know what you're talking about."

She held her hand out like a traffic cop yelling "STOP" and then let that same hand reach up and stroke her own face. She rubbed her face several times, first one side then the other. She began to hum, as if she were doing a chant. Suddenly she cried out and her eyes flew open wide. Her countenance was different now. She had a faraway look about her. Then, she set her jaw again, and placing both hands atop the walking stick she pounded it on the surface of the red clay road twice, like a judge would his gavel once sentence had been pronounced. She gave a dramatic bob to her head and stood there, staring at me. She seemed very satisfied with herself.

I stared back, blankly. I had no idea what had just happened.

She hissed, like a cat, and waved a hand at me dismissively.

"You don't have no idea what I'm talking about, do you? Are you thick in the head? What you been lookin' for out here all night?"

I was stunned. Was she talking about Turner? How could she know anything about me or what I was doing?

"Ma'am," I said. "I want to get your name and information. Excuse me just a second."

When I had returned to the car earlier, I had pulled my sweat soaked shirt off and was now wearing only my white tee shirt. I reached inside the car and fumbled around in my shirt pocket for my tablet and pencil. I stood back up.

"Ma'am, tell me…"

She was gone. She had simply vanished. I didn't see her. I didn't see any of the dogs. I stepped away from the car and listened for leaves rustling or twigs breaking. Nothing. I reached inside the car and got my flashlight. I shone it into the woods all around and on both sides of the road but the batteries had gotten weak and the beam didn't sweep far. I couldn't see or hear her anywhere. After all that I had seen and heard today, I was in no shape to go looking for her. I drove home nearly in a state of shock.

CHAPTER 25

CHIEF CALLING

I arrived home about seven o'clock in the morning. I was too tired to eat. Rose hadn't heard about Wallace or Turner and I only gave her the basics. I didn't mention my meeting with the old lady. I couldn't get my mind around it myself. I took a quick bath to wash off the swamp and the sweat, and fell into bed, hopeful that the world might make sense when I woke up.

I had asked Rose to wake me at noon. I'd been so tired that I hadn't turned down the bed or even changed positions. I got up stiff and sore. I gulped a couple of mugs of coffee and Rose fixed me a plate for lunch. For some reason, after waking, I no longer felt there was a chance to save Wilson Turner's life. I couldn't be sure whether my meeting with the old lady had anything to do with that. Still, I decided to go back and look for Turner, or his body, right away. I was wrapping my gun belt around my waist when I heard a knock at the door. There was a bad wind blowing through our area and I didn't want Rose to answer it.

"I'll get that," I called out to her.

"I've got it," she reached for the doorknob before I could stop her.

"It's Doc," she said opening the door.

I breathed a sigh of relief, but tried not to let Rose notice my concern.

"Doc, I think Kid left a swig of coffee in the pot if you want a cup."

"No thank you, Rose," Doc said. "Too hot outside for me to drink any after about seven o'clock. Besides, Ollie Bell and me just ate lunch. Bacon, lettuce and tomato sandwiches. Mighty fine this time of year."

"I love those too, Doc," Rose said. "I think you've just inspired me as to what I am going to fix for supper. Kid was out all night so our meals have gotten flip flopped a bit."

Doc looked over at me quickly. I had gone out again without him and he was hurt by it. We had had disagreements about this in the past. Doc couldn't understand why sometimes I just operated better by myself. This time was more sensitive however, because it was the first time I had seen Doc since our argument over Mark Anthony.

Rose looked from me to Doc and back again.

"I'm going to take Judy out to the swing for a bit," she said. "I'll see you later Doc."

"So you were out all night last night, were you?" Doc asked.

"I was," I said.

"Did it have anything to do with this mess up at Coweta County?"

"It did." I answered.

"So are we ridin' together anymore or what?" Doc asked. "You gonna just go it alone full time now?"

"I don't know Doc, you tell me?"

"Aww hell, Kid! You still sore about what happened after court the other day? That wasn't nothin'. You know how I get sometimes."

"Yeah Doc, I know how you get, and sometimes I need a break from it. And sometimes there's stuff I need to do that you might not need to be a part of. And when those times come again, and they will, I don't want to keep having this same conversation. Now that's just the way it is. If you can live with that, then we ride together. If you can't, then I'll talk to the Chief."

Doc jerked his head to one side as if I had slapped him. I liked the old boy. I didn't want to hurt his feelings. But these were serious times and our work was dangerous. I had to do the job the way that was best. I couldn't worry about feelings.

"I can live with it, Kid," he said reluctantly. "But you need to know that the Chief is the reason I'm here. He can't get through on your phone and he told me to come and find you and have you call him right away."

"Doc, if you called him on me…"

"I didn't call him!" Doc nearly shouted. I had offended him again and I was instantly sorry. "Hitchcock called him!"

I looked down at the floor of my den. "I'm sorry Doc," I said. "I should have known. What did Hitchcock say?"

"I don't know. Chief didn't tell me anything other than he wanted you to call right away. He's been trying to call here and the town switchboard is acting up again."

Before I went to the phone, I pulled open a drawer in the kitchen and took out my checkbook. I tore out a check that I had written while I was eating and handed it to Doc. Then I stepped over to my phone.

"Holy Moses!" Doc exclaimed. "This is a check for nine hundred and thirty two dollars. What in the world are you giving me this for?"

"That's your half of what I sold that confiscated Chrysler automobile for."

Doc stood there with his mouth open for a minute before saying, "Kid, I don't know what to say. I wasn't there that day. You made that bust."

"We're partners aren't we?" I asked. "The only thing I was waiting on was to hear what you just said a minute ago."

Doc shuffled from one foot to another. Maybe a part of him wanted to tell me to keep the money. Maybe his pride wanted him to turn it down. But times were tough and he couldn't.

"Kid, I uh…" he stammered. "I, umm, really appreciate uh… Hey, I hear you busted up ol Punkin pretty good. You're gonna save everybody in this county or die trying, aren't ya?"

He was teasing me now, but it was good natured and I smiled. I started telling him about Punkin, as well as the bust I had made at Roxanne Coleman's house in Manchester, but the phone rang before I could finish.

"Hello," I said.

"That you Miller?" It was my Chief. He had called me before I could call him, which would not be good.

Chief Edgar Thompson had come up through the ranks of the Atlanta Police Department. He was used to big city life and big city crooks. He was tough as nails. He came over to the Department of Revenue to start up the enforcement division, the branch I worked for, back in '38. I had watched him build this department from nothing. I had been with the Chief since the beginning. He liked me and trusted me. That wouldn't even slow him down, however, when it came time to chew me out.

"Miller, what the heck are you doing down there? Are you going maverick on me 'cause I'll bring you to heel so fast it'll make your head spin."

"Chief, I didn't…"

"Hitchcock called me," the Chief interrupted. "He says you were up at Coweta County yesterday poking around an ongoing assault investigation that might turn into a murder case. I pay you to find liquor stills, not to work for the Sheriff's department. Is that understood?"

"Yes Sir, I was only…"

"You want to do a good deed? Go find Wallace's still and leave the rest of it to Pitts or Potts or whatever his name is. So that's item one. Now for item two."

There was going to be an item two.

"I got a call from the administrator of the Warm Springs Foundation. He says you brought two black children in there, one of them burned pretty badly. Then you threatened one of the doctors if he didn't take care of the two of them. Later, the kids told him you took their Daddy away."

"I did take him away. I took him to the Greenville jail. He's there now. I was going over to the courthouse to file charges against him today."

"The kids said you had their daddy in the trunk of your car. That's a little out of order, wouldn't you say?"

"I figured it would be best if he didn't ride up front with the two children he abused, but maybe I'm off base on that, sir," I said.

"Don't get smart with me, Miller," the Chief said.

"I had intended to have the Sheriff take custody of Woodley and the children but he was indisposed and then I got all caught up in this Wilson Turner case."

"Well, get un –caught up in it. That case is not your affair. I suspect the local Sheriff will be calling for volunteers to look for the victim's body soon. If he does, you and Cook can go help. Maybe you will find Wallace's still while you are looking for the body. You sure haven't found it any other way. And stop trying to rescue every poor child in the state of Georgia will you? Get back to doing *your* job! Find stills and bust bootleggers and moonshiners. That's it. That's all your job is supposed to be."

I didn't like his comment about not finding Wallace's still. I started to invite him to come down and stomp around Wallace's two thousand acres as much as Doc and I had, and see if he could do a better job of finding it. But I knew better. I figured he had said all he had to say so I decided to go fishing.

"You told me the Turner case was none of my affair. Did Hitchcock bother to tell you how he happened to see me there?"

"This is the second time I have told you not to get fresh with me, Miller. There will not be a third. I know Hitchcock was there. Potts called my office and asked for Hitchcock's help. He went through what you might call, 'the chain of command' or 'proper channels.'"

"Hitchcock...proper channels?" I asked sarcastically.

"Look, I know you don't like Hitchcock. Heck, I don't like him either. The guy can be a jerk. But he's the closest man I have to you as far as skill in the woods and tracking, and Potts asked for him by name."

"I'm sure he did. The two of them seem to have quite an affection for one another."

"You're outta line, Miller. I'll handle Hitchcock and what he does. You focus on what I am telling you to do. Get back to what you do best. Go find some moonshine stills."

He hung up on me. I didn't have time to tell him about busting Roxanne Coleman or that she probably had 200 gallons of 'shine in her garage.

I set the phone back in the cradle deliberately and turned to look at Doc. He was standing with his arms crossed.

"I heard most of it. He wasn't exactly quiet," he said.

"Doc," I said. "Let's get the axe out of my trunk. I'm going to Greenville to get the County Attorney to file charges against Punkin Woodley. And after we're done there, we've got a lady's still to bust up."

CHAPTER 26
ROXY

We rode in Doc's car in an awkward silence. I had just been dressed down pretty good by the Chief and I had some things to sort through. Finally I made a decision. I told Doc everything. Well…almost everything. I told him that I had been working on Turner to become an informant. I told him about meeting with Wallace. I told him what I saw at the truck stop and about the search I did for Turner's body. I told him about Daniel Godfrey coming to see me outside my church, but Doc had already heard about that. Then I told him exactly what had happened with Punkin Woodley, and that I knew to within a half a mile of where Daniel Godfrey's still was. I even thought about telling him about meeting that old lady, but I decided to keep that private for now. By the time I got finished, my dander was up again and I was feeling re-energized.

"We need to set up a raid on Godfrey's still soon. I would love nothing better than to lock him up for moonshining before he can screw up the courage to come after me. First things first, though. Chief said we could look for Turner while we were looking for Wallace's still. Right now that matters more to me than Godfrey's empty threats."

I looked through the windshield at the road ahead. I could feel Doc looking at me more often than he was looking at the road.

"Kid, do you hear yourself? What in the world are you talking about 'empty threats'? The Godfrey brothers don't make empty threats and you know it!" Abruptly he pulled the car over onto the shoulder of the road.

"Kid, I've been doing some thinkin' myself. We've known each other for twenty years. We've rode as partners for eight. And ever since the beginning, I have deferred to you on cases; let you pretty much call the shots. And I gotta admit that has worked out awfully good for me most of the time. I know I complained about you leaving me behind, but the truth is, I don't mind it as much as I let on."

"What do you mean, Doc?"

"Kid, you're startin to meddle in stuff and go into places that I don't want no part of. You go off on your own half the time and every time you do it seems like you kick a hornet's nest. This thing with Punkin ain't the first time you've gotten involved trying to help some kid or rescue some poor wretch. You never clue me in till it's all over, or you've gotten yourself in hot water, like today."

He waited for me to say something but I didn't know what to say. He went on.

"Aww hell, Kid, I would never admit it outside this car, but I know we're different kinds of agents. I'm not the tracker you are, I'm not nearly the woodsman, and I can't come close to hanging with you handling a gun. I'm trying to get by, that's all. I'm trying to take care of me and mine. This is a job for me and it ain't no more than that. You on the other hand, you're on some kind of darned crusade or something. And I'm gettin real concerned that you are going to end up dead. Now if that's the path you wanna take, that's strictly your business. But it ain't my path. They just barely pay us enough to make a living. In my mind they don't pay us enough to walk through doors to bust up a poker game outnumbered four to one."

"Doc, I told you about that right after it happened, and made sure you got your cut …"

"I know you TOLD me about it Kid. And sooner or later, with the way moonshinin' is going, and the way you're going, you aren't going to be telling me about it—you are going to be dragging me with you."

Doc looked out the side window for a minute and stared at the cars passing by on the blacktop. Meanwhile, I tried to think of something to say.

"Now, you want to go stomping around up at Wallace's place looking for somebody he beat to death? John Wallace would just as soon shoot us as look at us. And we haven't even talked about Sivell yet. When all you wanted to do was find stills and bust em up with an axe, I was right there with ya. But now if you want to go head to head against Wallace for some vendetta, or to save some sharecropper or save the world... well...maybe this is another one of those times that you don't need me along. They don't pay us that much, I tell ya."

I didn't want to hear what Doc was telling me, but before I could respond, the radio crackled. "Calling Agent Cook or Agent Miller," the Dispatcher said.

Doc nodded at me and I picked up the Mic.

"This is Agent Miller, over."

"Agent Miller, you know that lady you arrested over at Manchester? Miss Roxanne Coleman?"

"Roger, Dispatch," I said.

"Well, she's out. The charges were dropped. And she wants to talk to you, over."

I rolled my eyes. I didn't know how she beat the case so quickly, but now I wouldn't have the pleasure of smashing her still to pieces.

"I may talk to her sometime later. Agent Cook and I are on a more urgent case at the moment."

"No you're not Miller, over," the dispatcher was enjoying himself. He continued. "This lady knows some folks. The Chief called here and said you are to drop whatever you are doing and go talk to Miss Coleman right now. She claims to have some good information for you."

I could hear the dispatcher laughing as he spoke. This was just what I needed, that loud mouth glorified desk clerk starting some kind of rumor about me and this lady moonshiner.

I let out a deep sigh and keyed the mic. "Tell the Chief we are on the way. I will have Agent Cook stand nearby as a witness when I talk to her OUTSIDE her house, over."

"Enjoy yourself Agent Miller, over and out."

• • •

Doc pulled the car up to the curb of Roxanne Coleman's big, red brick house. We both got out. Doc lit a cigarette as he stepped up the sidewalk to the front porch.

Just as I put my boot on the bottom step of her front porch, Miss Coleman stepped outside to meet us. She had that same slow, deliberate walk that I had admired before. Click…click…click…went her red high heels. She had traded her sundress from the other day for a snug black skirt and a white top. A necklace of what looked like rubies adorned her neck. I wondered if there was ever a time when this lady wasn't dressed up.

She stopped at the edge of the steps, folded her arms across her midsection and cocked a hip against the nearest column.

"I thought the next time I saw you, you would be wearing wide black and white stripes, not that outfit," I quipped.

She laughed with a throaty, alto, laugh. The lady was definitely intriguing.

"Why Agent Miller, you should have expected that I would be released for good behavior." She winked at me.

I couldn't help but smile. Then I looked down at the steps. I had to admit that Miss Coleman made me uneasy and she seemed to enjoy that.

"We were told you had some information for us," I said.

She looked up at Doc who was still smoking and standing a few steps behind me. The smile left her face.

"I have some information, but I won't tell him." She jerked her chin toward Doc. "I don't like him."

"You don't even know him," I said.

"Call it woman's intuition," she said.

I thought she was being unfair to Doc but he didn't protest. He just held up his palms and said, "I'll wait by the car." He walked over, threw a hip up on the front fender and looked down the street, focusing on some kids playing baseball in a field about a block and a half down.

"Miss Coleman, I..."

"Please, call me Roxy. Would you prefer that I call you, Kid, or must we stick with Agent Miller?" Her smile was back and I wondered who had told her my nickname.

"Agent Miller will be fine, Miss Coleman."

She pouted briefly then wrapped an arm around the column and swung herself all the way around it, like a little girl.

"So that's the way it's going to be," she said, in her best little girl voice.

"Miss Coleman, I really have some pressing matters I need to get to."

She stopped swinging, and her manner changed in an instant. For the first time since I had met her, I thought I saw a twinge of vindictiveness in her eyes.

"You're looking at everything all wrong!" She said it as if she were a disappointed schoolmaster lecturing an errant child.

I frowned and started to ask what she meant, but she didn't give me a chance.

"I hear you're good at what you do Miller, but you're still just a two-bit small town cop when it comes right down to it. And you're thinking small town. You should get out more. Maybe leave the boonies once in a while. There's a big world out there." She waved an arm towards the horizon.

I was starting to feel my face flush. I felt blindsided by her sudden change in demeanor.

"That big world you're talking about," I said. "Is that where you learned to be a crook? Is that where you learned how to sell folks poison?"

She ignored the insult.

"You're looking at the thing from the wrong end," she said. "It's not always important where it comes from. You need to focus on where it's going. Find out who is getting paid."

Her words stopped me cold. Now we were finally getting somewhere. But I had to admit I didn't know where. She saw the puzzled look on my face.

She came down the steps rapidly and stepped up to me almost as if she wanted to fight. She put her hands on her hips and looked up at me.

I could smell her perfume again and for a moment wondered what Doc thought of this. Wow, her eyes were beautiful.

"The liquor, Miller," she said. "The liquor! Do you honestly think that John Wallace buys those registered cattle and all that land from money he makes off these hicks?" She nearly spat the last word and I started to think that I might not like this woman.

"Wallace is way beyond just selling around here. You want to bust Wallace? Cut him off from his buyer. Cut off his shipping."

She tossed both hands in the air as if she was talking to an idiot. I squinted at her. Why was she telling me this now? She didn't need a "get out of jail free" card. She had already talked herself out of jail. Was she trying to get rid of me? Throw me off her trail?

"You know, I see that the drive going back to your garage is pretty worn down," I lied. "Looks like maybe somebody hauls a real heavy load out of there pretty regular. That's probable cause. That means I might need to take a little stroll back there and have a look."

She didn't back down one bit. "Go right ahead, Miller," she said. "You see how long they held me in jail the last time. My stay this time will be even shorter, since all you will find is an empty garage. For that matter maybe you would like to tour my basement. I'll even let you in. Nothing down there but a few jars of canned vegetables."

I didn't need to look. I knew she was telling the truth. She was daring me to do a search. So somehow, this woman, who had only been out of jail for less than twenty four hours, had unloaded and hauled away a couple of hundred jugs of moonshine, disassembled and removed a working still, and cleaned up all traces of both from her property? There had to be someone helping her. There had to be more to this woman's business than just a little supplemental income from some homemade liquor.

Roxanne Coleman was standing here trying to give me a tip for one reason and one reason only. She was trying to take out her competition. Still, no matter her motives, what she was saying had my interest. She could see the wheels turning and she took a step back, let her hands drop from her hips and began to walk methodically back up onto her porch. She had been mad for a minute, now she was going to turn on the charm again to finish making her pitch.

She turned toward me, her blonde hair whipping around and falling across her shoulder. She smiled brightly once again. Something told me she had practiced that move in a mirror a time or two, and that she had used it with a great deal of success in other negotiations.

"I hear you made a big bust a while back. I hear you confiscated a fine automobile. Go back and talk to the man that used to drive that car," she said, now walking slowly toward her front door. "Find out where the merchandise is going. Then you might learn where it came from, and a whole lot more."

She opened the door and didn't look back again. "Lovely day to you, Agent Miller. It was just delightful chatting."

The door closed. Then I heard the lock turn. Our conversation was over.

CHAPTER 27
PRINCE ALBERT

As I walked toward Doc's car, he slid off the fender, walked around, and got into the driver's seat. He started his Dodge's big V-8 and looked over at me. "Where we going?" he said.

"You still on board for trying to find Wallace's still? I mean if we are just looking for the still." I asked.

"Yeah, I suppose so," Doc said.

"Then let's ride to Stovall."

Doc let out the clutch and accelerated out past the kids playing baseball. I leaned out the window as we drove past. I couldn't help but think back to a simpler, happier time in my life when I'd played the game for money. Sometimes I missed it so that my chest hurt. I watched as a little shortstop did a nice job of cleanly fielding a hot grounder then throwing a kid out at first. I craned my neck out the window and watched till the game faded from sight.

We were headed to Stovall and John Wallace's place. I was going to let Doc do what he felt right about doing. I was going to let him look for Wallace's still. I wanted to do that too but I was also determined to find Wilson Turner, dead or alive. I had found a button and a thread and I was going to follow it till I found the entire shirt. Maybe Turner would still be in it.

"You remember that time we walked over the section of Wallace's place that used to be the old Ivy Plantation? We found that little cold water branch there, remember?" I asked.

"Yeah, I remember," Doc said. "We liked it pretty good as a place where Wallace might draw water for whiskey makin'. But we never got time to follow it very far."

"That's the one," I said. "I'm gonna let you drop me off on the side of the road so that I can cut across his place and bisect the upper part of that branch about a half a mile up from where we were that day. I'll work my way downstream. You go to the corner of his property where we first located the branch and work your way upstream. We'll meet somewhere in the middle."

"Alright," Doc said. But I sensed worry in his voice. He wouldn't admit it to me but he didn't want to be on Wallace's place by himself.

I stepped out of Doc's car along a desolate stretch of road. It was only mid-morning but the sun was already hot. I reached in the trunk and got one of Doc's army canteens. We both kept several filled in our cars. The only difference was, I put fresh water in mine every few days. With Doc, you never knew when you might be grabbing a canteen that had been rattling around back there since last summer. "Oh well," I thought. "If a man gets hot and thirsty enough he can drink it, I suppose."

As I watched Doc's brake lights fade around a distant curve, I have to confess there was a real feeling of loneliness for a few seconds. Rather than dwell on it, I sought the cover of the woods. I would rather be in deep woods where I could make myself nearly invisible than to stand here on the side of this road where Wallace or Sivell could drive by and make trouble.

I bounded quickly down the embankment and felt an extra wave of heat as I entered the stagnant air of the woods. Honeysuckle vines pulled at my feet as I walked the first quarter mile, making the going difficult. Then the woods opened up a bit. Wallace owned all of this now but a hundred years ago it had all been part of a huge Southern plantation owned by the Ivy family.

The way I had it figured I was about a quarter mile due west of the spot where I had found the button and thread. Since I had thoroughly searched the thicket last night, I wanted to move toward the thicket but focus my search on the perimeter of forest around it. My hope was to find some new sign there. Once I found something, I would use that spot as though it were the center of a clock.

From that center I would walk outward towards every number on the clock until I found a second sign. At that point I would have a general direction of the trail and could narrow my search area to that compass direction.

I did better than I thought I would because I came upon my own tracks where I had briefly entered these woods after I found the button. I used that as the center, then started walking toward my clock settings. I found nothing out towards noon, one o'clock or two but in the direction of three o'clock I hit pay dirt.

As I walked along slowly, scanning the ground and the tree trunks up to head high, a glimpse of red caught my eye. I walked past it for a second before it registered in my brain that I had seen something. I retraced my steps and saw it again. I knelt down and brushed away a layer of oak leaves to find a Prince Albert tobacco can. My mind immediately went back to that night at the still when Turner fell and then complained to me about denting his can of Prince Albert. I reached in my pocket for a handkerchief and tried to grasp the can without wiping any potential prints off it. It was only when I lifted the can out of the leaves, that I saw the blood.

There on one of the leaves by the Prince Albert can was a tiny speck of what looked to be dried blood. I was just about to reach down and lift up the leaf when a voice startled me.

"Agent Miller!" the voice boomed.

I jerked my head up. I had been too caught up in what I had found to be aware of anyone approaching. I had let my guard down a bit. The first thing I noticed when I looked up was a big roan horse. The second thing I noticed was the pearl handled Colt .45 John Wallace was wearing on his hip.

CHAPTER 28
WE MEET AGAIN

I felt my entire body tense up. Then I caught myself. The worst thing I could do now was to have a big reaction. I determined that, no matter what I had to do, I was coming out of these woods with this tobacco can. I wondered if Wallace was willing to shoot it out with a lawman to get it from me. Rather than find out, I decided to try something.

"Morning John," I said calmly. I was still kneeling near the spot of blood so I reached into my shirt pocket and took out my own rolling papers, careful not to show the pouch of my own tobacco in the same pocket. I rested Turner's can on one knee and then took out a paper. As I had done a thousand times on my own, I held the paper curled between my thumb and forefinger, pressing down on it lightly with my index finger to form a trough. Then I popped open the lid of the Prince Albert can with my thumb. I prayed a quick prayer that Turner had tobacco left in his can or else this ruse was going to end badly. He did, so I shook out some tobacco into the paper, snapped the metal lid closed, and wrapping the can in my handkerchief, stuffed it into my hip pocket. As I finished rolling the cigarette Wallace kept talking. He seemed to take no note of my activities.

"So what brings you out to visit my land this fine morning?"

Wallace was all smiles. He specialized in charm when it suited him, namely when he wasn't in a rage over something, or demanding I run someone out of the county, or pistol whipping an unconscious man.

"Now, John," I said. "As hot and humid as it is what do you suppose would bring me to take a walk in these woods? You know I ain't bird watching."

Wallace laughed, and it almost seemed genuine. "Well, Miller (for the first time that I could ever remember, he didn't call me Mr. or Agent) you might as well be bird watching 'cause there's nothing else to see down in these woods."

I licked the paper to seal it and popped the cigarette into my mouth. I was going to take my time lighting it. Something bothered me about smoking a dead man's tobacco.

"You riding your fences this morning?" I wanted to lighten the conversation a bit, see if I could read Wallace's state of mind.

"Just checking on things," Wallace said. "I like to make sure I don't have trouble with trespassers."

Now Wallace had changed the tone, and I didn't like where it had gone. I also didn't like being lectured about trespassing by a man who possibly just committed murder. I took out my Zippo lighter and decided to make a show of lighting the cigarette. The lighter would give me a reason to have my hands in motion. That in turn would give me a jump on Wallace if it became necessary to draw on him. I glanced briefly at Wallace's Colt. He wore it in front of his belt with a cross draw set up. He would be a half second slower than me on his best day. If things went badly, I was pretty sure I could shoot Wallace right out of that saddle.

"Well, it pays a man to keep riff raff off his land. I can appreciate that," I said. "Folks that don't have a right to be here shouldn't be here. Of course that don't include me, does it John? As a state agent, I got every right to be just about anywhere in Georgia I want to be when I suspect moonshine is being made. So I've got a right to walk around till I find your operation."

I smiled back at Wallace.

"Well, Miller," Wallace said, a faint smile of his own creasing his face. "I hope you're in the mood for a mighty long walk," Wallace's jaw was tightening as he spoke. I had challenged him for the second time and he wasn't used to that. He wheeled his horse around, rested a hand on the back of the saddle and looked back over his shoulder at me. "Cause you're going to walk the rest of your days on this farm and you ain't never gonna find no liquor still. I left that business behind long ago, as I told you on the night we met in your automobile."

With that, he dug his heels into the sides of his horse and started to ride off. "You have a nice day Agent Miller. Make yourself at home," he called back to me.

I was all but out of a sticky situation. I had the Prince Albert and as soon as Wallace was out of sight I could pick up the leaf, I could have just let it go. I don't know why I didn't. I guess I just didn't like Wallace's big shot attitude. I spoke up loud and clear.

"Did you do what you told me you would do John? Have you done gone and killed that boy?" I shouted.

Wallace pulled his horse up sharply. He didn't turn around.

"I knew this wasn't the only time you had been out here looking around," Wallace said. "Miss Mayhayley told me she ran into you out on the road real early this morning. We kind of figured you weren't just looking for a still." Wallace was looking straight ahead, his back to me. I felt like he was deciding what to do, like he was thinking about shooting me. I made a mental note of the name Mayhayley so that I could tell Potts that she might know something about all this. After another moment, Wallace turned his horse around and was facing me again. Just as the horse came around, I decided to go ahead and light that cigarette. I let the Zippo burn in my hand as I talked. I wanted it to capture Wallace's attention.

"You haven't answered my question, John," I said. "You told me you aimed to kill Turner. Now the Coweta Sheriff tells me that they suspect Turner is dead. I know he was in the Greenville jail just yesterday. I saw you and Sivell on the square acting real funny. Then folks up at Coweta tell me a man dressed just like you were that day I saw you at the bank came and beat Turner and took him away. So, I'll ask you again, did you kill him, John?"

I continued to let the Zippo burn. Several times I saw Wallace's eyes dart toward it. That's what I wanted. If Wallace even looked like he was going to pull on me, I was going to shake my hand as if I had burned it. As Wallace watched the lighter fall, it would give me another half second to clear my holster and shoot. Didn't really think I needed the extra time but it paid to be cautious of a man who packed around a pearl handled Colt. He must at least *think* he was good.

Wallace squinted at me. I doubt any man had ever talked to him as directly as I just had and lived. What's more, I was on his property.

Suddenly, Wallace's face creased into a bright smile once again. And at that moment, I knew we would both walk out of here. A minute before, I had been pretty convinced that only I would.

"Mr. Miller, you take me too seriously sometimes," Wallace said, chuckling. "Yes, I get my dander up, and I admit Turner had me mighty upset the night I met with you. But I never meant I would literally kill the boy. I was just acting out in front of you because I *did* want him out of the county. As far as all this other affair you're talking about, I hadn't heard anything about it. Sheriff Collier got word from the Carrolton Chief of Police that Turner had been arrested up in Carroll County. The police up there had seen one of my Guernsey cows in a pasture near Carrollton. They staked out the pasture and caught Turner red handed trying to load my cow up in his truck."

Wallace continued, "Collier got Turner moved to Greenville jail. I suppose he did so because the theft was committed against a resident of Meriwether County. I told him I wanted to press charges. Turner stole some of my registered cattle and I aim to have satisfaction over it. But all that other, why I don't recall the last time I was up at Coweta County. As for you seeing me, I am up at the square conducting some business or other pert nigh every day. I wish I'd had more time to chat with you there in the savings and loan, and take you to lunch."

I snapped the Zippo closed against my holster. Wallace wasn't going to pull on me today. He also knew I didn't have anything on him and no basis to make an arrest. Everything I had just mentioned was circumstantial at best.

I nodded slowly. "Well, I've got plenty of looking yet to do. So unless you want to just show me where your still is, I guess I had better get back to looking."

Wallace laughed again. "Nope...nope," he said, still smiling broadly. "I'm afraid I have a farm to run. No time to ride around looking for phantom stills with you." He wheeled his horse around again. As he rode off, he called back over his shoulder once more, "You're a persistent man, Agent Miller. Someday I hope you find whatever it is you're looking for." The sarcasm in Wallace's voice was apparent.

I watched him ride away. Then, I said under my breath, "I hope so too, John...I sure hope so too."

CHAPTER 29

NEW STILL SITE

An hour later I was heading along the stream where Doc and I had agreed to meet. I came to a section where the stream gurgled over some large flat rocks, then ran clear across smooth pebbles till it made a sweeping oxbow. I checked over my shoulder several times as I walked slowly along the bank. I still half expected Wallace to come after me once my words to him had sunk in. If he came after me again, he might have help. As I rounded another bend in the branch, I was relieved to see Doc kneeling at the center of the oxbow.

He was bent down looking closely at the ground, but he looked up when he heard me approach and I thought I saw a look of relief on his face. "Hey Kid," he said. "Come and have a look at this."

I walked over and saw right away what had his attention. Though there was a thin layer of pine straw scattered about, it was pretty apparent that the ground had been leveled and cleaned up a bit, perhaps by a tractor with a box blade on it. We were almost at the middle of Wallace's big woods. He wouldn't have been building a barn or a cattle pen way out here.

"Cleaning off an area this size, right next to the bend of a flowing branch," I said. "Doc, we may not know where Wallace's still is now, but I think you just found where a new one is going to be."

I looked up at Doc and he was beaming. He had a right to be proud.

"Let's ease out of here without leaving much sign," I said. "We'll come back one night in a couple of weeks, and I would say this one will be built and in operation."

We began the long hike back to Doc's car, hoping not to be spotted. We remained silent as we walked, but as we got close to the car I spoke up.

"I met up with Wallace not far from where you put me out," I admitted.

Docs head snapped back like I'd thrown a jab at him. "How did he react?" he asked.

"He didn't like me being on his property, of course. But then he laid on the charm. He came across as calm, but some of what he said had a bite to it. I think he's desperate, Doc. And I think that makes him even more dangerous."

We moved on back up the branch towards Doc's car. By the time we arrived and were headed up highway 18 back towards Chipley, it was nearly 1:30. Neither of us had eaten lunch so we headed towards town to get a bite.

"Kid, don't Wallace still have family up here at Chipley?"

"Yeah, I think his Mama still lives up here," I said.

"You think she's got any guilty feelings about what her boy has been up to lately…like maybe guilty enough to tell on him?"

"Doc, you're on a roll today, boy," I teased. I had to admit, I had never thought about trying it.

As we arrived in Chipley, a little diner was off to the left. We pulled Doc's sedan into the dirt and gravel parking lot, parked, and went inside.

"Whatch y'all want?" The waitress was testy. "The special was chicken and dumplins but we done cleaned all that up. We're gettin ready to get supper fixed. It's mighty late to come draggin in here wantin lunch."

"Will you quit bein hateful?" The male cook was leaning down and looking through a framed opening where he would sit the completed orders for the waitress to pick up. "You're gonna run another customer off! What can I fix you boys? I've got time to grill ya a hamburger steak, maybe fry ya some hashbrowns, how bout that?"

I smiled at him. "That'll be mighty fine," I said. "I know we are late coming in and I apologize." I looked over at the waitress and smiled at her as well. She looked me up and down with a look of disdain, but I thought her face softened a bit.

"Y'all drinkin sweet tea or you want a Co-cola?" she asked.

We both ordered sweet tea and she brought it over to us.

"I've passed by here before. Y'all stay pretty busy. I imagine a place this size with one waitress must keep you hopping." I kept smiling.

"I don't do a whole bunch of sitting around, that's for sure."

"No, I don't imagine you get many breaks," I said sympathetically.

"Y'all the law?" she asked.

"Yes ma'am," I replied. "We're law men."

"Well, we're happy to have your kind in here. I didn't mean nothing by what I said earlier. It's just that we get folks draggin in here all hours…"

"No explanation needed. I thought you were well within your rights to be a bit put out with us. Believe it or not, my wife and I used to run a little lunch counter at a drug store. Nothing aggravated my wife worse than for someone to come in long after she had cleaned up wanting something to eat in the middle of the afternoon."

Over the course of the meal, the waitress and I carried on small talk several more times. When she came to clear the dishes, I made sure she saw me getting ready to place a generous tip by my plate. Doc did the same.

"Say," I lowered my voice a bit. "We are kind of needing to talk to a Mrs. Myrtice Wallace. Would you happen to know where she lives?"

The waitress frowned. "Yeah, I can tell you. You best check the Methodist Church cemetery seein as how she's been dead for seven years. What kind of lawmen are you?"

I felt my face flush. I had made a stupid assumption that Mrs. Wallace was still alive and now we looked silly.

"I uhh…"

"What would two lawmen want with Miss Myrtice anyway? Are you two Revenuers? Is that the kind of law you two are? I'll have you to know that Mr. John Wallace is one of the finest men in the state of

Georgia. If it ain't the federal revenue boys coming around asking about him, it's you state pukes."

I stood up. "Okay, here we go," I said to Doc, knowing that I was about to hear yet another local brag to me about how Wallace had given her money or something when she was in a jam.

"Your durned right, here we go," she said.

I threw down enough cash to more than cover our meals. With the tip money, she had enjoyed a pretty lucrative hour off the two of us.

"Maybe we don't want your revenue money around here," she said as she followed us toward the door.

"Mabel, shut up, will ya?" the cook hollered from the kitchen. "John Wallace don't own this diner, I do! And I like revenuer money just fine."

I hit the front screen door of the place and it flew back against the stop. The heat of the parking lot hit me like a wall but I was steadily walking for Doc's car.

"Ya'll boy's come back and eat with us again real soon!" The cook was still hollering. Mabel stood just inside the door with her hands on her hips, as the spring slammed the door closed.

"That went real fine, Kid. You done a beautiful job of calming the contact and carrying on the interrogation there," Doc said.

"Shut up, will ya Mabel," I said.

CHAPTER 30
COMPARING DATES

We asked around Chipley a bit more for information about Wallace's still, but people were even more tight lipped than the waitress. We came up empty. We then drove over to Coweta County and I turned in the Prince Albert can and the leaf containing the spot of blood that I had picked up after Wallace rode away. The deputy on duty said he didn't think the spot was big enough for the lab in Atlanta to be able to determine if it was even human or not.

I got home in the early evening for a change and had some time to walk out in the yard barefoot and set up the sprinkler so Judy could play in the cool water. I enjoyed the rare opportunity to be home in time to have dinner with her, Rose and my grown son Buddy. Buddy had been in the Navy since the war. For now he had decided to stay in but was on thirty days leave. He had come home for a couple of days but would soon head back down to Florida to spend a week or so at Panama City Beach with some of his buddies before shipping back out.

After dinner, I packed a pipe, brewed a pot of coffee, and took a cup out onto the screened porch. Buddy followed me out there. I unfolded a couple of full sheets of an old newspaper and got out all five of the little carvings I was presently working on. I was keeping them in an old beat up tackle box and had been taking turns getting one out each day and slipping it in my pocket. That way, whenever I got a few idle minutes, I could give it some individual attention. Now I took turns working on them one at a time.

Buddy came out and set in the chair across from me, watching me work. We sat quietly for a time, me puffing my pipe, sipping the scalding coffee, carving, and Buddy just rocking methodically. Those moments were precious with only the sound of the rocker creaking, the tree frogs outside, and tiny slivers of wood falling on my lap and onto the newspaper.

"Daddy," Buddy finally said. "You know I only have another year left in the Navy on this hitch. I don't think I will reenlist. I think I am ready to do something else. I want to open a shop or something. I want to build motors, maybe even get into racing somehow."

I didn't say anything. Buddy and I had not been close in the last few years. I liked the woods, fishing, and hunting. He had always been nuts about cars and motors. I often wished we had tried a little harder to meet halfway. Now, even though I thought chasing some dream about race cars was foolish, I wasn't of a mind to say so.

"You ever think of doing something else, Daddy?"

I looked over at him and I thought I saw him flinch in the darkness. He was expecting me to get mad, but I wasn't mad.

"I think about it quite a bit," I said. "I have been thinking about it more than ever lately."

"What would you like to do?" he asked.

"Play for the Crackers," I said. Buddy scoffed.

"I don't think the Atlanta Crackers sign very many forty year old first basemen," he chuckled.

"No, I don't suppose they do."

We were quiet again for a time.

"Mama worries, Daddy. She worries every night and I don't think it is good for her health."

Now I felt my jaw clench. Did he think I didn't know that? Then I reminded myself that he was only looking out for his Mama.

"I know she does son, and that bothers me too. It weighs on me quite a bit."

"Then why don't you quit?" Buddy said. "Get a different job. Do something safe."

"Because I am good at what I do," I said. "I can help people. I do help people. I protect them by getting bad men locked up."

"I don't mean any disrespect Daddy, but is it worth it? Is it worth what you go through to lock some guy up for five years or less? Is it worth it when they don't even stay locked up? How many of them get back out and just go right back to what they were doing?"

I didn't answer for a long while. Finally, I promised to think about other opportunities. Buddy didn't seem satisfied, but he eventually stood up and I heard the front door close as he went inside.

His phrase, "they don't stay locked up" kept rolling over in my head. Then I began to think about Wilson Turner being locked up in the Greenville jail. I wondered if he had known that Wallace and Sivell were laying for him. The mental image of that jail log book kept flashing across my mind's eye. I could see Turner's signature and the date scrawled across the lined page…

The date! I got quickly to my feet and went inside. I went to the back room and grabbed my gun belt. There was a pouch there where I stored my tablet and a few other affects whenever I got off duty. I retrieved the tablet and thumbed the pages back to the night I had staked out Turner's still. July 12th 1946. Still holding the tablet in one hand, I went to the bookshelves in our living room. There on the top shelf was a green metal tackle box that I kept a padlock on and used for important papers instead of fishing tackle. I fumbled in my pocket for my keys.

I opened the lid slowly. I almost didn't want to see John Wallace's letter. I didn't want to be wrong about this. Finally, I sat the tablet down on an end table and turned on a lamp. Then I sat Wallace's letter down beside the tablet. I had interrogated Turner at the still on July 12th. Though Wallace's letter had been delivered to me on the 13th, the letter was dated July 8th 1946. John Wallace had written me the letter asking for a meeting with me in which he talked about killing Turner long before I had ever talked to Turner at his still.

Sheriff Potts had been right. Whatever had Wallace so mad at Turner, whether it was cows or skimming money or whatever, had nothing to do with me.

I stared down at the two pieces of paper on my table. Turner's wife, his father-in law, and even Potts had tried to tell me but I had still carried guilt about getting Turner into trouble. I leaned my head back and let out a long breath of relief. It seemed as if a weight that I hadn't known was there lifted off my chest.

With that weight gone I felt like I could sleep for a week if I could just get myself to relax. Sometimes I thought about stealing just one jug of moonshine from one of the rare "clean" stills that I raided. I would use it to knock myself out on nights like this. I scoffed to myself. I would never go through with that, but sometimes I could understand the attraction. The sound of little running feet caused me to open my eyes and sit up.

"I wissen to Wed Skelton Daddy," Judy said. She walked over to our radio set and turned it on. It would take a minute for the set to warm up. Judy was only three years old, but she already knew how to turn the radio on and she loved Red Skelton. We all enjoyed it. Soon Rose came in. As she walked by me she placed a hand on my shoulder and squeezed. I took her hand for a moment as she passed over to her usual spot at the end of the sofa.

It wasn't long before Red broke into one of his routines. He was doing "Junior the Mean Widdle Kid". Judy laughed and laughed. I wondered sometimes if she really got the humor or if she just laughed because her Mamma was laughing. I laughed too and the tension began to leave my muscles.

At some point however, I lost my concentration on the show. As I watched Judy and Rose enjoying the program, I realized that I had to get my focus away from the Turner case for a time. I had to protect my two girls. I wanted to nab Daniel Godfrey and it had to be soon. I hadn't made a move yet on the information I got out of Punkin Woodley.

Everything had happened so fast with the Turner case since then that I hadn't had a chance to pursue the lead.

It would take me some time to put things together. First Doc and I would have to slip in and stake the place out. We had to figure out when they were running and who was working the still. I wanted to set up a raid for a night that Daniel Godfrey would be there. With Godfrey and possibly his crew out to get me, it would only make matters worse to just bust up his still.

If I did that he would surely come after me with all that he had. He might even come after my family. Daniel Godfrey didn't see moonshining as wrong. He saw it as his right. Just like he thought he had a "right" to kill me if I tried to stand in his way.

CHAPTER 31
LATE NIGHT CALL

As I thought about how I would carry out the surveillance on Godfrey's still, I was jolted by the phone ringing. Decent folks didn't disturb someone's evening this late unless it was bad news or official business. Rose looked at me, a twinge of dread in her eyes. I got up a bit stiffly and walked to the phone. I picked up the heavy black receiver and held it to my ear for a full ten seconds before saying, "Hello".

"Agent Miller, this is Lamar Potts," the voice said.

"Sherriff Potts," I said.

"Miller, I know you have some interest in the Wallace case. I just want you to know that we arrested him this evening on suspicion of murder. We believe he killed Wilson Turner."

I let out a long sigh. I didn't know if I was relieved or just sad. "I thank you for letting me know," I said.

"I do have one problem," Potts said. "As you know, the state of Georgia is a Corpus Delicti state. If I don't have a body, I don't have a case. And right now, I don't have a body. I think that is something you can help me with."

"Don't you have Hitchcock?" I blurted. It was petty on my part and I regretted saying it as soon as it came out of my mouth.

"I do have Hitchcock," Potts said. "But I could sure use you as well. In fact I think I am going to be assembling a pretty big search party for Turner's body the day after tomorrow. Tonight's Wednesday, some of the law officers that are going to help can't get here till Friday. But I am trying to get as many people as I can to assemble in the morning at 0700 outside my office there at the Coweta courthouse. Can you be there then?"

"I'll help you all I can Sheriff, but I have already been whacked once by my Chief for spending time on your investigation, and I have to tell you, I have a very pressing matter on a case I am working over here in Upson County."

I was thinking of Daniel Godfrey but I didn't want to share that with Potts. I didn't know him that well and I didn't want to take a chance on word getting back to Godfrey.

"I understand. I hope you don't mind but I already gave your Chief a call. I met him a time or two when he was on the Atlanta Police Department. He told me to let you know that you have his okay to help on this."

"That's fine by me. I'll help as long as I can," I said.

"Thank you Agent Miller."

The line went dead. I started to sit the phone back in the cradle. Then I heard some background noise on the line.

"Miss Burter Mae," I spoke into the phone. "You better hang up your phone right now."

Nothing happened.

"Miss Burter Mae, I know good and well that is you listening in on this party line. Now this is official business and you are about to get into trouble."

Still nothing.

I walked over to the window and pulled open the curtain. I looked at the large antebellum house on the opposite corner from my much smaller home. I could see Miss Burter Mae sitting by her little table lamp with the curtain open. She was holding the phone up to her ear with her hand over the receiver.

"Miss Burter Mae, I can see you sitting there listening from my house." She looked up abruptly. She hadn't thought of that.

"Now I am going to walk right over there and throw you in jail for the night if you don't hang up this phone, right now!" I was trying to hold back a smile. Miss Burter Mae was Woodland's unofficial news service.

"Dadgummit Cullen!" she exclaimed as she slammed down the phone.

I chuckled to myself and watched her snatch the curtains closed.

So now me helping with the Turner case was official. A few days ago I would have been glad for the opportunity, but now I wondered how I was going to go after Daniel Godfrey in the middle of all of this. I felt someone staring at me and turned around to see Rose with a worried look on her face. I smiled my most comforting smile.

"Nothing to worry about," I said.

"Cullen, are you sure?"

"Well, nothing I can't fix," I smiled again.

She smiled back but then said, "You can't fix everything you know?"

"I can fix this," I said.

Rose fidgeted with her hands and looked at her wedding ring for a second. Then she went back to the sofa, sat Judy on her lap, and turned up the radio a bit.

I watched my girls for a while. Then I prayed a little silent prayer. "The Mangum children counting on me to keep their daddy straight, two little black children abused, another child's Daddy lying dead out in Wallace's woods someplace, a vindictive moonshiner wanting me dead, and a lady in Manchester trying to get me fired or take over the liquor business in the area or something…

"Lord," I mumbled under my breath. "Please forgive me for lying to Rose. I can't fix all this."

CHAPTER 32
SET UP

I picked the phone back up and dialed Doc. It took four tries but I finally got connected to his phone. Doc answered on the first ring.

"Doc, it's me," I said.

"What's up, Kid?" he said.

"Listen, I just got a call from Sheriff Potts up at Coweta County, he wants us to help him look for Wilson Turner in the morning."

"We ain't got enough going on? Potts want you to hit the campaign trail for him too? I told you when you started nosing around in this it was gonna cost you."

"I know you told me," I smiled to myself. "But it's not politics. The Chief told us to help if we were asked so we gotta go. Listen, I need your help on something else too."

"Yeah, okay, I'm listening."

"Doesn't Spence Martin owe you a favor from when you helped him with that raid over at Macon?"

"Yeah, he kind of owes me one."

"Good, he's got a boat up there. See if you can get him up here by late tomorrow afternoon with it. The three of us are going to take a little trip up the Flint River."

"You goin after Godfrey's still tomorrow?" Doc asked.

"Yeah."

"Probably best," he said. "Waitin' only puts you in more danger. How many nights we gonna stake out?"

"One," I said. "Just Thursday night. We can help Potts again for a while on Friday. That gives us one evening to find the still from Punkin's directions. And we gotta be extra careful while we're looking not to leave a trace of sign. Godfrey sees a leaf out of place, he will move the whole operation before we know what happened."

"Yeah, he won't miss much," Doc agreed. "So you're gonna raid after just one stakeout? Kinda risky, ain't it? You might raid on a night that Godfrey's not there."

"Yeah, I know. I'm goin' with my gut on this one. Tomorrow is Thursday. If we find him there tomorrow and he doesn't have the numbers on us too bad, we take him that night. If he's not there, he surely will be the next night. He won't leave that operation up to his hired hands on a Friday night. That's a big production night for him."

"Okay Kid, you're the boss."

"So you get Spence to bring the boat and tell him we will meet him at the shoals of the Flint River by Double Bridges at 5:30 tomorrow afternoon. We can put the boat in there and not risk being seen. As hot as its been that's too early to be a good fishing time so maybe nobody will be out there at that time of the day. It'll take us a full hour to float down the Flint, hopefully that will give us three hours of good daylight to find the still and set up our stakeout."

"Okay," Doc said. "I'll make sure he is there and ready at 5:30."

I looked around for Rose or Judy. Neither of them was close-by.

"Doc," I said.

"Yeah."

"We gotta get this one right."

"Yeah," Doc said. "I know.'

CHAPTER 33

SEARCH PARTY

Thursday morning I woke up before daybreak, ate breakfast, got dressed and swung by Doc's house so he could follow me. He would need his car so he could leave early and set up things with Spence and the boat. We arrived at the steps of the Coweta County Courthouse at seven AM sharp and talked about how we would go about finding Godfrey's still. After about twenty minutes L. Z. Hitchcock rolled up and we stopped talking.

"Miller," Hitchcock said, as he pulled on his black cap. Hitchcock always wore a black ball cap.

"Hitchcock," I answered without smiling.

"What you here for?" he asked. "They need somebody to hold the leash on the spare blood hound while the rest of us track?"

I looked at the ground and smiled, but there was no joy in it. I wanted to knock that cap off his head.

"No." I said. "No, L.Z. they wanted me here so I could come and find you when you got lost. We wouldn't want your mama to worry."

Doc laughed out loud at that one. Hitchcock tried a weak grin of his own but it didn't last long. Soon others began arriving. Eventually, Sheriff Potts stepped out onto the entryway of the courthouse and gave us a short send-off speech. I was only half listening. I had been after

Wallace long before Potts ever knew who the man was and I had known Turner. I didn't need to hear any speech.

After he finished his little talk and the search party began to head out in groups of two or three, Potts came down the steps towards us

"L. Z. how bout you come with me?" Potts said. "We'll work together."

"Fine by me Lamar," Hitchcock said, and he turned to walk away. Potts hesitated a moment and looked back at us.

"I appreciate you boys comin' over here to help." Sheriff Potts said. "Miller, I wanted to let you know we only got a partial print off that tobacco can you found. Forensics in Atlanta may not be able to positively identify it but they are saying it's possible it might be Turner's. Still, it won't be admissible seeing as how Turner worked for Wallace, there's no telling when he dropped that tobacco. Now you boys take the Northwest corner of Wallace's place. I know that's mostly cow pasture but there's some broken sections of woods too." Without waiting for a response, he followed Hitchcock to his patrol car.

"Kid," Doc said. "I didn't like the way he said that."

"What do you mean?" I asked a question I already knew the answer to.

"Well, he acted like that can you found wasn't nothing. I'd dare say he don't have much else from them woods with a partial print on it. On top of that, it seemed to me like he was talkin down to us. And why is he stickin us way out on that far corner of the place?"

I squinted at Potts and Hitchcock as they got into Potts' patrol car temporarily lost in thought. "You're right," I finally said. "He was talking down to us. But he ain't stickin us on no Northwest corner, I can tell you that. I knew where we were going to look before I ever heard from Sheriff Lamar Potts."

As we walked back toward Doc's car I took a moment to look at the scene unfolding around me. Since we had been early to arrive, and near the steps of the courthouse, I hadn't taken much time to look around. I had never seen anything like it. There were sheriffs and deputies from other counties, state troopers, half the revenuers in the state, and even some city police from various communities around Georgia. There had to be five hundred lawmen here, all for one murder case. I had to admit it was a testament to the clout Potts had around the state. Then I wondered how much of this was being driven by the attention this case was getting in every major paper in the South?

Doc and I had to wait a bit before we could pull my car out of the parking place. We sat with the windows down and watched one type of patrol car after another drive past us heading for Wallace's land. That was the first time the full weight of it hit me. All these lawmen were trying to help find the victim of a murder. It gave me a cold feeling inside to think about that word…murder. Turner was actually dead at Wallace's hand. Then something occurred to me that gave me an even worse chill. The other day with Punkin, I had been on the verge of committing the same act myself.

CHAPTER 34

TRACKING

A Pickens County squad car and a Georgia State Patrol car were already parked when Doc and I rolled up to the end of the trail I'd made the night I had searched for Turner. We pulled off to one side of the trooper car and walked directly to the edge of the thicket where I had found the button. Just inside the edge of the woods, I pointed back toward the thicket.

"Doc, you see that piece of white handkerchief tied up high on that blackberry vine?"

"Yeah," Doc said.

"I left that there the other night when I found that shirt button. From here where would you say we were when I found the tobacco can and ran into Wallace?"

"Gosh, from here?" Doc hated it when I quizzed him like this. "I don't know, Kid. I would say it's more or less that way."

Doc stretched his arm out in a northerly direction. I reached up and, grasping his forearm, turned him like a giant weathervane until his arm pointed due east.

"No, now Doc, from here its due east. Now imagine if we was to draw a straight line from that hankie to where the can was found. Somewhere along that line might have been where they hauled Turner. The trick is, we could be off just a degree or two on the compass and miss the whole trail. So from here we need to fan out side by side and walk a hundred yards or so toward the east. Then we can come back to this starting point, move over five or ten yards left and right, and walk another line east. We'll keep doing that till one of us finds something."

We searched that way for the next couple of hours without finding anything. We saw other officers off in the distance a time or two and waved a greeting.

But persistence paid off because I found my next clue on the rough bark of a Chestnut tree. There I saw a few strands of black hair. I stopped and took a small manila envelope out of my pocket and lifted out the hair between my thumb and the back edge of my pocket knife blade. I called Doc over and held the strands up for him to see before putting them in the envelope. Then I notched the tree bark where the hair had been.

"I'm six feet tall," I said. "Wallace is probably six two, so close to the same height. Now if we assume that these black hairs came from Turner..."

"That's a pretty big assumption there, Kid," Doc said.

"Yeah, I know. But if we do assume that, then the hair was too low on the tree trunk to have rubbed off if Turner was walking or had been pushed up against this tree trunk in a standing position. But imagine if I had you flopped over one shoulder like so."

I stooped over before Doc could react and slung him over my shoulder. His belly ended up across my shoulder with me having an arm wrapped around the back of his legs, his upper body was draped over my back.

"Hey easy there, Kid," Doc said. "My hat just fell in the dirt."

"Quit complaining" I said. "Look where your head hits on that tree trunk. That is just about where the hair was."

I eased Doc back down to his feet.

"If Wallace carried Turner from that logging road, then walked by the spot I marked with that white handkerchief back there, and continued on in this direction," I said as I pointed from the road, then swept my arm past us and pointed off in the distance, "he would end up walking right across the spot where I found that Prince Albert can."

I stood there like that for a minute, holding my arm out and looking down it like the barrel of a rifle. I was identifying landmarks that I would walk to so I could keep myself aligned. Once I had those landmarks in mind, I let my arm drop back to my side.

"So you think Wallace packed that kid's body all the way across his place and the tobacco can eventually fell out of Turner's pocket?" Doc seemed suspicious of that theory.

"I know, it don't make sense to me either. There is a whole lot of ground between here and there. Why not bury the body somewhere in between? And why wouldn't the Prince Albert can fall out of Turner's pocket long before where it did? Why would he pack the body so far?"

Doc pushed his hat back on his head and grimaced for a second. "No, that don't hold water to me, Kid."

"Yeah, me either. Unless…unless he was in a panic. Unless he didn't know what to do with the body. Oh well, at least we have a trajectory. Let's head that direction. If we find more sign we will know we are on to something anyway."

It took us a solid two hours to make it a hundred yards. With every step we looked all around us. We needed something to catch our eye, a depression in the grass or in the matted leaves left over from the prior fall. Our job was made all the more difficult by a thunderstorm we had experienced last night. Anything along the surface of the ground had been washed away.

I stood up and took out my pocket knife. I cut a little green twig off a nearby maple at a sharp forty five degree angle. I quickly stripped the leaves and the thin layer of bark off it with my knife. Then I stuck the sharp end of the now nearly white twig into the ground right in line with our path.

"There's our marker," I said. "Let's keep looking."

We searched on for two more hours. The sun rose high and hot in the sky. We found a couple more things including an indention in some soft soil where it looked like the toe of a man's shoe had dug into the ground. It was just past a thick vine that caught my ankle as I walked past. If I nearly tripped over it, I figured someone carrying a load and not watching the ground close would surely stumble there. We put another marker right next to the toe print.

Further down and about an hour later we came to a stand of pine trees. The first tree we came to had a fresh twig broken and hanging down. It too was at about the right height to have been contacted by a load being carried over my shoulder. Soon we came to another broken twig and then another. All were at a similar height and all were along the same straight line we had been walking. We made new markers and placed them at each one.

By now it was noon and time to take a break. Off to one side was a cluster of granite boulders that would have been here when the Indians lived here. We walked over and found one to use for a seat and a neighboring one to use for a table. We were both pretty worn out by now. I had a pouch with me and I lifted the strap over my head and sat it in my lap. I pulled out a can of sardines and a little foil pack of saltine crackers and handed them to Doc. Then I pulled out one more of each and sat them beside me. I took the canteen off my belt and took a long draw of what was now lukewarm water.

"Much obliged Kid," Doc said about the sardines. "All I had was this here bologna sandwich that Ollie Bell fixed me." He produced a sandwich wrapped in wax paper from the cargo pocket on the side of his pant leg. Doc was wearing a pair of green fatigue trousers he had picked up at Army Surplus. The sandwich looked like it had endured a hard journey.

"Tear that thing in half and give me some," I said, "Since I gave you my sardines."

Doc did so without protest and we had a tolerable lunch sitting there on the stump.

"Mighty slim pickin's, huh Kid?" Doc said, nodding back toward the trail.

"Oh it's fair to middlin I'd say. Now Doc, I want you to look back along that line. Look at all them sapling markers we have got up between here and the loggin road. Forget for a minute that you are looking for a murder victim. If you had found that much sign when we were looking for a still you would think we were really on to something."

Doc pursed his lips and nodded his agreement.

"I'd say this trail is getting pretty hot. The bad news is, we can't stay with it much longer. We got to leave to meet Spence to go after the Daniels still here in a while. Let's search till one o'clock and then make sure Potts knows what we found. He can send more men over here later today or tomorrow. I may have a couple of visits I want to make on my own in the morning."

"You ain't going to see that Roxanne again, are ya?" Doc winked.

"No, not her. I am going to go talk to the driver of that Chrysler."

After lunch we started our search again. However, the trail went cold...ice cold. We didn't find another thing. We even searched in circles around the markers but we found nothing.

As we had planned, we pulled out of the woods at one o'clock and drove over to where Potts had a command post set up. We found Potts there. He wore muddy knee boots and it was clear he had been doing some searching of his own across the swampy area of Wallace's property.

He looked up at us, acknowledged us with a barely perceptible nod, and waited for our report. We gave the envelope with the hairs to his deputy/brother. I then reminded Potts about the button and told him about the trajectory of that, the hair, the broken twigs and the tobacco can. After telling him what we had found and where, and mentioning our markers to him, we waited for his response.

He looked at me eye to eye and then simply said, "Well, thanks for coming over, but that ain't much, now is it boys?"

Doc started to puff up his chest. He didn't like Potts' comment one bit. Neither did I, but I was more interested in gauging why Potts had said it than I was in expressing my displeasure.

Potts had the reputation of being a pretty fair Sheriff and he should certainly know that in a search like this, what we found was not insignificant. I placed the back of my hand on Doc's chest to stop him before his protest began. He caught my drift and stopped himself after saying, "Now wait just a minute..."

Potts looked over at him. "Sorry if that hurts your feelings, Cook," he said. "But quite frankly, I don't have time to worry about your feelings right now. I have got a murder to solve and a killer in my jail who is going to get sprung by a lawyer if I don't find a body soon. So I need a little more than a few hairs that might belong to a cow or a deer, and a button. Maybe if you two had looked where I told you to look you would have found something a little more useful."

I could feel Doc looking at the back of my head, waiting for my response. I didn't like Potts' attitude but more than making me angry, it struck me as odd. Finally, I spoke up.

"Alright Sheriff, we will be tied up on other cases this afternoon but we will be back over tomorrow and see if we can't do better for you."

"That'll be fine I suppose," Potts said. "Report to me in the morning at the courthouse and I'll give you an assigned area. Maybe you can look where I ask you next time."

I cocked my head, started to tell Potts what I thought of his assignment, and then decided against that. Instead, I turned and headed back to my car.

Once we were driving away Doc said, "What the heck is that guy's problem? I am about half tempted to go back over to him and show him what I think about him."

Doc wasn't going anywhere. That type of bluster was par for the course for my partner. "Keep your shirt on," I said. "Potts is probably feeling the heat. This case is in all the papers. Even Atlanta and Birmingham are covering it. And with this search party it's going to draw even more attention. If I were him I might be hard to deal with right now, too."

Even as I spoke the words, I knew they rang hollow. Potts should have been all over our trail. He should have pulled a few men from some other location and sent them to pick it up while we were there to show it to them. I thought about Hitchcock riding out this morning with Lamar Potts and the surprising friendship between those two. I hoped that friendship wasn't going to mess up what had up till now been some pretty fine police work by the Coweta County Sheriff.

CHAPTER 35
TRAIL GOES COLD

Doc headed back to Woodland to take care of a couple of things before he was to meet Spence and the boat. I decided to ride into Stovall to see if I could connect with anybody else on the search party that I might know and trust.

I was passing across the rail road tracks next to the Stovall depot. The depot was about all there was to Stovall, with the exception of a little country store. As I looked to my left I noticed a rail road maintenance crew. They had a small maintenance locomotive pulling a flatbed car loaded with new cross ties. Two men were working with a pry bar while another man was digging an old cross tie out from under the track. The work caught my eye so I pulled my car over.

"Howdy," I called out.

"Hey," the man who appeared to be the foreman called back reluctantly.

"You boys have got a hot job to do there. Southern Railway ought to let y'all save that work for fall," I said.

"We ain't with Southern," the foreman said. "We work for the Dixie Line. Dixie don't care how hot it is."

"Trains gotta run I suppose," I said smiling.

"We thought you were coming over here to fuss at us for having the track closed for a while. Everybody else around here has."

"Yeah, I guess folks don't like having Stovall commerce interrupted," I replied sarcastically. Say, what are you gonna do with those old ties you're removing?" I asked.

"Pile em up along a remote section on up the line. Railroad will pick em up and burn em eventually, but they'll probably sit there a year or more rotting till somebody gets around to picking them up."

"Well if it's not too much trouble, would you leave me about ten over here around the depot somewhere? I promise you I'll pick em up in the next few days. I like to use them in my garden to box off tomato plants and the like."

"Sure thing," the foreman said. "No problem."

We exchanged a little more small talk and then I saw J.C. Otwell's State Trooper car coming toward the crossing. I flagged him down. But as I was walking his way I stopped and turned back to the rail crew.

"Say, fellas, how long you been on this particular section of track?" I asked.

"Oh, I'd say a little over two weeks now," the foreman said.

"So no train has run through here in two weeks?"

"Nope," he said. "They haven't been able to run this line since we started. That's why folks around here keep rushing us. We'll be done in another three or four days though."

"Much obliged," I said making a mental note. Then I walked over to J.C.'s car.

"Boy I wish I had a big V8 in my car like they give you boys," I said smiling. "maybe all these bootleggers wouldn't outrun me so easy."

"Howdy Miller," J.C. said. "You been helping with the search too I suppose."

"Yeah, my partner Doc had to go get some things ready for another case we are working so I just rode up here to see what I might see. Hey, J. C. unless you got somewhere particular you were going to look, I'd like to show you something we found."

"Sure, be glad to. I haven't found anything so far anyway."

I got back into my car and Otwell fell in behind me as we headed for Wallace's farm.

I led him out to the logging road and we walked around the thicket and into the woods. I half expected to see other lawmen, maybe even Potts himself, working my trail but there was no one there.

It only took a few minutes for me to show Otwell my trail markers. We looked for another forty minutes and neither of us found another hint of sign. After another thirty minutes we were discouraged.

I sat back down on the big boulder where Doc and I had previously eaten lunch and took a long pull off my canteen. Otwell plopped down beside me and did the same from his.

"Maybe Potts was right," I said. Maybe this ain't much of a trail."

"I wouldn't go that far," Otwell said. "You've got to consider, Wallace would have been careful. Plus, we've had a big rain since the day Turner was killed. But I will say this, I am about ready to give up on finding much more today."

"Yeah," I said. "Me too. In fact it's nearly three o' clock and I've got to be over in Upson County by 5:30. I may start heading for Woodland and eat some of my wife's cooking before I head back out for the evening."

I shook out a handkerchief and tried to wipe off my forehead and my hat band, but my handkerchief was about as wet with sweat as they were.

We sat there silently for a few minutes, looking around from the stump as if a clue would jump out at us. Finally, I asked the question that had been on my mind for quite a while.

"Otwell," I said. "Why do you suppose Potts doesn't have anybody over here looking into this area after what I have already given him?"

"That's a tough one, Miller," Otwell said. "I don't know Lamar real well. I have worked with him on a case or two. I have to admit I am still trying to make up my mind about him. I think he is a pretty good Sheriff overall. He grew up in Coweta, he knows the county over there like the back of his hand. But he definitely has his own way of doing things. Sometimes I think he's just got a pretty small circle of people that he trusts."

"Well, he ought to be more selective about who those people are then. Otherwise he is only going to hinder his investigation," I said. Otwell nodded his agreement.

"What led Potts to go ahead and arrest Wallace, do you know?" I asked.

"Potts got enough probable cause that he got a search warrant for Sivell's car and Wallace's house. He found blood stains in the back floorboard of the car and a bloody khaki work shirt in Wallace's dirty clothes hamper. Also somebody on the highway crew pointed out both Wallace and Sivell as being the men that drove by chasing Turner's truck and shooting at him out the side window. I don't know if Steve Smith from the diner made a positive ID yet or not. But the identification from the highway crew members and the physical evidence was enough to make an arrest."

"What the heck happened to that boy, Otwell, I mean, what did Wallace do? All I know is what Steve told me that day at the truck stop."

"I don't know much more," Otwell said. "Apparently Potts believes Hardy Collier was in cahoots with Wallace on this. He thinks Collier was ordered by Wallace to release Turner at noon so that Wallace could follow him."

I punched a fist into my palm. I told Otwell about how I had seen Wallace, Sivell and Collier that morning. I told him Wallace and Sivell were wearing Khaki work clothes as would match what Potts found in the hamper. "I remember looking at my watch when I headed out of Greenville to question an informant on another case. I had made a report to Collier at eleven thirty. I was within half an hour of stopping this thing from happening and yet Collier sat there and lied to my face. He made out like he was going to check up on the information I gave him about Wallace, and he was playing me the whole time."

"Well, that's not all," Otwell said. "The jailer, Jake, he was told to drain gas out of Turner's truck. Turner wasn't supposed to make it nowhere near the county line. He was supposed to run out of gas somewhere on the way to Stovall. I guess Wallace was going to take care of him there."

I shook my head again. "Poor Jake," I said. "That's why he had a swollen eye. He was all upset and talking about doing his best. Collier or someone punched that old man because he didn't drain out enough gas. I would bet a paycheck on it."

"After Turner got released from jail, he apparently saw Wallace following him. He took off running in that new pickup of his. Wallace and Sivell chased him to Steve Smiths place and beat him," Otwell said. "From there, you know as much as I do. I guess the district attorney is going to try to prove that Turner died in the parking lot there at Smith's diner. That way the case stays away from a biased or intimidated Meriwether County jury."

"And from there they could have taken Turner anywhere. From this property the only solid evidence we have is a Prince Albert can with *maybe* a partial print on it that *might* have belonged to Turner. But Turner worked for Wallace. He could have dropped that can a long time ago. I don't know if that button even belonged on Turner's shirt or that the hair was his."

"Maybe the state crime lab can do something with the hair."

"Where is he Otwell?" I said. "Where the heck is Turner? And how does this story all add up?"

"Miller, your guess is as good as mine."

We sat there a while longer and I told Otwell about my meeting with Turner at his still that night.

"You know," Otwell said. "If Turner had cooperated with you, and if your hunch about Wallace's liquor making is right, Wallace would already be doing time for moonshining and Turner would probably be alive today."

"Yeah," I said. "That thought has been eating at me."

I leaned forward and placed my hands on my knees. Then I stood up stiffly. I had been going pretty hard for several days and had spent a good bit of time crouched, hiding, or sitting on the hard ground near one still or another. All of that was taking its toll.

"You know Otwell," I said. "I haven't told anyone this, but a really odd thing happened to me the morning after I found that button."

I told him about meeting the old lady on the dirt road on the morning after my first search at Wallace's place. I told him how Wallace had sat on his horse that day and used the name Miss Mahayley.

"So, do you think I'm crazy, or that I was just running on fumes and conjured this old lady up in my imagination?"

"Oh no, you didn't conjure her up, and I don't think you're crazy," Otwell said. "John Wallace already gave you her name. Miss Mayhayley and the old lady you described are one in the same. I know her pretty well. And she's told lots of folks lots of things that left them in awe."

CHAPTER 36
VISITING MAHAYLEY

I followed J.C. out of Stovall to a gas station where we both filled up. I left my car there and got in with Otwell. We drove onto highway 27 and headed up to Heard County to see Miss Mahalya Lancaster. I told J.C. that I absolutely couldn't stay long. I was already going to miss out on having supper at home. By the time we talked to Miss Lancaster it would be all I could do to meet Doc and Spence on time.

"Mayhayley is quite a character," J. C. said. "I have gotten to know her pretty well over the last few years. She lives in a little cabin with her sister Sallie Mae. Sallie Mae has some kind of physical disability and she is in the bed a lot of times.

I have responded as a backup to the deputy Sheriff several times in the past few months because Mayhayley has been robbed four times. Turns out she had money stuffed all over that shack. She had money buried out in the yard."

"You mean buried in jars or something?" I asked.

"No, I mean buried in the dirt. I mean corners of twenty and hundred dollar bills sticking up out of the dirt in the crawl space under that shack. I mean bills just thrown in a pile in the yard and covered with a foot or so of dirt. I never saw nor heard of anything like it," Otwell said. "It got to be a security problem for the neighbors. Word was getting around amongst thugs from all the way up to Atlanta. When Heard County elected their new Sheriff, first thing he did was had me go out there with him. Mayhayley kind of trusts me. So I stood by and he talked to her. He had to force her to put that money in the bank.

A whole bunch of people in the community came and helped. I was there, all the deputies and the sheriff were there. It was like a treasure hunt. Mayhayley knew how much money she should have but she didn't remember where all she had buried it. Folks would find a stash, dig it up, and then bring it in the house and just pile it on the table. Another group sat there at the table and flattened out the money and put it in flour sacks. I want you to know that lady had over twenty four thousand dollars in cash and change!"

"You've got to be kidding me," I said.

"No, I am serious. And she knew within a few dollars of how much she should have. Even with all those people handling her money, not one dollar came up missing. Now here is the kicker, we give her an escort to the bank, it was like we were escorting an armored car or something," Otwell smiled.

"We get her and the money to the bank and the banker won't take it! Say's we are not putting that nasty money in his bank. So the people in the community took the money across the street and a store owner let them use his big sink he had in the back and donated some laundry powder and they washed and dried that money for her. Everybody in this county loves the old gal and they believe in her. They washed it, dried it, ironed it out, and she deposited every dime that we left that house with. Nobody took anything from her."

"Well I'll be…" I said laughing.

"Beat anything I have ever seen in my life," Otwell said.

After turning off the paved road, we wound down a dirt road, then took a left onto another made of red clay. Finally, after what seemed like a hundred miles but was only about twenty, we pulled up into a dirt yard. There was a weathered one-room shack with a ramshackle porch on the back. Mayhayley Lancaster was sitting on the old backseat of a car that she was using for a porch sofa. She had a corncob pipe in her mouth. There were dogs of every size and description lying all over the porch, on the car seat with Miss Lancaster, and in the yard.

As we got out of the car, she gave me a real once over. She stared at me for what seemed like minutes, as she puffed on her pipe. She still wore her army hat and brogans. This time her dress was store bought, not made from flour sacks, and she wore a drab grey apron over it.

"Miss Mayhayley," Otwell waved and smiled, "how are you doing this afternoon? This here is…"

"How many of y'all goin to come out here asking me questions?" Mayhayley said. "I done talked to that Sheriff Potts, I talked to you, I've had reporters already come out here being a botheration and knockin' on my door. And every dang one of you wants to talk about the same thing. And this one here," she wagged a crooked finger in my general direction, "he already tried to run me down with his car one time."

"Now, Miss Mayhayley, that is not exactly how it happened," I said, smiling slightly.

She dismissed me with a wave of her hand.

"Dollar and a dime," she said.

"What do you mean a dollar and a dime?" Otwell asked, but by the way he was smirking at me, I had a feeling he already knew the answer.

"Dollar for me, dime for my dogs if you want to know somethin'. I ain't tellin' no more to nobody for free. I got to get by too, you know? I got to take care of me and mine."

"Now Miss Mayhayley, we…"

I stopped Otwell in mid-sentence by reaching in my pocket and getting the money. I stepped up onto the steps and thrust it out for Miss Mayhayley to take, which she did, placing the money in an apron pocket.

"We were kind of interested in seeing if you knew…" I began.

"I tol you walls was pressin' in on him. Tol you about the water long ago. I tol you what I seen. Come in the house!"

I didn't believe in this woman or any so called magical powers. But I must admit, hearing her say those words again gave me a cold shiver. I looked at Otwell and he looked at me. Then I walked on up the steps. The screen door slapped against the doorjamb when Miss Mayhayley didn't wait for me. There was a cookfire burning in the fireplace making the house stifling, even with the windows open. A kettle suspended from a cast iron hook was hanging over the fire, something that smelled like vegetable soup simmering slowly inside.

The walls were almost completely covered in old newspapers that appeared to be pasted into place. A plain wooden table and four chairs adorned the center of the room. Two black leather chairs with chrome metal arms, the type I had seen in many barber shop waiting areas, were pulled in front of the fireplace. As promised, Miss Sallie Mae was lying in bed. She had a white cotton sheet pulled all the way up under her nose. Only her eyes and fingers were visible, but her eyes were smiling. A shock of long white hair lay across the pillow and spilled over the top of the sheet. I guessed Miss Mayhayley to be in her seventies and Miss Sallie Mae at least ten years older.

"You two sit down at the table. I will attempt to consult the spirits to get you your answer. I would thank you to keep your roving eyes off of my sister, as she is in her dressing gown and not attired to receive callers."

"Uh...yes Ma'am," I said awkwardly. "But respectfully, we haven't asked a question yet. I would like to start by asking you why you left so abruptly that night..."

"I know what you came here for!" she cut me off, slamming a palm down on the table. "I know what it is you seek. Now, first things first."

With that she reached over on a counter and grabbed two oven mitts. She reached down into the coals of the fire and, using the two mitts doubled together, grasped the handle of an iron skillet. Only the handle was visible. The rest of the pan was buried under the coals. She pulled the pan out to the stone hearth, and using an old piece of board, she carefully scraped red coals from the lid of the pan.

She then sat the pan onto the top of a wood stove that wasn't lit. Finally she carefully lifted the lid off with the mitts and sat it over in a sink to reveal the golden brown top of a cornbread cake.

"Looky there, Sallie," she said, picking up the pan again and lowering it so Sallie Mae could see the bread. "Finest chef in New Orleans couldn't of cooked it no better. Don't you two get no ideas. Dollar and a dime's for information, not for supper. Me and Sallie Mae's got to eat on this for a couple of days yet."

"We're fine Miss Mayhayley," Otwell said.

"Hush now! The both of ya. I will need quiet."

She then squatted down at the hearth and reached for a fireplace poker. She began to stir the coals in an area near the center of the fire. She stirred and stirred. Then she began to sway slightly and a low humming sound came from deep within her. Suddenly, she leaned forward and spat into the fire. The coals hissed and sizzled. Miss Mayhayley leaned her head back and her eyes rolled back in her head. Sallie Mae sat full upright in the bed, the sheet still pulled up to her chin. She giggled at her sister, mumbled something indiscernible and pointed at Mayhayley.

At that moment, Mayhayley shook her head vigorously, and using the poker as a cane, pushed herself to a standing position.

"He ain't there no more," she said matter of factly.

"What do you mean?" I asked.

"When I met you on the road that night, I only saw walls...stone walls like would make a tunnel. I tol Potts he was in a hole in the ground. By the time I talked to him I could see that it wasn't no tunnel, it was an old well. He was throwed down in an old well. But he ain't there no more."

"Are you speaking of Turner...Wilson Turner?" Otwell asked.

"YES, TURNER!" Mayhayley shouted loudly enough to startle us both. "Who did you come up here looking for? Who else would I be talking about?"

"Well, where was the well and where is he now?" Otwell asked.

"I told you people already I don't see that. I don't see where the well is."

"Did you tell Potts that he wasn't in the well anymore?"

"Well no, ya idgit," Mayhayley said. "He was still in there when Potts came. Gone now though. They put him on a mule. Mule was covered in mud. Don't know where they took him. Don't know where he is. Just know he is gone from where he was before."

"Who took him? You keep saying *they* took him. Who is they? Is there anything else you can tell us?" I asked.

I didn't believe any of this. If this old lady knew anything it was only because someone had told *her*. I didn't have time to sit out here in the middle of nowhere and be toyed with.

Now Mayhayley Lancaster looked at me with a big frown on her face. She seemed to almost pout as she stared at me. Then, as she had on the morning I saw her on the road, she hissed at me like an angry cat.

"I know nothing more to tell you and I don't care to talk to you no more on the matter."

"Did Wallace tell you all this?" I asked.

Miss Lancaster slammed a bony palm down on the kitchen table.

"I am the Oracle of the Ages. I see. I don't tell things people tells me in confidence, I tells what I see. And I seen he was in a well and now he is gone and now I have told all I have seen and all that I will tell."

With that she stamped a foot, pursed her lips and furrowed her brow. She was staring a hole through me. She was through talking.

"C'mon Miller, let's let these ladies eat their supper," Otwell said as he stood up.

I nodded respectfully at Miss Mayhayley and stepped toward the door.

"He's got a good heart, J.C.," she said. "He's just a might hard to please. You can bring him back sometime though."

"Thank you Miss Mayhayley," I said. Then I nodded toward the bed, "Miss Sallie Mae, hope you feel better."

Twenty minutes later we left the dirt road and pulled back onto the highway.

"You don't believe her, do ya?" Otwell said.

"I believe she either saw something, or somebody, maybe Wallace, told her something. I don't believe there is any such thing as an Oracle. No, that part I don't believe. Do you?"

"Sometimes I am not sure. No, really I don't guess I do. But this is not the first time she has helped the law out on a case. She has helped folks find stuff they lost. People around here sure do believe in her. They believe she sees things."

We rode in silence for a time. We were nearly back to the turnoff that would take us to the gas station and my car. Finally, I spoke up.

"You know," I said. "Something she said does make sense. If they dumped that boy's body down an abandoned well in the middle of those woods, that would explain why a fairly hot trail might abruptly go ice cold."

CHAPTER 37
FLINT RIVER

I left Otwell and the John Wallace case in my rear view mirror and tried to clear my head. I needed to start thinking about the Daniel Godfrey case again. I was somewhere on the South side of worn out from the day I had put in already and I even had to fight sleep a time or two while I was driving. I stopped at my house in Woodland, and since I was in a hurry Rose put on a pot of strong black coffee, filled up a thermos with it, and made me a sandwich for the road. I kissed the girls and headed out. I arrived at the shoals of the Flint River just off highway 36 at 5:15. Even though I was a few minutes early, Doc and Spence were there and had the boat in the water. We had four hours of search time.

"You boy's do good work," I called out, smiling. "I thought I was going to be too early."

"We does what we can," Spence said, tossing his cigarette butt into the edge of the river. We piled into the boat. Spence brought along a sawed off Winchester twelve gauge double barrel. I knew why he had the extra firepower. We had as good a chance of getting shot at tonight as we ever would have. I even pulled my Smith back out, turned the cylinder to make sure it was ready, and holstered it again. I had an extra hundred rounds of ammunition in an ammo pouch on my belt. I had never brought that much ammo on a raid.

I had to hand it to Godfrey, the information I got from Punkin Woodley proved one thing. This was one well-hidden operation. And it was defensible. From what I had been able to piece together from Punkin's reluctant tip, and from my own knowledge of the area, Godfrey had located this still such that it would be almost impossible to approach on foot from any direction. The still was in the center of a triangle, so to speak Thunder Road made up one side of the triangle with Pigeon Creek as the base. The third side of the triangle was the river. Thunder Road followed some steep ridge tops and had very narrow shoulders. Anyone wanting to search for the still, or set up a raid, would be unable to park a car alongside the road without their car being obvious.

No matter how subtle or quiet an agent tried to be from the road, Godfrey and his men would be ready and waiting. They would either lie in wait for the revenue agents and ambush them, or at the very least, move the still operation. That's exactly why I wasn't going to use the roads.

I was going to float upriver and then ease the boat into the mouth of Pigeon Creek. We would portage the boat and hide it as best we could. Then we would ease up the creek toward the still. My gut told me that Godfrey had yet to hear about Punkin being arrested, and he sure wouldn't know that Punkin had given me anything. He wouldn't be expecting anyone to know his location well enough to try an approach by water.

Punkin had told me enough to get me within a half-mile or so of the still. That was much closer than I had ever been before. Still, it was a considerable distance in heavy woods. To make the search more challenging, Pigeon Creek had a fork. Punkin didn't know if the still was on the north fork or the south fork of that creek because he had always walked in from the road.

The Flint was going to give me a back door access to "Over the Top." And deep in the heart of that country, far back in the thick piney forest, was where I was going to find Daniel Godfrey and his still. Godfrey wanted me dead? That was going to be hard to accomplish from the state prison.

CHAPTER 38
ROCK HOUSE MOUNTAIN

We rowed slowly into the mouth of Pigeon Creek.

When the water began to get shallow, I rowed us over to the bank. We drug the boat up onto the shore, hiding it beneath some saplings in a dry ravine. We moved up the creek together slowly and deliberately. We stayed away from the soft sandy deposits along the bank of the creek, careful not to leave tell-tale footprints. Finally, we came to the fork.

"Alright, here we are," I whispered. "You boy's take the South fork, I'll take the North. If you haven't found anything within a half mile you probably aren't going to. At that point, come out the way you went in. We will meet back at the boat at eight. If either of us hasn't shown up by eight, the others will know we are on to something."

"So you're doin' it again?" Doc said. "You goin' it alone?"

"Doc, there's two forks and three of us. Somebody's got to be on their own."

Doc made a face but said no more about it. Spence opened the action on that double barrel again and looked around suspiciously. The boys were nervous and I didn't blame them. I could have brought more men, but that would mean more possible sign and more ways to tip off Godfrey.

We moved out. Spence was really good with navigating in the woods so I wasn't worried about Doc. I didn't say anything to them, but I was confident the still would be on my fork somewhere. The South fork of Pigeon Creek, where they were going, ran through some bottoms, thus it contained more silt and was shallow. The North fork ran straight out of rocky ridges. It was deeper and had more flow, a much better place for a big still.

I picked my way carefully along the creek bank, stopping every few steps to listen to my surroundings. More than once I stepped out on a rocky outcropping, dipped a handkerchief into the water and doused my head and face to cool off. I was completely in my element doing this part of the job. The woods were a part of me. I got to know Pigeon Creek and the depth of the North Fork a few years ago when I made several trips here looking for a smaller still. I hadn't known of the Godfrey brothers back then, but that early bust started a chain of events that eventually led me to pursue them. When I thought back on it, I had been working on this case for years. I had a feeling I was close, really close to finally closing it out.

I continued along the creek, going further upstream than I had ever been. Suddenly I felt a blast of cool air. That could only mean one thing. I was nearing a cave. The air from underground would be a constant 60 to 65 degrees. I had always heard of a cave back in here called Rock House Mountain but I had never been to it. The place got its name from the true story of a Cherokee Indian family that once lived here. The family ran away from the Trail of Tears and hid out in the cave. From what I had heard, they lived there for several years.

As I stood there, the cool air washing over me, I had a hunch. I moved toward the flow of air letting it guide me like a beacon. The woods were thick and honeysuckle vine created a nearly impenetrable wall but I slowly worked my way through. Finally, I saw the cave opening. I stopped to look for trip wires. Moonshiners would tie a wire to a wad of tin cans suspended from a sapling as an alarm. The sound of those cans would stand out like a bomb going off in the quiet woods. Sometimes they would even set traps for unsuspecting revenuers. The traps might cause a pile of boulders to fall on him, or a snare to yank him upside down by the feet.

I finally made it all the way to the mouth of the cave without incident. I sat there and listened for a full ten minutes. When I felt certain that no one was inside, I turned on my flashlight. Jackpot! The cave was full of barrels. I pulled a nearby cork and smelled the moonshine. I had to be close to the still. I had spent the past four years trying to shut down the Godfrey brothers' liquor operations. I had finally gotten Harry. Now, brother Daniel's operation was close by.

CHAPTER 39
FOUR TURNIPS

I left the cave and continued to work my way upstream. I didn't expect anyone to be at the still this early in the afternoon, but I couldn't take any chances. I moved as slowly and steadily as a bobcat stalking its prey. Suddenly, I froze. There running about an inch over the ground was a trip wire. I let my eyes follow the wire first in one direction, where ten yards down it was secured tightly to the trunk of a small sweetgum. As I followed the wire in the other direction, it disappeared several times beneath the oak leaves. Finally, looking up a little wet weather feeder stream, I saw where the wire ended.

It was tied off on a heavy stake that was jammed against a sturdy two-by-six board. The board was holding back a pile of boulders big enough to break both my ankles. It was a booby trap. I stepped over the wire carefully, stepping on rocks whenever possible so as not to leave tracks.

I eased along a bit further and finally, up ahead, I saw the trough protruding out of a waterfall about six feet high. Unless you've been where I have been I cannot describe the feeling to you. Some stills you find after one or two tries. Sometimes you get a tip that leads you right to a still almost without looking. On this still however, I had questioned countless informants before Mark Anthony had sent me to Punkin. I had spent endless hours in the woods looking for Daniel Godfrey's still. And now I had found it. This time, not only was there the thrill of accomplishment at ending the production of moonshine, there was also the satisfaction that I was going to keep my family safe.

The trough was a waterway that was present at every still. It captured cold creek water and funneled a portion over to the still. I had to resist the urge to charge ahead. In a few more careful steps I finally saw it. The still was hidden between two small ridges with about two acres of flat ground in between. Then I saw black thread. The bootleggers would check to make sure the thread hadn't been broken before they would fire up the still. I avoided the thread and finally stepped into the flat.

There spread before me was Daniel Godfrey's design. And it was a beauty. There were four what were called "turnip boilers," the name coming from their odd shape. The mash was cooked inside the turnip boiler, and if the head piece was on, the cooking mash would pressurize, allowing alcohol vapors and a little bit of mash to boil over. The head piece for each of these boilers was missing. Godfrey and his hands probably took them home with them when they were not in use.

The head piece would be one of the most precious parts of the still to a moonshiner. They had to be custom made by a coppersmith and securely fastened to the turnip in order to allow the mash cooking in the boiler to work properly. The head piece also included a long spout that flowed to the "thumper." The thumper would be about one fourth full of liquid, usually beer, and would trap any solids that boiled over from the mash. The thumper got its name because it would make a "thumping" sound as the moonshine vapors momentarily condensed and then flashed back to steam.

From the thumper, the vapors flowed into the other precious commodity of the moonshiner, the worm. Worms, like headpieces, were usually fashioned by coppersmiths and thus were difficult to obtain. The trough that ran from the waterfall carried cold creek water into four smaller troughs. Each small trough ran to a worm box. The worm box would contain the copper "worm." Hot moonshine vapors flowed through the worm, or coil, which was bathed in cold water. As 'Shine traveled through the coil, it would condense and flow into what was called the "money piece." After the money piece was some type of filter through which finished moonshine would flow into jugs or mason jars.

Daniel Godfrey had four pretty good sized turnip boilers here, each with its own thumper and worm. From the look of it, he could produce at least one hundred and fifty gallons a night. He could sell the stuff for about two dollars a pint so he was generating about twenty four hundred dollars in income for every night he ran. That's a whole lot of money in this day and time. That was money worth shooting a man over if you were Daniel Godfrey.

By taking the boiler heads and the worms each time his men left, Godfrey protected them from being stolen by competitors or damaged by the likes of me. His precautions weren't going to work out so well for him however. At the appropriate time, I would make him drive an axe through them while I watched. I began to look for a place to get comfortable. I might have to wait here for up to a couple of hours before the hands showed up and fired the still. Doc and Spence would have to wait until I could slip out without being detected.

I found a spot about sixty yards away from one of the turnip boilers and nestled back into a wild grape vine, making sure that I was well hidden. I took out my notepad so I could write names of anyone I recognized or any name I heard called out by the workers. The grapevine was growing around the base of a pin oak and I used its trunk as a back rest. I had only been there five minutes when I heard distant voices.

I was surprised. It was still not quite dusk and at least an hour early for moonshiners to be getting started. I thought for a few moments that perhaps the voices were just someone out on one of the ridge roads walking and talking. But no, the voices were already getting closer. In fact, they were closing fast. These folks weren't that far away. I didn't like the situation. I was well hidden, but I wouldn't have the cover of darkness to help me. In this much light I couldn't afford to move even an inch. That being said, I wasn't in a good position. There was a root or a sharp stone or something sticking me right in the rear. I was going to have to sit dead still for at least two hours. I couldn't sit on a root for that long.

I had to hurry. I reached beneath myself and tried to move whatever it was. It was a stone and it was buried deeply in the ground. I tried shifting over but this was rocky ground and the next spot I sat on was worse. The voices were getting closer. I could almost make out what they were saying. They were talking very loud for moonshiners. They had gotten cocky, thinking they would never be found.

I looked to my left. I only had about two or three minutes where I would still be able to move. There was a good heavy stick nearby. I would use it to dig out the rock and then I would be able to sit still. As I reached over and wrapped my hand around the stick, my hair stood on end. There, an inch from my hand was an eastern diamondback rattler.

CHAPTER 40
RATTLER!

I knew I had to get my hand back before the rattler got coiled. I did so, still clutching the stick. Then I took a quick glance toward the voices. At the top of one of the ridges that bordered the still, I saw a man's hat. His face would be visible in seconds. I looked back at the rattler. He was coiled now and starting to rattle. I'd made him mad. In the midst of all the adrenaline my instincts took over, and I put my right hand on the butt of my pistol. I had no doubt that I could draw, fire, and decapitate him from here, but then I would have armed moonshiners on me, one of whom wanted me dead.

Now I could see the first moonshiner's torso. He was still one hundred and seventy five yards away and not looking in my direction. He was focused on the still or either on the men following him. They were loose, laughing and talking, not on alert. I had to do something and it had to be now. The rattler was really shaking his rattles. I used to do a little switch hitting back on the baseball diamond so I gripped the stick with a death grip in my left hand. I only had one chance at this or I was going to die, one way or the other. I swung the stick in a tight arc as hard and fast as I could. The snake struck. I had a half-second head start. I hit him in the head as he struck and diverted him. While he was stretched out, I reached over and slammed my right hand down just behind his head, pinning it to the ground. Then, using the stick like a hatchet, I chopped down hard repeatedly until I saw blood and the snake stopped squirming.

I could barely catch my breath. I looked up expecting a whole lot of guns to be pointed at me but that didn't happen. The first moonshiner was just getting to the still and was reaching for the lid to the mash pit. I had pulled it off. I couldn't believe it. I tilted my head back against the tree trunk, nearly knocking off the pith helmet that I wore on raids. For the first time, I realized I could hear my heart pounding. I took several deep breaths and then looked at the snake. He was writhing a bit but that was just nerves jumping. He was dead alright.

I watched the still closely. Every time they did anything to make a noise, I took my stick and made a movement to create a shallow grave. I couldn't take a chance that someone might find this dead snake, or see flies buzzing around it tomorrow. I had to be able to come back in here with a raiding party. It took me some time, but I eventually got the snake buried, even putting a double fist sized rock on the snakes head, just in case.

It took a good twenty minutes after that for my pulse rate to get anywhere near normal. It was finally starting to get dark and the cover of that darkness allowed me to relax a bit. I didn't relax for long. Just about the time I gathered myself, and prepared to start writing down the names of the six workers at the still. I heard footsteps behind me. The left over leaves from fall were heavy and I heard the unmistakable shuffling gate of a man coming up to my rear. I dare not turn around for fear of the movement being detected. After sitting motionless for what seemed like an eternity, the man came up alongside my right and stopped about five steps in front of my position. I cut my eyes over there. It was Daniel Godfrey.

Had he stopped because he had seen me? From his body language I didn't think so, but I wasn't sure. After the snake incident I had rested my right hand on the ground right beside the pistol in my holster. Ever so slowly, I moved my hand to the butt. If Godfrey had seen me, I was going to make darn sure to take him out first when the shooting started. Again, the adrenaline flowed. This time however, my heart rate stayed steady. I felt more comfortable in a gun fight than in trying to out strike a rattler.

I watched Godfrey. He kept standing there. He wasn't more than thirty feet away. He was watching the still intently. Suddenly he shouted so loud that it startled me a bit. "Dang it, Beanie!" he called out. "I have been standin here listenin to you, and you ain't going for no six draws. How many times have I got to tell ya, that sixth draw don't do nothing but waste time and labor."

With that, he stomped into the creek and crossed over to walk into the firelight of the still. He didn't know I was here. Now I knew I was going to beat Daniel Godfrey. I had him.

Sometimes the sixth draw was too weak and would water down the whiskey too much to be used. Some moonshiners would use it in the thumping pot to make it stronger. Other, more unscrupulous guys would "jug it up" with beading oil as Wilson Turner had attempted a couple of weeks before with his spoiled liquor. Beading oil caused weak whiskey to form beads as if it was stronger. Beanie could use that to sell worthless whiskey to unsuspecting customers for the same price as the best stuff.

Nothing eventful happened over the next hour. I took names. Once I heard the name Beanie I knew that was "Bean Pole" Johnson the store clerk I had busted when I made the poker game bust. I had done some digging and found out that Beanie had been a petty thief and general scalawag his whole life. Some of the others I knew as well once I heard them talk more. I had the names. I had done all I could do. It was time to go. But how would I get out of here without being seen? Suddenly a way was provided. An unexpected bolt of lightning lit up the woods, followed within seconds by a loud clap of thunder. Everyone jumped. Godfrey looked skyward.

"You boys stick it out here and finish this run. As soon as you get it jugged you can put out the fires and leave. And you better not leave my worms or heads down here, I don't care how wet you get."

"Where you goin Godfrey, to sit in the house and hold hands with the little lady?" Bean Pole asked.

Godfrey wheeled on Beanie and cuffed him hard. Then he slapped him twice more.

"You talk to me like that again at my still and I'll beat your sorry ass to within an inch of your life," Godfrey said. "And if I ever hear that you even thought about my wife again, I'll shoot you through the gizzard for it. You understand me, you foul mouthed wretch?"

The other workers froze. Bean Pole only cowered and nodded in the affirmative.

"I got important business to attend to," Godfrey said. "It's somethin' I have to do myself. I don't trust nobody to do it for me." He looked up at the sky again. Then he stomped across the creek and walked right past me until the sound of his footsteps disappeared into the night. It thundered a few more times and the still workers mumbled to one another about how they would soon be getting rained on.

In a few more minutes I heard a vehicle start up out on Thunder Road behind me. I wondered what business Godfrey had to conduct. Finally, rain began to fall, softly at first then much harder. The sound of the rain in the canopy of trees would cover me so it was a good time to move out. I had to meet Doc and Spence at the boat.

CHAPTER 41

STORMY NIGHT

Daniel Godfrey had the advantage of having his pick-up truck parked within a mile of his still. Because of that he was standing in Miller's back yard in the pitch black of a summer thunderstorm within forty minutes of leaving the woods. The rain had let up for a bit so the conditions were perfect for taking care of his task without being seen.

He walked slowly but steadily up to the Camilla bush and squeezed between it and the wall of Miller's house. There was a metal bucket near an outdoor water faucet. Daniel moved it under the bathroom window. Standing on it with one foot he peered into the lower right corner of the window. At first he only saw a distant shaft of light coming into a far bedroom from what looked like the kitchen. Then he saw a little girl run into the bedroom just off the bathroom door. She tip toed up to flip on a light in the bedroom. Godfrey didn't move. She picked up a baby doll from a toy crib, wrapped a pink blanket around it, and turned the light off as she left the room. Godfrey hoped she wouldn't be within sight of her Daddy when they conducted their business. A thing like that could scar a kid.

. . .

The rain was soft when we got into the boat and only a drizzle fell as we rowed back to the landing. By the time we got to our vehicles, it began to come down hard once again. Doc's house was less than a mile from my own and I followed his Dodge back towards Woodland. As we approached the Talbot County line, the rain began to pound so hard that I could barely see his tail lights in front of me.

As we drove along slowly, something was gnawing at me. We had what we wanted. I'd had a good productive stakeout. I had made Godfrey as the boss at the still and I knew Godfrey owned the land that the operation was on. This raid would be the final blow to the more violent branch of the Godfrey brothers.

I couldn't enjoy that success however, because I couldn't forget what Godfrey said about business he had to handle. The closer we got to Woodland, the more I found myself anxious to get home.

• • •

Daniel Godfrey was miserable. Crouched down behind the Camilla bush, he had his slicker pulled up tight around his neck. The rain was pouring down now and he was starting to think he might wait and do this another night. No. He was here now. He was going to do what he had to do and get it over with. He didn't want this hanging over him. The wind was blowing and now lightning began to flash, followed within two seconds by thunder. Just his luck, it had barely rained all summer but now he had to sit out in this. The fires back at the still were surely quenched by now. He would be a full night behind on production.

"If I could just do something to take my mind off being wet," he thought. He reached inside his slicker and then inside a dungaree jacket he had on underneath it, to find his pipe and tobacco. He probably shouldn't under the circumstances, but by God he was going to have a smoke. That is if he could keep the durned thing lit. Where the hell was Miller?

• • •

Little Judy Miller tip-toed to reach the bathroom light switch. Before she could flip it, something caught her eye. There was something outside. A firefly? Leaving the light off, she pushed the little step stool over toward the window and climbed up to peer out. For a split second she caught a glimpse of an orange glow that looked strangely familiar. She assumed that it was the lit end of her Daddy's pipe.

• • •

Godfrey had seen a silhouette appear inside the bathroom and moved quickly around the corner. That had been close. He angrily snatched the pipe from his mouth, knocked out the burning tobacco into a puddle near his feet, and watched ruefully as each little orange speck went out. He had only gotten two puffs. His jaw muscles clenched. He didn't deserve to have to sit out in this crap like a petty burglar.

• • •

"Mama," Judy called into the living room. "Daddy's home." She was clearly pleased.

Rose Miller looked up from her knitting. "Why do you say that?" she said. "I didn't hear his car."

"Me saw hims pipe outside the bathroom window."

Rose tossed her knitting aside, jumped up from the chair and swept Judy into her arms. "Daddy only smokes a pipe when he is here sitting out on the porch drinking his coffee." Rose ran to fetch her husband's shotgun. "She tried to calm her voice for the sake of her little girl. Judy had already begun to whimper. With her toddler on her hip, Rose picked up the phone to call Sheriff John Henry Ferguson.

Rose loosened her grip on the phone. The receiver dropped loudly to the floor. Rose Miller's eyes were wide, her face pale.

"I can't call the Sheriff" she said blankly. "The phone is dead."

CHAPTER 42
EYE FOR AN EYE

I watched Doc's turn signal come on and as he took a hard left into his driveway. I drove on past, did a rolling stop at the corner, and took a right onto Pleasant Hill, the street my house was on. I said a short prayer. Then I got a lightning bolt, literally.

As I rolled down my street, only a half mile from my house, I passed by old man Pie's house. Vernon Pie prided himself on never having owned a "motor car" as he called them. He was strictly a mule man. Even now he had an old barn behind his house where he stored a wagon. His mules pulled him to town in that thing once a week. At the very moment that my side window was in line with his barn door, lightning struck nearby. I don't think I would have noticed that the door was open except that I saw the red taillights of a pick-up truck. I happened to know that old man Pie was down with the croup. His daughter had taken him over to Columbus so she could tend to him while he was sick. No truck should be in that barn.

I killed my headlights and snatched the Ford over into Vernon Pie's driveway. I opened my glove box and took out a box of cartridges. I drew my pistol, opened the cylinder and let the wet rounds fall to the floorboard. I replaced them with fresh ones. I holstered the pistol again and reached into the back seat to retrieve my crumpled black rubber slicker. I reached for my Stetson, knowing that the wide brim would shed water away from my eyes. This seemed like a good night to walk the rest of the way home.

• • •

Daniel Godfrey took one last look into the bathroom window. He hadn't seen anyone the last three times he looked and now he heard thumping inside the house, as if someone was rearranging furniture. He had had enough of this! If Miller was on a still somewhere and it wasn't raining there, then no telling when he would get home. He reached down and rested his hand on the butt of the .44 he had jammed down into his belt just beside the buckle. Any other night Godfrey would have waited for as long as it took, but the weather was brutal and he had had all he was going to take of it. He turned abruptly to head toward his truck. A brilliant flash of lightning lit up the night sky. That's when he saw C. E. Miller standing twenty feet away.

• • •

I stood facing the man who had told me just days before that he was going to kill me. Now I had caught him peeking in the window of my home where my wife and little girl were. A stiff wind was at my back and the rain poured off the brim of my Stetson. I didn't let it steal my focus. My eyes were locked onto Godfrey's as I spoke evenly.

"It ain't gonna be no big deal Daniel," I said, loudly enough to be heard above the wind. Godfrey turned his head to one side a bit and looked puzzled. His eyes shifted downward for a second and then came back to mine. He was considering making a move.

"What are you talking about Miller?" he said. "What ain't no big deal?"

"Did I ever tell you how I made it through the depression, Daniel?"

"What? What the hell…"

"I painted houses." My hand was hanging loosely by my side. My grip was open and relaxed. My breath was steady and even now. Godfrey was thinking about what I was saying.

"I must have whitewashed half the houses in this county. I didn't like the work much. Sometimes I painted a whole house and only cleared thirty or forty dollars. But it was work. It gave us grocery money, you know?"

"What the hell do I care..." Godfrey began.

"You're thinkin about pullin on me Godfrey," I interrupted again. "I can see it in your eyes. And when you do, I am going to blow your brains all over the side of my house. But it ain't gonna be no big deal, because I've still got my drop cloth and my brushes. I can just white wash that wall tomorrow. Be good as new."

There was a long silence. Daniel Godfrey wanted to try me. He wanted to prove that he was better than me, wanted to prove to himself how tough he was.

"Go ahead Godfrey. You came to *my* home. You looked into my window near where my little girl plays. I want ya' to try it. You might clear before I do...maybe."

There was a long silence. My gaze never wavered from the spot on the bridge of Godfrey's nose where my slugs would enter. I didn't allow myself to focus on the rain or to get distracted by the flashes of lightning or the peals of thunder. I noticed Godfrey's right elbow begin to crook ever so slightly. He was shortening the distance between his hand and the butt of that big forty-four.

"That's a whole lot of pistol your packin' there Godfrey. A man could do a lot of damage with a cannon like that. Course, that's supposin' he could clear his belt in time with all that iron." I let that sink in.

There comes a point in these situations when a man makes a choice. He either realizes his limitations, or he makes a decision that gets him killed. Godfrey decided he wasn't ready to die. I saw him relax his arm at the elbow.

"You're a little bit smarter than I thought you were Godfrey. Now I want you to reach up with your left hand and real slowly, I want you to unfasten that belt on your trousers and just let that Colt drop off to the ground there." Godfrey clenched his jaw muscles, but in his heart he knew he had just come close to dying, and that took a whole lot of the mad out of him. He did what I told him.

"Miller, so help me, the time is gonna come that I am gonna…"

"Shut up Godfrey. You ain't gonna do squat. You had your chance and now it's over between us. You're goin' to the state pen where you can visit your brother Harry. That's all you're gonna do."

CHAPTER 43
MAKING THE CASE

It was just as I was about to step over and kick Godfrey's gun off to one side, that I saw Rose come out of the shadows to my left. She wore no coat or hat. She was soaked to the skin, and her normally neat hair hung limp about her face. She was holding my Browning shotgun and walking slowly toward Godfrey.

"Rose," I said. "I need you to give me that shotgun and go call John Henry."

"I can't call John Henry," Rose answered. Then she jutted her chin toward Godfrey. "I can't call anybody because he cut our telephone line."

"Well," I said calmly, "then take the girls with you and go over to the Pie place. You'll see my car there. The key is in it. Y'all drive down and bring Doc back here. We are going to take Godfrey here to the jail house."

"I'll do no such thing. I am not budging and I am not giving up this shotgun, until I know you have got handcuffs on him. I am not leaving here wondering if he knocked you in the head with something before you could get him secured or if you changed your mind and just shot the man in cold blood."

I didn't like this situation at all, but I couldn't help but smile. Nobody threatened Rose Miller's children. Then the comment she had made about me shooting Daniel sunk in and the smile left my face.

With Rose holding the shotgun on Godfrey, I soon had him tightly in handcuffs and sitting under the shelter of our little front porch. Then Rose drove down and fetched Doc. We put Godfrey in the back of his car. I walked around to our back door to step inside a moment and check on the girls. As I reached for the door, Rose burst outside and jumped into my arms. She held me so tight that I thought she would squeeze the breath out of me. She kissed me several times on both cheeks.

"Cullen Miller you are the bravest man I know," she said, surprising me. Then without warning she let me go and took a step back.

She slapped me. Then she balled up her fists and punched me in the top of my arm and then in my chest. There was fire blazing in her eyes.

"But you dare to draw this white trash to my home!" she fumed. "You put my child in harm's way, Cullen, and that I will not allow."

She pointed a finger at me. She was still soaking wet and her hair hung down like strings of wet yarn around her face.

"You were egging him on. Don't look shocked. I know you too well. You are changing before my eyes, Cullen. You were standing out there like Wyatt Earp or something. You wanted Godfrey to draw. You wanted to shoot him down. I will not have my children live in fear in their own home. I'll not have them live in fear of the men you spend your nights chasing around in the woods and I'll certainly not have them fearful of their own daddy.

"Somewhere along the line something has changed. I am starting to wonder if you are out to get justice anymore. Remember who you are, Cullen Miller. Remember *whose* you are. Vengeance belongs to the good Lord, not to you Kid. You better think long and hard about what you do for a living and how much it means to you. Because as God is my witness, if anything like this ever happens again, I will leave you where you stand and I will that little girl in there with me."

There was nothing more to say. I just stood there stunned but not surprised, if that makes any sense. Rose turned on her heel and went into the house, slamming the door behind her.

CHAPTER 44
PONDERING

After a hot shower, I sat in the living room alone. Rose lay in bed with Judy, the two of them having fallen asleep as they comforted one another. I was still far too charged up to lay down myself. We had taken Godfrey to the local Talbot County jail and after waking up a judge, managed to convince him to deny Godfrey his one phone call until we could conduct a raid tomorrow night.

I had made a pot of coffee, strong and black, and sipped on a steaming cup of it as I thought. With everything I had been involved with today, I had nearly forgotten that I had promised to help with Sheriff Potts' search party in the morning.

Now I began to roll Turner and Wallace over in my mind once again. I might be able to find the body, but there was another way I could help Potts. I finally had The Upson Liquor Gang just about shut down. If I could find their stills, I could find John Wallace's. A liquor case against Wallace might convince a judge to hold him without bail. Maybe that would give us time to find the body. And if Turner was not found, at least a second liquor conviction would keep Wallace from hurting someone else for a few years.

The old clock on the wall tick-tocked rhythmically. The house was so quiet I could hear myself breathe. A fan whispered a humid breeze in through an open window. I took another sip of coffee from the white ceramic mug.

The storm had passed so I flipped on the radio, keeping the volume low. The game was probably over but maybe I could at least catch the score from my favorite baseball team, the Boston Braves. They were playing the Cardinals and so the broadcast would be coming out of St. Louis. Our house was high up on a ridge that ran half way across Talbot County. When the weather was just right, and sometimes cloudy weather was better, the elevation would let us pick up A.M. radio broadcasts from hundreds of miles away.

The game had gone into extra innings so with a little adjusting of the dial I was able to hear the 11th inning. I got my carvings out and worked on them as I listened. The Braves went on to win the game, but it didn't lift my spirits much.

There was some mail on the table and I went through it. My paycheck from the state revenue department was here and I tore open the brown envelope. The $200 check was for a month, and it was much needed.

I switched off the radio and turned off the lamp. We kept a nightlight on for Judy and I stepped quietly into her doorway guided by that light. I leaned against the doorjamb and watched her sleeping. A few auburn curls were matted to her forehead. The summer storm had cooled things but it was still muggy. Through the screen of the open window the tree frogs outside were in full voice after the welcomed rain.

What was I doing? For two hundred dollars a month I *had* put my little girl in harm's way. What's more, she barely knew me. I was dead tired when she wanted to play and was headed out to a raid or stakeout most nights right after supper. I turned and looked into the floor length mirror that Rose kept in Judy's room. I stared at myself a moment standing there in my white sleeveless tee shirt. Rose had been right. The man in that reflection didn't look like a thug or a heavy. Yet I had been fully prepared, and perhaps even a little eager to take Daniel Godfrey's life just hours before. Three days ago, I all but appointed myself a vigilante against Punkin Woodley.

Something was changing. I had gone from an agent who had only drawn his gun three times in my first few years to one who had nearly used it for lethal purposes three times in as many days. What was this job doing to me? I was getting harder, less compassionate, especially toward anyone involved with moonshine. I wasn't the loving and kind man I wanted to be for my family anymore. I used to be full of laughter and jokes. Now I seldom smiled. I was always focused and scanning those around me. I was more suspicious of human nature than I ever thought I could be.

Then again, I knew it wasn't just the job that had given me a hard edge. The truth was, I had carried a burden with me since I'd been a small boy. It was a secret that I'd never even told Rose. It was the secret that more than anything else drove me to this work. I sat down heavily in the rocking chair where I used to rock our babies and stared at my toddler as she slept. Eventually, sleep overtook me and the nightmare came back to me as it had so many times before…

It was the 4th of July, nineteen hundred and twelve. Papa had warned me to stay away. But there was a dance that night over at old man Buffington's barn, and even from our house I could hear the fiddle and the banjo and the raucous sounds of a square dance. So I used the same "secret" escape that I used when I ran out to coon hunt half the night. I jumped from my window and grasped onto the limb of the big cypress at the corner of the house, then slid down the trunk. In ten minutes I was slipping into the arc of light cast by a dozen lanterns hanging from the barn rafters. Folks were dancing, stomping and sweating in response to the orders of the square dance caller. I smiled as I watched through a crack in the wall. But as I eased around the corner, my smile faded.

The barn had an elevated platform along the front where Mr. Buffington's men loaded wagons with crates of oranges during the day. Now that platform was filled with men and women of every age. I had never seen folks behave the way I did that night. They were falling all over each other and pawing at one another.

They were swilling a clear, strong smelling drink from mason jars or sipping it from jugs. I'd heard tell of "moonshine" or "white lightnin" as some folks called it, but I'd never been near any. Somehow I knew that the moonshine had a whole lot to do with how these folks were acting. The whole thing made me uncomfortable, even a little scared, and I remembered

Papa's words of caution. I knew right then that he would whoop me good if he caught me here. I turned to leave. That was the first time I saw her.

Sitting over on a pile of firewood, just on the edge of the lantern light, was a young girl. I guessed her to be the age of my sister Lucy, not more than three or four years older than my ten years. She wore a beat up man's hat and a dress made out of burlap orange sacks. She was playing with a pet raccoon that had a little string tied around his neck. I smiled at that and walked over to her.

"Howdy," I said.

"Howdy," she replied, looking up for a second then at the ground and finally over at the coon. She was even more shy than me but I noticed a slight smile too.

"He ain't much more than a baby," I said. "Must a been born this past spring."

"Yep," she said, smiling a little more. "I had his Ma since she was a pup, but the fever got hold of her and Pa put her down. This one here is the only one of her young'uns that lived."

Me and the girl got to talkin, and she was real nice. The coon was full of mischief and we had fun laughin' and playin' with that little fella.

Then, all of a sudden, some men came out of the dance.

"Gal young'un!" one of the men shouted. He held a mason jar of strong smelling moonshine in his hand. The girl jumped like she'd been shot with a gun and closed her eyes really tight.

"I gotta go!" she said abruptly, taking the coon in her arms. But it was too late. One of the men grabbed her before she got two steps. He seemed not to see me, like I wasn't there at all.

"You gotta go wid him to the corn crib," the man said, nodding toward his partner. He grabbed the girl's arm in a hard grip and drank from the jar, then turned to his partner again with a wicked laugh. The other man took the jar and had another swallow too.

"I ain't goin to the crib no more, Pa. I tol you that. I'd rather die than go back in there with one of your sorry-assed friends again!"

The girl fought to get away, but the man she called Pa hit her hard enough to knock her hat off and then hit her again and knocked her to the ground. He grasped that little coon by the scruff of the neck and threw it out into the brush somewhere. I thought I heard it yelp.

That was the first time I saw tears coming down the girl's face. Finally, the men each grabbed her by an arm and lifted her up off her feet. I didn't understand what was happening but I knew something was terribly wrong. I had no idea what to do but I knew I had to try to help her.

I was sickly and scrawny, but I ran after the men. I wrapped myself around her Pa's leg. He stank of sweat and moonshine and soured tobacco juice. "You let her go," I shouted before biting through his filthy overall pant leg and into his flesh as hard as I could. Her Pa hollered out in pain but then grabbed me by the hair of the head, peeled me off and lifted me up to his eye level. I swung my fists wildly at him and then fear overtook me as I saw rage in his eyes. Holding me out away from him, he punched me once, a short powerful punch in my stomach by a fist that felt like iron. I felt all the air leave my lungs. Then he tossed me alongside the dirt road like I was a rag doll. I lay there like that, trying to get a breath, trying to get my feet under me. Then I looked up and saw the girl once more.

Before she disappeared into the Florida night, they let her reach down and pick up her hat. She looked down at me as I lay there. She wasn't herself no more. Something was suddenly gone out of her eyes. It seemed like she was staring at something far, far away.

I struggled to my knees, still unable to get a breath and stared after her. The three of them disappeared into the darkness. It seemed like a long time before I could breathe and for a minute I wondered if I might die there. Finally, I stood on wobbly legs.

A few seconds later I saw that little coon running up the trail the same way they had taken her. I thought that string around his neck might get tangled on something and choke him so I tried to catch him up to untie it, but I couldn't catch him. He knew a place somewhere, deep in that swamp, where they had taken the girl and he wanted to get to it. I found myself hoping for a moment that they would laugh and play again soon. That's when it came to me that I hadn't thought to ask her name or where she was from and that I had no way of finding her.

I walked home that night with hot, silent tears streaming down my cheeks. Instead of sobbin' like a baby, my jaw set and my face and neck burned like fire. Once back in my bed I stared out the window and I prayed to God. I prayed for that little girl. Then I prayed that I would grow up healthy and strong. And I prayed through clenched teeth that I would see those men, or at least men like them again someday, and when I did, that I'd know just what to do.

I woke suddenly and nearly leapt up from the rocker. It took me a moment to realize it had been the dream again, that I wasn't back in Florida. After I calmed a bit, I stepped over to Judy and kissed her lightly on the forehead. She stirred a bit.

I stepped back out to the table, picked up the brown envelope and slid the paycheck out. I looked at it once more by the dim yellow bulb of the nightlight then tossed it back onto the table flippantly.

I walked over to the window and pulled back the curtain. Only a few wisps of thunder clouds were left and the rain seemed to have cleansed the air. The stars were brilliant. The moon was at three quarters. Mrs. Burter Mae's house was dark. Everyone in Woodland would be asleep by now. I looked down the street at the Pie house. Godfrey's truck was still in the barn. I had locked the doors and confiscated the key when I took him to jail.

I stared at the moon for a long while and thought once more about that girl's empty eyes on that night long ago. Then I let Rose's words about killing in cold blood and vigilante justice sink in. I had given my life to Christ long ago. Yet, I was dangerously close to walking in the valley of the shadow of death and perhaps never coming out. I grasped the window ledge and I prayed right there. I stared into God's heaven and called out to him. "Dear Lord," I prayed. "I want to be used for your work. I want to be worthy to do battle with the children of darkness that you have given me the eyes to see. But dear Father, though I must walk into the valley of the shadow of death to find them, let me not lose my way. Lord, don't let me become one of them."

CHAPTER 45

COURTHOUSE VISITOR

The next morning, having only had three hours of restless sleep, I was too late getting to Coweta Courthouse so I could get my assignment from Sheriff Potts. Doc had work on two smaller liquor cases we were trying to close so I returned to Wallace's place and to my trail markers alone. This time I didn't look for tiny clues. Instead I looked for a well. Since I was looking for something much bigger and more obvious, I was able to cover a good deal of ground in a couple of hours. When this had been the Ivy Plantation they had dug multiple shallow irrigation wells and cisterns so that they could water the cotton crop. I found one abandoned well covered by rotting boards. The well was shallow and my flashlight shone all the way to the bottom, I probed the bottom with a long stick, nothing down there but silt and a few inches of muddy water.

I returned to my stump as the sun was setting. I sat there, sipped from my canteen, and just thought. I realized that I might well be sitting within yards of Turner. It was an eerie feeling.

I had indulged my curiosity about Mayhayley Lancaster and her "vision" but it really didn't tell me anything concrete. So, according to her, Turner's body was at one time in a well. A well where? And if I found the well, and Turner's body had truly been moved, would there be any evidence left there? If not, how would I know I had found the correct well?

I had to face it. I was spinning my wheels trying to find Turner. It was time to go back to what I did best. I decided that I wouldn't be deterred again. I had been searching diligently for John Wallace's still since the spring. I had originally sought Turner out to help me find that still. It was past time to return to my original plan.

I thought about what Roxy Coleman had said. No matter what her motives were, she was right. If I found where Wallace's liquor was going, I could trace it back to the source. Her saying that to me had set me to working on a little theory.

Miss Coleman had suggested I go back and talk to the driver of the Chrysler. I had some ideas about that driver that might connect to a theory I was working on that involved the rail crew. All I needed was for the driver to answer one crucial question. I decided to take a break from my search and go pay Mr. Dantonio a jailhouse visit.

• • •

I stopped back by the courthouse to check in with Sheriff Potts office. Only a clerk was there and I told her to let Potts know I would try to come back. To tell the truth, I got the impression that they had so much manpower on this search that they had no idea who was where. Sheriff Potts wasn't around the courthouse but as I walked down the granite steps, the sun so bright that it nearly blinded me, I saw the shadow of a man approaching me. It was L. Z. Hitchcock.

"L.Z." I said, without holding out my hand to shake his.

"I hear you found a trail, decent work on this one, Miller," he said. I suppose L. Z. expected me to blush at being complimented by a legend. Instead I stood poker faced, my hands still in my pockets.

"Look Miller, I want to talk to you about this Wallace deal," Hitchcock began.

"What's the matter, Hitchcock? You lose the Chief's phone number? I figured you would just call him again and try to get me run off the case. It almost worked last time."

"I never tried to get you run off any case," Hitchcock said.

As he was speaking to me, I noticed a black man standing behind one of the large oaks in the yard of the courthouse a few feet away. He looked very nervous and he was motioning for me to come to him. I thought I recognized him, but I wasn't sure.

"Scuse me a minute L.Z.," I said as I shouldered past him. I walked down the steps and headed towards the black man. He met me halfway.

"Agent Miller, I'm Charlie Anthony, I'm Mark's cousin."

"Pleased to meet you, I've heard..."

"Mister Miller, I can't stay. Matter o' fact I'm scared to stand here wid you now. I got a message for ya and den I got to get away from here. Mark has got to see ya. He want to see ya tonight at midnight. It's got to be tonight. He caint take no more chances. Meet him at the Stovall depot at midnight. He say he's got real important information for you in dis mess over at Stovall."

"Okay Mr. Anthony, I understand. You tell him that I'll be there."

Anthony didn't shake my hand or say goodbye. Instead, he turned and rapidly walked away ducking through the live oaks of the courthouse yard. I turned to go back and talk to Hitchcock but he was no longer on the steps of the courthouse. He had walked down onto the sidewalk and was now standing ten feet away with his back to me.

"Hitchcock, now you wouldn't eavesdrop on a private conversation would you?"

"What?" Hitchcock scoffed. "Don't panic Miller, I was just about to head to my car, that's all. I didn't hear anything."

I didn't believe him and it must have shown on my face.

"Look," Hitchcock pointed toward the cars parked on the streets. "My car is right there, I was going to wait for you by my car, keep your shirt on will ya?"

"What did you want to talk to me about?"

"I hear you and Cook put some markers out on your trail at Wallace's."

"Potts tell you that?" I asked.

"I don't remember it might have been him. Where is the trail?"

"Why do you want to know?"

"Because I want to go see if I can pick it up again. I can…"

I cut Hitchcock off. "You can't. I lost the trail and you will too."

"Miller, I always have been able to out track you and you know it. Now quit being bullheaded and tell me where the trail is," Hitchcock said.

"You're not talking to the newspapers now L.Z.," I said. "You're talking to someone who knows what's going on. The only thing you are better at than me is talking big to reporters. But feel free to go have a look."

"Miller," Hitchcock said. "Sometimes it's a little hard to tell when you are kidding a fellow agent and when there is some genuine resentment going on."

I had spent all the time with Hitchcock that I wanted to so I told him where he could pick up my trail. I started to tell him about Mayhayley Lancaster and what she said about the well, but he had already heard about that from Sheriff Potts who had talked to Miss Lancaster himself.

Hitchcock jotted down the directions I gave him, gave me a hard look, turned, and walked away. If Hitchcock could find Turner so be it. If he was busy looking for Turner's body he wouldn't be coming along on my raid of Daniel Godfrey's still.

CHAPTER 46
THE CUBBIES

"Sorry to interrupt your lunch but I'm here to see that boy I caught last week in the poker game," I said. "Name was Dantonio."

The jailer was busy unwrapping wax paper off a sandwich. He had the paper and sandwich sitting on a small brown bag soaked through with grease. There was a wax paper ball sitting on his desk blotter in front of the bag. It had soaked grease into the blotter paper. Apparently this was sandwich number two. The jailer didn't look up.

"He's in the exercise yard. I been lettin' him go out in the mornin's by himself. He don't get along with the other inmates." The jailer vigorously shook a pepper shaker over the sandwich. He still hadn't looked at me.

"Do you uhhh, want to know why I want to see him or maybe look at my badge?"

"Huh?" the jailers tone and facial expression made it clear how annoyed he was. "Oh, okay…yeah…I see it on your shirt there. Go ahead and see him if you want."

I walked out through the cells. One contained a guy lying on his back with his arm crooked over his eyes at the elbow. A second one on the opposite side contained an older man who was probably only five feet four. As I went by he did a "pssst," and asked for a smoke. I gave him one and lit it with my Zippo.

I stepped into the bright late morning sun through a door made of metal bars. Before I even walked through the threshold I heard a steady thudding sound. When I got out into the yard I saw Dantonio sitting on the concrete floor, his back against a post that held a basketball hoop. He hadn't seen me because he was throwing a baseball off the far wall, letting it bounce once and then catching it in a glove that was nearly dry rotted.

I took a look around and saw some other pretty pathetic recreational equipment in a corner. There was a mitt lying on a wooden shelf that looked worse than the glove Dantonio was wearing. I stepped over quietly and put it on.

On the next bounce of the baseball, I stepped in front of Dantonio and snagged the ball. Then I tossed it to him, using a little behind my back flip I used to show off when we were warming up before games. I still had a little touch, because the ball landed right in his glove.

"Well, if it ain't the cow-tipper that put me in here," he said. "You played ball?"

"Florida Grapefruit League," I said. "But that was a long time ago. You play back home?"

"You better believe it. I used to be pretty good too. I might have made it to 'the show' if I had stayed with it," he said.

"Where'd you play?" I asked.

The man started to speak as he threw the ball to me, stopped himself, and said, "Nice try," with a big grin on his face. He held the ball now.

I smiled back. "Come on, toss it here," I coaxed.

He fired one hard at my nose. He had a pretty good arm but he was seated and I caught the ball easily. Now *I* held onto the ball.

"You may as well talk to me," I said. "I could still put in a good word for you."

"You just wanna help me out huh?" he said. "Is that it? You just such a nice guy you going to help me out?"

"I need some information. You need some help. Me being a nice guy's got nothing to do with it."

"I ain't talkin," he said. I threw the ball back to him and he threw it back again. We tossed it three or four times before he held it in his glove.

"It is tempting though," he said.

"Why's that?"

"Cause, its been over two weeks since you nabbed me and I still ain't seen nobody. They told me they would look out for me. They told me if I ever got pinched that a lawyer would come and get me out, no charge, but..." he looked around the fenced exercise yard and held his arms out wide to indicate the whole area, "here I am. I'm still here."

"Yeah," I said, "I can see how that would upset a man pretty bad."

He looked at me a long minute. He started to smile but then he just squinted.

"Yeah, you feel real sorry for me," he said, "You're my best pal."

When I threw the ball back, he caught it, tucked it into his glove and then pulled the glove off. He stuck the ball and glove under his arm.

"I don't want to play no more." He stood up and turned his back to me.

I paused a second. Then said, "Suit yourself."

I took a few steps towards the door. Ever since the day I busted up that poker game I had been really keyed in on his accent. I'd been rolling it around in my head off and on ever since. Then the other night, while listening to the Braves game I had come up with an idea. It was time to play my hunch.

"Yeah, you probably better rest that arm," I said. "You were starting to throw more like Russ Meyer than Warren Spahn." I knocked hard on the barred door to alert the deputy to let me out.

Dantonio wheeled around as if I had snatched him by the arm.

"Warren Spahn? He's a gimmick, a flash in the pan. That high leg kick and all that junk? Hitters are startin to figure his stuff out already. Why, by the end of the year, Meyer's ERA will be half of Spahn's."

I didn't turn around. I didn't want him to see the big smile come across my face. I had gotten what I came here for.

"Yeah," I said as the deputy rattled the big key in the lock. "You're probably right."

CHAPTER 47

GOODBYE ROXY

I wasn't sure what led me to do it. Maybe my motives weren't totally related to my duties, but I decided to drive back over to Manchester and see Roxanne Coleman again. As I drove up her street, a cool front began to blow in and the humidity dropped rapidly. It was a welcome relief, though I knew it was temporary. It was far too early for fall.

As I rolled up to the curb in front of her house I saw her in the driveway. She wasn't as dressed up this time. She wore dungarees, her pant legs rolled up to the middle of her calves, soft soled canvas shoes, and a light denim shirt tied at the waste. Her blonde hair peeked out from a red kerchief tied to her head. She looked like a prettier version of Rosy the Riveter. She was stacking brown pasteboard boxes into a trailer hitched to the back of her car.

"Miss Coleman," I spoke as I tipped my hat. She had been so caught up in what she was doing that she startled a bit.

"Why, if it isn't Agent Miller," she said with only a slight air of sarcasm. She looked up briefly and then continued her loading. "Sorry Miller, it's not a good day for a visit. As you can see, I am getting out of this dreary little town."

"Where are you headed?" I asked.

"Oh, I don't know," she said as she turned to face me, placing a hand in each hip pocket, "I suppose I'll go West, probably Northwest. I am only sure of one thing. I am getting far away from this state." With that she swept one hand nervously at the bangs that had fallen from under her kerchief. When that didn't work she pursed her mouth and blew, moving her bangs out of her eyes.

"You were right," I said.

"Nice to know I have some value to you, Miller. I guess I don't always just pedal, what was it you called it…poison? You know, moonshine is not the big devil you think it is Agent Miller. The devil is in how people abuse it. Why, I enjoy a little nip myself at least once a day, and I don't look any the worse for wear do I? She swept her hands down her sides and then turned her palms upward. She stood there with her hip cocked, waiting for my opinion. It briefly occurred to me that if she was the result of a daily drink of moonshine, maybe I should try it.

I smiled then said, "Maybe moonshine is just a little devil, but it's a little devil whose throat I can get my hands around and maybe choke out. These little towns around here can use the relief. Besides lots of people don't handle it nearly as well as you."

She smiled at that. "So what exactly was I right about?" she asked as she went on with her work.

"I *was* thinking too small when I was here before. I think I am on to something now."

"Don't feel bad," Roxy said. "Apparently, I wasn't thinking big enough. At the same time I appear to have grossly overestimated the depth of my own friendships."

I reached over and grabbed a cardboard box off the front porch. It was heavy and I distinctly heard the sound of glass clinking together inside. I wondered if it was Mason Jars filled with Shine, but I didn't even want to peek in the lid. I had enough to contend with just now. I sat the box in the trailer at the same time that Roxy was adjusting the box she had just placed there. Our faces ended up an inch apart. Our eyes met for a moment and I felt butterflies flutter in my stomach. Roxanne looked surprised to receive the help.

"Thanks, Kid," she said genuinely.

When she stood and walked back over for another box, I was surprised to see a slight crimson tint begin at the exposed skin of her chest, and spread rapidly up her throat to her cheeks. I forced myself to focus on what I came there to discuss. With that re-focus, thoughts that had been floating around in my brain like random puzzle pieces suddenly began to click neatly together.

I stopped half way between the trailer and the porch, still holding a box.

"You called someone at the state capitol to beat the charges I arrested you on, didn't you?"

"I'm certain that I don't know what you're talking about," Roxanne said. "How would a small town girl like me possibly know anyone all the way up at the state capitol?"

I ignored her. "But the call did more than you bargained for. You got out of jail alright, but somebody up there talked to someone else. And that someone has an interest in the store where I busted up the poker game."

I sat the box in the trailer.

"You have a vivid imagination, Miller," Roxy quipped.

I reached out and took her arm. "Who is running you out of Georgia? What all do you know?"

She looked at me as if she was sizing me up once more. Then she turned and looked back at her house.

"Did I ever tell you about this house?" she asked. "This was my grandmother's house. You see Mr. Miller, I wasn't always a hardened criminal," she laughed sarcastically at her own joke. "I had family here. I had roots. After my grandma died and the money ran out I did what I had to do to hang onto this house and those roots. But things grew bigger than I ever intended and I am going to have to leave it all again now. I thought I was back home, but now I don't know where home is going to be."

I felt sorry for her despite myself. "I thought you said this was a dreary little town a minute ago."

"Yes," she was pensive now. "I did say that, didn't I? I've been angry, perhaps embarrassed as well, but I didn't mean it when I said it." She looked into my eyes again. "I didn't mean what I said about you either, Kid. You're one of the good guys. I'm glad, because there sure aren't many in your business."

"My business?" I said. "What about your business? And, thank you by the way."

"At least on my side of the fence you know what to expect," she said. "With the bunch you work for, I never know what's coming."

"Who are you running from?" I asked.

"You can't help me, Kid. So don't try. This is bigger than anything you can reach around." She stopped a moment, dusted off her palms and said, "I think that's the last of it." She shut the door firmly on the trailer and slid the bolt closed. "You'd best not worry about me. I'll be somewhere on the other side of Alabama by tonight. You're better served to worry about watching your own back."

Then Roxanne Coleman turned on her heel, walked up the front steps, and grasped the doorknob on her grandmother's house.

I took off my Stetson and bowed slightly at the waist. "I hope you have safe travels and much success in a new line of work," I said.

The corners of her mouth turned up slightly. "Goodbye Kid, tell your wife I said she's lucky."

I took a few steps toward my car before she called out, stopping me once again.

"You know what your problem is, Miller?" she called.

"No," I said. "But I'm pretty sure you are about to tell me."

"You assume that most of the men you work with are like you. You think they do the job for the same reasons as you, but you're wrong. There are very few men like you. Even the ones you trust the most will disappoint you someday. It makes me sad because that's what will bring you down in the end. It's what always gets your kind."

Then she stepped in the house and closed the door.

CHAPTER 48

GOLDSTEIN'S WHOLESALE GROCERY

Though it stuck in my craw, Roxanne Coleman was probably right. Something was afoot with Wallace's whiskey, the Godfrey brother's whiskey, and the store where the poker game was. That something was likely bigger than me. However, I had no intention of giving up on my investigation. As for her comments about the men I worked with, well, I tried not to think about those anymore.

I went home for a couple of hours and had a late lunch with Rose and Judy. I changed into my olive drab and got all my gear together for a long stakeout. I headed on into Manchester and drove to the outskirts of town to the Goldstein Wholesale Grocery Company. I drove on past the big red brick warehouse and crossed the railroad tracks behind it. There was a loading platform made out of heavy timber built next to the rail lines. Goods were unloaded from trains onto this platform before being moved into the warehouse. Ever since my talk with the rail crew I had known I would come here eventually.

I drove my car far over the railroad tracks which were elevated atop a three foot gravel bank and pulled my car well past, finding a perfect hiding place for it on a small gravel area behind an outbuilding. The outbuilding appeared to belong to the railroad and probably contained tools and repair parts for boxcars and track. Past the outbuilding, and on the other side of my car, were a vacant lot, a rusty chain-link fence, and then an open field.

I got out of the car, opened my trunk, grabbed my black slicker, and strapped on my gun-belt. Then I walked back towards the warehouse. The grocery company had a fence around their place, but the gate was meant to keep vehicles out, not a single man, and I squeezed easily between the gate and fence post. I crouched behind the rail embankment and moved toward the loading platform. After a quick peek into the yard of the warehouse, I moved toward the loading platform and hid behind it.

The outside walls of the platform were covered by a wooden lattice work and a section was missing on one corner. I ducked into the opening and nestled in. Using my rolled up slicker for a cushion, I made a passable seat. As my eyes adjusted to the darkness, I took out three of my carvings. I had two in one pocket and one in the other. These three were almost complete.

I had brought a little homemade tool along that was like a tiny ice cream scoop with a sharpened edge. I could get some detailed carving work done with it and soon my carvings really came alive. I looked down at them and was proud of them. They made me smile. Next, I took a piece of sand paper I had cut to size and began to quietly sand them in the direction of the wood grain. As I did so, I rolled them over and over in my hands. Over the hours I had worked these pieces, the oils from my hands had darkened the grain a bit. I always liked that. It made me feel that a part of me was in the wood and thus a part of the carving. It would feel good to give a little part of myself away to someone else.

Finally, I put the little figures away. I had been sitting for a while and I wasn't real comfortable but I had set my mind for a long wait. It was certainly possible that no one that I was interested in would show up here for days. I determined I would wait till eleven PM or so, and then I would need to head toward Stovall Depot and my meeting with Mark Anthony. I didn't have to wait nearly that long.

I looked up to see a mule drawn wagon approaching driven by none other than Bobby Rogers. Rogers had been smacked by Turner the night I had staked out Turner's still and he had spent most of his adult life working directly for John Wallace. Rogers pulled the wagon up to the warehouse loading dock, and within a couple of minutes the big wooden doors of the warehouse opened.

It didn't strike me as odd that Wallace's men were using a mule and wagon. A truck that could haul as much as this big wagon would be expensive. For that reason lots of folks still used them for farm work. Around here, a mule drawn wagon didn't raise any suspicions. A new large truck would get the attention of any revenuer worth his salt. If he was nothing else, Wallace was subtle. I suspected one of the many things that made him mad at Wilson Turner was Turner's insistence on driving a new truck and buying lots of new doo dads for his wife and baby. Those types of purchases drew folk's attention in a small town.

"You ready for another load already, Bobby?" the man in the warehouse asked.

"We ready alright. We doin a heap o' work. We ain't out there playin around."

Both men laughed and soon other warehouse workers were moving dollies loaded with fifty pound sacks of sugar onto John Wallace's wagon. This is what I had hoped for. The other day in Stovall, the railroad foreman had told me that they had had the rail down for two weeks. Roxanne had told me I was thinking too small and she was right. If a man was running some kind of huge still, he would need a whole lot of sugar. As long as the railroad was running, Wallace could have arranged for the train to deliver sugar to the Stovall Depot. But if the rail line closed it could really limit his whiskey making. With all the lawyer fees Wallace was probably incurring, he wouldn't want his moonshine income dried up. Wallace would need sugar, and he would need it in pretty big quantities, bigger than any he could get from a regular grocer. That's why I staked out Goldstein's.

I sat there and couldn't help but shake my head at the audacity. Sugar was very hard to come by, even this long after the war rationing. There were weeks that Rose still couldn't get enough sugar from Mr. John Goolsby's Supermarket to bake Judy a cupcake. There was one thing I was certain of. Bobby Rogers wasn't interested in doing any baking. He was acquiring a primary ingredient of liquor mash, and he was doing it in broad open daylight.

I watched as the loading was completed and wrote down first names of any warehouse workers that I heard used. At an opportune time, I would come back here and listen to these fellows try to tell me that they had no idea what all this sugar was going to be used for. I might try to lock a couple of them up.

In the meantime, I let the wagon drive away and the warehouse doors close. Then I gathered my things and jogged back to my car. There was no need to tail the wagon. I had a general idea where it was going. I started my car, drove back across the rail road tracks and drove out of town toward Stovall. I actually passed the wagon along the way but resisted the urge to wave. I drove at a leisurely pace, as I would have plenty of time to wait for the wagon to come down the Durand road.

CHAPTER 49

UNTOUCHABLES

I had a good head start on the wagon so I took the time to stop at the Warm Springs police station. I knew the officers there so they obliged me when I asked to use the phone in the chief's office. I closed the door and called Earl Lucas. Earl was a federal revenue officer I had worked with on a few cases where we did a joint task force between us state boys and the feds. The operator connected me to the Treasury Building in Atlanta, but the switchboard operator there had to track him down. Finally, they got him to the phone.

"Lucas," his baritone voice came through the receiver.

"It's Miller," I said.

"Hey Kid," his voice picked up an octave and it was clear he was glad to talk to me. Lucas and I always enjoyed working together. "Whatcha got going down in your neck of the woods?"

"Oh, nothin much," I said. "Say, I've got a question for you. You remember that stakeout we did outside of Fayetteville that time? We ended up sitting on that shot house up there for four or five nights."

"Yeah, sure, I remember."

"I got to thinking about some of the stuff we talked about when we were sitting there in your car for all those hours."

"Yeah, seems like we covered about every topic we could think of," Lucas chuckled.

"Yeah…yeah we did. Say, don't I remember you saying that you worked under Elliot Ness for a while back when he first started in on Capone?"

"Yep, I was one of the original fifty "Untouchables" but I got transferred out before things got really hairy up there in Chicago. Would you believe Ness is working as a clerk in a bookstore right now? That's the last I heard anyway. Bottle got to him after a while. He always liked the juice. Even back when we were first breaking up speakeasies, he wasn't afraid to take a sample or two home."

"Yeah, I thought you had said he was drinking a little bit too much lately. Say, you just said the magic word. That's why I called you. What happened to Capone's speakeasies. He went up in '31 right? So I guess all those places shut down?"

"Oh no," Lucas said. "They're still very much in business. They don't have to call them speakeasies anymore of course. No, now the mob really thinks they are big shots. They've got bars galore in Chicago that all the respectable people go to. Doctors, politicians, lawyers, even judges, drink in mob bars every weekend."

"I suppose since they can get legal booze now, they don't have much demand for moonshine, huh."

"Well, like I said Kid, I don't ever work up there anymore, but when I've talked to my old squad they tell me they are still moving a couple hundred thousand gallons a year up there. Those city folks still like their fruity drinks mixed with good ol' fashioned moonshine. I guess they think it's quaint. Why are you asking about all this now? Are you on to something down there?"

"Yeah," I said. "Yeah, I probably am. I'll let you know as soon as I know. I'll be seein' ya, Earl."

I sat the phone down in the cradle and I couldn't help but smile to myself. Now it all made sense.

Warren Spahn is my favorite pitcher on my favorite baseball team, the Boston Braves. Spahn led the big leagues in ERA last year. He is an

All-Star pitcher. Russ Meyer, who I mentioned to Dantonio while we were playing catch at the county jail, was a solid pitcher but only in his second year. His ERA was over 4.00, the kid was a journeyman and nothing more than that. I threw those two names out there in front of Dantonio and he went nuts telling me that Meyer was better than Spahn. Yet Dantonio had said he played ball himself, that he played the game at a high level.

No knowledgeable baseball man would even compare Spahn to Meyer. That is unless that man was following his heart, not his head. Meyer pitched for the Chicago Cubs. That accent of Dantonio's that I couldn't figure out, it was northern all right, as I had suspected that day at the store. But there had been something else in it that I couldn't put my finger on. Now I had. The other part of his accent was Sicilian. So Dantonio was Sicilian and a passionate Cubs fan. To top it off, on the day I arrested him he kept bragging about the people he worked for and how they had influence and how they would get him out. But they'd left poor Dantonio hanging out to dry. Instead they had used their influence in more industrious pursuits at the State Capitol.

They had somebody inside the capitol, maybe even somebody in the attorney general's office. They didn't care if Dantonio rotted in jail. They weren't going to call in a marker for him. Instead, Roxy Coleman's phone call to the capitol alerted someone that my bust of the poker game was putting that store, Gibbs Junction, in jeopardy of being closed. And Gibbs Junction was more than just a country store. It was an important link in a supply chain of moonshine to thirsty customers in Chicago. Dantonio sure had driven a long way to buy Wallace's moonshine. He'd come all the way from the mafia formerly run by Al Capone.

CHAPTER 50
CHESAPEAKE LUMBER COMPANY

When I got to Durand, I pulled past a little inconspicuous lane and backed my car into it. From where I was parked, I could watch the road for the wagon as it went by with very little risk of being spotted.

A good pair of gated mules can pull a wagon at about eight miles an hour. Considering that it was twelve miles from Manchester to Durand, Wallace must have had a good pair of mules, because in an hour and a half on the dot, the wagon rolled past my position. I looked at my watch and made a note of the time. I wanted to wait and leave here so that I could pull into Stovall just behind the wagon as it arrived. Once again, my estimate was spot on because as I pulled into Stovall, the wagon was just turning off the main road, to a nicely graveled lane that led to the Chesapeake Lumber Company.

"Well, I'll just be darned," I couldn't help but say aloud. Now it all came together for me. I had been searching for a year for a still that John Wallace swore he didn't have. I had searched day after day and night after night, walking every creek and nook on Wallace's place. I had wanted desperately to shut down what I thought might be the largest supplier of moonshine in the state of Georgia. All those hours of sweat soaked searching had been in vain. I couldn't find Wallace's still because it wasn't hidden in the woods. He didn't have a faint trail leading to a still deep in a swamp or woods like other moonshiners did. He had a first class gravel road. He had mass quantities of sugar delivered to his still in broad daylight because he knew he had hidden it perfectly, he had hidden it in plain sight.

When I had peeked underneath the Chrysler that day, I noticed it had spring stiffeners on the back springs. The car was rigged to carry a heavy load and it had been loaded to the maximum with kegs of moonshine. The kegs had been stenciled with the initials C.L.C. I didn't know what those initials meant then. Now I did…Chesapeake Lumber Company.

I had been wrong on one thing but right on a couple of others. I had been wrong to think that busting Wallace's and Godfrey's stills was going to get lots of moonshine out of the market in Georgia. That wasn't going to happen because their liquor wasn't primarily being consumed in Georgia. Dantonio had been down here enough times that he knew where he could get in on an illegal poker game. I was an agent that prided myself on keeping up with what the local thugs were up to and I hadn't even known about that game 'till I busted it. That told me that Dantonio was pretty familiar with the area. He had made trips down here many times. Wallace and the Godfrey's were regular suppliers for Chicago, not for Georgia.

I had been right in suspecting that Wallace was lying to me about being reformed and being out of the liquor business. I had also been right to suspect that the still where I met Turner that night was a small side operation and that the majority of his income was coming from a much larger still he was running for Wallace. This still at the lumber mill had to be generating big money…very big money.

For now I kept rolling down the road. I had busted enough stills around Stovall that people were getting to know my car. If I pulled over anywhere near that lumber company somebody was going to alert the boys and they would be long gone when I got there. I had begun to think that I would have to poke around tonight after meeting Mark Anthony, but then I got a big break. As I cruised slowly down the road, I saw a little old lady all dressed up to go shopping. She had her car backed out of an old wooden garage. The car was idling with the door opened while she tottered around to close her garage door. She fastened the door with a hasp.

I drove on slowly past her house and then turned in a side road before stopping for a few seconds. As I watched in my rearview, I saw the lady's black Plymouth roll past. I then backed my car out and headed for her garage. I got out and opened it up, parked my car inside, and shut the door. My car would be completely hidden. Next, I managed to move from her yard, through little patches of woods here and there, until I was all the way to a strip of pines beside the Chesapeake Lumber Company.

I stood well back in the shadow of the pines and observed for about half an hour. I got a feel for how many men were there and what their patterns were. There were three men, two white and one black, working the sawmill. There were another couple of guys moving stacks of lumber from the sawmill to the lay-down yard. After a bit I saw the doors open on a huge warehouse building and out came the empty wagon that had contained the sugar. Albert Washington, the other black man that had been at Turner's still the night he spoiled the moonshine, was now driving and Bobby Rodgers rode beside him. Wallace was still likely calling the shots for this operation from his jail cell, communicating through visitors to his cell who were relaying messages here.

I hid behind a large pine and let the wagon drive right past me. I watched until it turned back onto the main road. The two men would be headed to the barn where I had met Wallace on the night after he sent me the note. The other men were busy running the sawmill. This was my opening.

I remained behind the tree until one of the lumber yard workers brought a load of lumber out and set it in the yard. As he drove the fork truck back into the warehouse, I knew I had several minutes clear. I walked to a side door near the rear of the building, I didn't run. Running gets spotted by even a distracted witness. The back section of the large building had stacks and vents poking through the roof. This would be a small pulp operation. They were making pulp here for sale to a large paper mill just up the road toward Chipley. I drew my Smith, and in the same motion, stepped in the door.

I was at a disadvantage as my eyes adjusted to the dim light inside, but no one was there. It only took seconds for me to realize that this was the perfect hiding place for a still. The making of pulpwood can be a smelly undertaking. What's more, steam and hot water are involved to create the slurry that goes to the paper mill. That process would give perfect cover to a large still operation. And that is exactly what Wallace was doing.

I holstered my pistol and began to walk around in awe. Two huge submarine boilers dominated one end of the large wood plank building. I had seen some pretty big stills in my day, but I had never seen anything like this. I estimated the boilers to be twenty-five hundred gallons each. Huge copper lines ran to the biggest liquor vats I had ever seen. Everything was the biggest I had ever seen for that matter.

Two things in particular were the most impressive. The 2 inch copper pipe that was the equivalent of the "moneypiece", normally a half inch tube, ran underground. I looked past the point where the pipe entered and saw two hatch doors side by side made into the dirt floor of the pulp mill. I opened the first one, pulled my flashlight off my belt, and peeked inside. The smell alone would nearly make a man drunk but the tank was empty. The second tank was three fourths full of moonshine.

I closed and secured the hatches. It would take every revenuer I knew to come in here and tear down this still. Maybe I could get Earl Lucas to bring a dynamite crew and blow these tanks up. I couldn't help but chuckle to myself. Wallace had it all figured pretty well. A few seconds later my feeling of admiration evaporated. Past the underground moonshine tanks and along a far wall, there was a large set of doors. The right-hand door had a smaller man door cut into it. I walked up, turned the knob and pushed the door open. It led into a storage room.

Sugar had been rationed for the war effort. Even now, production still hadn't caught up. As I looked in the storage room, I realized Wallace must have planned on being acquitted quickly, and then getting right back to making a whole bunch of liquor. Aside from the wagon load of sugar Rogers had just put in here, the storeroom was filled to the rafters with empty fifty-pound sugar sacks tied in bundles. When the sacks were full, they would have filled at least a train box car, which proved another hunch I'd had was right. Sugar deliveries had formerly been coming in by train to the Stovall Depot. Those would have been transported here in short trips during the dark of night and much easier to conceal.

Maybe John Wallace would beat the murder charge, but I had what I needed here to build a case against him that would send him to the state penn for a long, long, time.

CHAPTER 51
CONSPIRACY CASE

It was a twenty-five mile drive back home from where the lumber company was, and I only had a few hours 'till I had to meet Mark Anthony at Stovall Depot. Still, I had no intention of killing several hours hanging around here. I decided to go home for a bit and make the drive back in time for my meeting. That would give me some time to think.

Wallace didn't own Chesapeake Lumber Company, a business associate of his did. But the state of Georgia had just passed a new law. I had the option of building a "conspiracy to manufacture moonshine" case against him. I felt like I could make a conspiracy charge stick.

As I arrived home I felt good. I felt a sense of closure and accomplishment. I had been after Wallace off and on since '44. For that matter, I started keeping an eye on him almost as soon as he had been released from state prison in '39. Wallace had sworn to me that he was a changed man and that he was out of the liquor business. I suspected it before but I knew it now, Wallace was a liar. With the operation I had just seen I was beginning to wonder if Wallace had ever had an entire year in the last several where he was not making liquor.

And then tomorrow night, I would raid Daniel Godfrey's still and cut it up into little pieces while he sat in jail awaiting another charge. I might not shut down that store, but I was about to take a big chunk out of the moonshine supply coming out of West Georgia.

Rose had made a light supper of her wonderful chicken salad, sliced tomatoes and onions, and pimento cheese sandwiches. Rose's mother, who everyone called Granny, joined us for dinner and would spend the night. She only lived across the street, but Judy adored her and got a big kick out of having Granny sleep over. After we ate, the four of us went outside to sit in our metal lawn chairs. There had been a thunderstorm somewhere out toward the Pleasant Hill community and we were getting a nice cooling breeze from it.

I let Judy take off her dress and put on her overalls and some little beaded Indian moccasins made out of soft deer hide. She loved that little outfit and I watched her and Granny laugh and play as though they were siblings. I pulled off my boots and socks and rubbed my feet on the soft green grass of our lawn. In that moment, I was about as content as a man could be. Soon, I tossed a cushion from one of the lawn chairs into our yard swing. I used it for a pillow and lay down. Judy came over and gave me a gentle push. The swinging motion soon had my eyelids droopy.

On the stroke of six we began to hear the chimes ring out from down at the Methodist church, the same church where Daniel Godfrey paid me a visit. My Papa broke ground on that church in 1927, five years after I had left my boyhood home in Evinston, Florida to try and make a life here in Woodland. By then he too had moved to Georgia. I had helped him lay the foundation for the church.

Every Saturday night the chimes played. My Papa had been so proud of that steeple. There used to be a real bell, but now there were four loudspeakers which broadcast chimes from a record. Still, it was a pleasant and a peaceful part of the week to hear them. Three hymns were the standard number and the second one tonight got my attention. It was one of my favorites, *Shall We Gather at the River*. For some reason as the chimes played, it was the last verse that ran through my mind. I had heard this hymn before, when I was only six years old.

Soon we'll reach the silver river...

My mind took me back again, back to my mama. Mama was so beautiful. Her people had been Castilian Spanish. Her olive skin, deep brown eyes and long black hair reflected that. Her family had been wealthy but she lost every one of them to the Asiatic flu of 1889. When Papa met her, she was living in an orphanage, penniless. But on the night I was thinking of now, Mama was pregnant with my little brother. The night before her labor pains had started, she'd been holding me and telling me stories as we sat in her rocker. I felt the same kind of contentment then that I felt tonight.

Soon our pilgrimage will cease...

I should never have looked into her bedroom door. Papa told me not to, but when the Doctor finally got there I wanted to see how Mama was. She had been crying out so loudly. That's when I'd seen the blood. It saturated the white sheets. The doctor, his shirtsleeves rolled up and perspiration beading his forehead, wrung red water and blood from a white towel into a porcelain basin. I saw Mama's face as she cried out. She was so pale that she barely looked human. I've never gotten that image out of my mind.

Soon our happy hearts will quiver...

I can still hear the rumble of the hearse as the two horses pulled it. It was an open hearse and I kept my eyes locked on Mama's casket as I walked along behind. We were headed to the cemetery and I remember how I kept laying my hand on the casket lid as if by doing so I could open it and Mama would come back to us. Papa never remarried. He was never the same man again.

With the melody of peace...

My eyes popped open now as I listened to the chorus.

Yes we'll gather at the river

The beautiful, the beautiful river

I looked at my watch. It was twenty after six. I would need to leave by eleven fifteen to meet Mark Anthony on time. I wasn't sure how many times through the years I had gone out alone at night to meet some informant, or to raid some still or shot house. It was funny, but in all those times, I can't remember ever feeling scared.

Gather with the saints at the river
That flows by the throne of God

But tonight for some reason I had a terrible sense of dread. I wondered if I would ever come home from Stovall. Of if I made it through tonight I wondered if I would be shot raiding Daniel Godfrey's. I wondered if I would see Mama again soon.

CHAPTER 52

GODFREY WALKS

Not five minutes after I had listened to the church bells, my phone had rang. My local Sheriff and Great Uncle John Henry Ferguson had called to tell me he had released Daniel Godfrey. I had slammed down the phone and was now standing in John Henry's office coming unglued.

"What do you mean, you kicked him loose?" I shouted.

"I didn't have enough to keep holding him. You didn't want him making his phone call. I was denying him his rights and he knew it. He was threatening to let some of his friends up in the State Capitol know about what I was doing. What was I supposed to hold him on? Carryin' too big a pistol? Daniel Godfrey's been carrying that pistol as long as I can remember."

"How was he goin' to call the politicians on ya John Henry? You weren't supposed to let him use the phone, remember? All I needed you to do was to keep him in here till Saturday night when we did the raid, and then I was going to file a liquor case against him."

"I didn't have nothin' to hold him on, Kid!"

Rose must have sensed my fury as I left our house and called Doc because now he stepped in the office door as well.

"You could hold him on the fact that he tried to hurt my family... which is your family too!" My face was hot and I was getting angrier by the second. Doc moved around in front of John Henry's desk and tried to step between us. I moved over to my right and came around behind the desk, bringing me closer to John Henry.

"Kid," Doc said cautiously. "Now you'd best take it a little easy."

"Yeah boy," John Henry said. "You better settle yourself down. I was sheriffin in this country long before you ever thought about wearin that tax man badge you wear. You might want to avoid tellin' me how to conduct my job in *my* county."

"Tell ya what, Uncle John Henry," I said sarcastically. "I'll take my badge off." I unpinned the badge from my shirt and tossed it on the desk. Then I pushed John Henry's government-issue office chair hard against the back wall so that a couple of outdated wanted posters fluttered down from a cork board. Suddenly, I made a move to grab my great Uncle by his uniform shirt, but Doc came over the desk and got between us.

"Now dammit Kid, you hold on," Doc cautioned. "You're about to get up to your neck in something you don't want. Then who is it gonna watch out for Rose and that little girl."

For his part, John Henry had never backed up an inch. Instead he reached over and grabbed his black billy club out of his duty belt that was hanging on a coat rack.

"Kid, I'm gonna let this one slide today on account of your family. But you had best know that I am too old and too smart to go to dukin' it out with somebody twenty years younger than me. You ever try to come at me like that again in my own office and I'd just as soon split your skull with this stick as look at ya."

Doc was holding me against a far wall with everything he had. Somewhere in the ruckus I had knocked his hat off and stepped on it. Now it lay crumpled on the floor. I felt sorry about that. I had no remorse about John Henry.

"Guess what John, you're going on your first liquor raid tonight. Me and you ridin' together, a regular family reunion!" I said through clenched teeth.

"I told you a long time ago Kid, I don't do liquor cases," John Henry said.

"Well, you're doin' this one." I shook Doc off and walked over and picked up his hat. I tried to reshape it as best I could. "You're goin' on this raid with me and you better darned well hope that Daniel Godfrey shows up at that still. And if he does you are putting your cuffs on him right on the spot."

"Boy, if your Daddy was alive to hear the way you were talkin to me…"

I ignored the reference. I snatched my badge off the desk and then pounded the desk once with my fist.

"I'll be by here to pick you up and you had better be ready."

"Don't waste your gas, cause I ain't goin," John Henry said.

The anger, which had only slightly subsided built up in me once again.

"What am I gonna do in Jack Marshall's county?" John Henry said shrugging his shoulders.

"He can't go cuffing somebody in Upson County, Kid!" Doc said.

I stepped back to the front edge of John Henry's desk and pointed my finger at him.

"If something happens to my family, you are responsible and you can rest assured I will be back here and deal with you on it," I said.

John Henry only stared back, but for the first time I saw a look of remorse in his eyes.

CHAPTER 53
DANIEL GODFREY'S LAST STAND

"You get Spence and the others, I'll see if J.C. Otwell from the State Troopers and a couple of county policemen will tag along. I want to get this still surrounded. If they see an overwhelming show of force, there's a lot less chance of any shooting."

"You gonna check in with Sheriff Marshall first?" Doc asked.

"I'll call him but I don't know if he'll come out against a Godfrey. That family represents a whole bunch of voters for him." I answered.

I was speeding towards my house. I wanted to know that Rose and the girls were safe before we did anything else.

"If I had to guess," Doc said. "Godfrey ain't going nowhere near your place for awhile. He knows the law is on to what he wanted to do. For now he's gonna go back to the moonshinin' business and get out of the hit-man business."

"I think you're right," I said. "At least I pray you are."

We found Rose outside taking down laundry from the clothesline. Judy sat nearby in the flower bed shoveling soil into a pail with an old spoon.

"Rose, I want you to take Judy and y'all go spend the night with your cousin Annie Glenn tonight."

Rose looked at me and then looked at Doc.

"Why?" she said with worry in her voice. "Never mind, don't answer that. I'll pack us a bag and have her pick us up in an hour." I could see her stiffen, steeling herself for whatever might come.

"I am pretty sure it is only for tonight," I said, trying to be reassuring.

Rose didn't look up at me. She only continued with her laundry as if we weren't there.

• • •

A few hours later, Doc, Spence, J.C. Otwell and a new agent named Cecil Durham, and county policeman Jack Caldwell were with me staking out Daniel Godfrey's still. It was almost 9:00 at night. I had to be at the Stovall Depot in three hours to meet Mark. I didn't want to miss that meeting but I wasn't about to be in Stovall with Daniel Godfrey on the loose. If Sheriff John Henry Ferguson didn't think sneaking outside a man's home with a loaded .44 was enough to hold Godfrey, I would make my own case and make sure it stuck.

We were positioned in a large semi-circle between the still and the Flint River. We weren't hidden as well as I had been when I staked out the still earlier. Instead, we lay flat on our bellies about a hundred yards from the still, waiting for the crew to arrive.

Dusk set in and then gradually darkness fell. My heart began to beat hard in my chest. If Godfrey and his crew didn't show up soon, they could be out looking for me. They might find Rose.

Just as I was getting concerned however, I heard a man in the distance walking through the woods. Unlike the last time I was here, none of the men talked or exchanged banter. I figured that Godfrey hadn't told them he got thrown in jail. That would have made some of his crew nervous but perhaps he had demanded extra caution.

One by one the men filed into the still. A lantern was lit, then another. Bean Pole Johnson was here again along with some others. Finally, after what seemed an eternity, and with cold sweat beading on my forehead, Daniel Godfrey stepped into the lantern light.

"Alright now, we are gonna make two runs tonight since we lost the whole batch last time," Godfrey said. Then he started, "We've got a lot of time to make..." I never let him finish what he was going to say.

I eased up to my feet as quietly as possible. One by one the men nearby did the same. Then I turned on my flashlight and shone it in Godfrey's face.

"This is a raid boys," I said, dispensing with my usual "prayer meetin" joke or scripture verse. I didn't feel much like lightening the mood tonight.

At my word everyone with me turned their own flashlights on. Daniel Godfrey just stood there, a smirk on his face. A couple of his men started to run in the direction from which they came, back toward the mountain and Thunder Road. They were met with multiple flashlights flooding their eyes.

"Some of you fellas may have met your friendly local Sheriff, Jack Marshall. He and his boys came along to help us tonight." The workers, realizing there was nowhere to run, stopped. They slowly, and dejectedly, walked back to the still.

"Miller, you just can't get enough of harassin me, can you?" Godfrey asked. "I hate to break it to ya, but you jumped the gun. You see there aint been no liquor run through this still tonight. And besides, until I followed ol' Bean Pole here just now, I didn't even know all this was down here. I never saw it before in my life. So you don't really have no charges against me anyway. It aint my fault Beanie started buildin' a still on my land without my knowledge."

"Hey!" Beanie exclaimed.

Godfrey stopped him with a look.

"I don't need to catch y'all makin moonshine tonight," I said. "I already did that last night. I got every one of y'alls names in my little notebook, and I will be testifyin about what I saw you doing here last night. You ran at least fifty gallons of shine while I was watching."

Daniel Godfrey looked confused. "There ain't no Revenuer ever been anywhere near this still before," he said. "Any man sets foot on my property in my woods, I would know about it. There ain't never been a Revenuer yet could hide his sign from me."

"Well, I guess this is a first then," I said. "I was here, and I will testify that I observed you directing liquor making operations at this still." I stepped over and pulled one of two axes out of a stump where the men had been splitting wood to fire the still. "I'm gonna let you do the honors of chopping up these caps and worms, Daniel," I said.

"Miller, you're lying. You ain't never been here."

"You knocked Beanie down last night when he smarted off about your wife. Then you said you had business you had to handle. I guess you and I know what that business was supposed to be, now don't we?"

Even in the dim lantern light, I thought I saw Godfrey's face flush. Still, he was committed to continue with his act.

"I'm here to tell ya, you are making all this up. I would have seen your sign if you had come in here, even if it had been last night."

"Trooper Otwell," I said. "Would you do me a favor and walk across the creek with me and Mr. Godfrey here. I am going to let him carry a shovel over there and dig a bit."

"What do you mean, Kid?" Otwell said.

"Well, if he digs around that wild rose hedge across the creek he is going to find a dead rattlesnake that I killed yesterday. By now the worms and grubs ought to be after him. I killed him just before you got here last night Daniel. Then I buried him so the flies wouldn't tip you off. That's my proof. I was here, I observed you making moonshine, and my testimony is going to send you to the jailhouse."

We found the snake just like I said and Daniel Godfrey knew I had him. He was none too happy about it. Just before Jack Marshall took him back up the mountain toward where his patrol car was parked, Godfrey decided to try and make me look bad. He had walked as far as the outer perimeter of the still site, with Marshall holding him by the crook of his elbow, when he pulled up short.

"Hey, Miller," he called. "You know you are always going around threatening people with that pistol of yours. But for the life of me I can't remember a single time where you ever shot anybody. For that matter, I don't know that I have ever seen you with the thing out of your holster. Everybody seems to think you can handle a gun, but maybe not. Maybe all you are is a bunch of big talk."

I took a quick glance over at the still. I was twenty five feet from it.

"Well, Godfrey, I always heard *you* were a prime moonshiner, always heard you took pride in your work. Why, I am ashamed to look over here and see that your worm is leaking and your money piece is loose. It's a big disappointment."

"What are you talking about Miller, I ain't never had a leak…"

I didn't let him finish. In a second my Smith was in my hand. My first shot cut the worm, which was a half inch in diameter, loose from the thumper keg. My second shot blew the money piece off the worm box. I got a bit cocky and went for a third shot to kick the money piece up from the leaf litter where it landed and into the air. I missed that one, but I don't think any of the fellas standing there with their mouths hanging open noticed.

I holstered my weapon and then watched Godfrey walk off with Sheriff Marshall. He had been right about one thing. I had never shot a man. I hadn't even fired my weapon in the line of duty, unless you counted just now. I didn't like showing off, but my reputation in this job was critical. Men needed to know what I *could* do and that I was willing to do it. That was enough.

By the time we got Daniel Godfrey and his boys to the Upson County Jail it was 11:00. And though I was proud to see him stand there in the cell when the door was slammed in his face, I was going to have my hands full to get to Stovall by midnight.

CHAPTER 54

THE DEPOT

Thunder clouds were still in the area as I drove toward the depot. I glanced at the luminous dial on my watch. It was 11:30 and I was about a mile out of Durand and fifteen minutes from Stovall. I had run my siren and driven hard until I turned off the highway from Warm Springs. Now the last thing I wanted to do was draw attention to a secret meeting. The siren was now off and I had to force myself to drive the speed limit.

Moonshiners, bootleggers, and moonshine drinkers, all trying to cut a deal, frequently wanted to meet at midnight. I guess they felt safer then. They were people of the night mostly. Mark Anthony couldn't afford to be seen talking to me in the daylight in John Wallace's back yard. Wallace might be in jail for now but you had better believe he had eyes and ears all over the county. So we would meet under cover of darkness. And this was one of the darkest nights I had ever seen. Despite my best efforts I was late. I finally coasted up quietly to Stovall Depot at 12:25.

I didn't use my flashlight. Instead I got out of my car and stood there a full two minutes, letting my eyes adjust to the dark. Then I moved toward the depot. I didn't see Mark Anthony yet. I stepped onto the wooden ramp that led up to the depot loading dock. I stood on the dock for a minute or so straining my eyes to see if maybe Mark was coming up the road towards me. Suddenly I heard a crash from the far end of the building. My Smith was in my hand half a second later, though I wasn't conscious of drawing it. I pointed it toward the noise and waited. I wasn't sure if I would see a muzzle flash before they shot or not. There was another crash. Somebody had fallen.

"Agent Miller."

The voice was weak and the words were garbled. I eased toward the sound. As I got to the edge of the loading dock, I saw him. Mark Anthony was lying on his side with his knees drawn up nearly to his chest. I hopped down off the ramp and went to him.

"Easy, Agent Miller, easy. I'm in awful pain," he mumbled.

"Alright Mark, alright. We're gonna roll you over nice and easy…" I rolled him onto his back as gently as possible. He cried out.

"I wasn't quite to the depot when somebody jumped out," Mark said. They were laying for me." As he said this, he leaned his head over to one side and spit out blood.

Now I shone my flashlight for just a couple of seconds. I could see that his nose was bleeding badly, his lips were split, and he was missing a tooth in front.

"Mark, who did this to you?" I asked.

"It was too dark to see, the first thing he did was hit me in the ribs with a two by four. I never had my breath taken from me like that in my life. I think it broke my ribs…it…it paralyzed me. I couldn't raise my arms to defend myself. Whoever he was he kept wailing on me with that board. I went down and then he kicked me in the face with a heavy boot. He stomped my nose with his heel.

"Did he talk to you? Was it a white man or a black man?" I asked as I folded a clean handkerchief and held it against Mark's bleeding nose.

"He made me tell him something Agent Miller. He made me tell him something that I only wanted to tell you. Get me to your car. We mustn't stay here. I'll tell you in the car. I know where Wilson Turner's body is."

I struggled to get Mark to my car. He could barely walk. The man weighed a good two hundred and twenty five pounds so I couldn't carry him either. Between the two of us, we eventually got him inside. It hurt him too much to sit up so I lay him across the back seat. I got in and started the car.

"I'm going to hit the siren and rush you to Warm Springs. I kind of got to know a doctor over there."

"You'll do no such thing," Anthony tried to shout. "Respectfully, Agent Miller, are you trying to get me and my cousin's family killed? That is what will happen if I am seen being delivered to any doctor by you. Take me to my cousin's house. They will care for me as best they can. My cousin's wife has the gift of healing."

I knew Anthony was right. Whoever had done this wouldn't risk him talking to doctors and once I took him to Warm Springs the risk was too great that they would discover he had been talking to me. They would likely come after him again and finish the job. I left my siren off and swung the car in a U-turn back toward his cousin's house.

"Now Mark, I am going to ask you again. Who did this to you?"

"He said he would come back and kill me and my cousins. He said he would make sure we never got a Christian burial... that nobody would find us. So you needn't ask me again who it was."

"I can't help you if I don't know..."

"You can't help me anyway Cullen!" Mark groaned with the effort of the words. Still, he forced himself to continue, "You have to disavow yourself of the notion that you can make everything right. Only the Almighty himself can do that and he will someday. But that day is not here. Until it is we must live in the world we have. Now please respect my wishes in this. You know how things are, Agent Miller."

I gripped the wheel with all my might as my car roared down the road. I didn't know what to say.

"He wanted to know why I was at the depot. He kept saying, 'What do you know, boy? Tell me what you know or I'll beat you to death!' I think he would have done it. Somehow he knew that I was going to be here."

"Hitchcock!" I said through gritted teeth. "He eavesdropped when I was talking to your cousin at the courthouse."

"I have not told you that it was Agent Hitchcock" Anthony said. "I have said that it was too dark and that I didn't know who it was. I am not even sure if it was a white man or a black man, and if asked in court that will be my testimony." Anthony was laboring even more to talk. But he had one more thing to ask. "Agent Miller, do you suppose he went after my cousins first?"

CHAPTER 55
THE TRUTH COMES OUT

We rolled up into Charlie's yard and I ran around to help Mark Anthony out of the car. His cousins heard the ruckus and came outside. Charlie had an old timey side by side double barrel shotgun hung over the crook of one elbow.

"It's Agent C. E. Miller," I called out. "I have Mark inside and he's hurt."

I opened the rear door, squatted down and reached inside for Mark. He grabbed both my forearms in a vice like grip and held me there.

"They burned that boy Mr. Miller," he said somberly. "They had him in a well deep on Wallace's place but Wallace got scared. That fortune teller Miss Lancaster told him that the police would find Turner's body. Wallace made Washington and Rodgers help him fish the boy's body out of the well. They strapped him on a mule and carried him down to the old Ivy Plantation place. Wallace owns that too. They took him down to Potato Creek where they had a place cleaned off where they were going to build a new still.

I thought back for a moment. Mayhayla Lancaster had said, "they put him across a mule, mule was all covered in mud." Then I remembered the new still site Doc had found.

"I know the spot," I said. "My partner found it the other day."

"They stacked up cord wood and built it up all around the boy's body. They covered him up with fat pine wood and gasoline and they burnt him up."

I grimaced at the notion, then gathered myself and said, "Alright Mark, alright. Don't worry about it anymore. I'll find him. Let's get you in the house."

By now Charlie had come around the other side of the car with a big heavy quilt. We rolled Mark onto the quilt and carried him inside like he was on a stretcher. I helped them get him to where Charlie's wife Rachel took over. I stayed for a bit and tried to help where I could. Mark Anthony was beaten about as bad as I had ever seen a man beaten. With every new bruise or cut that I saw, my anger at L. Z. Hitchcock grew. There was moonshine in the house and this was one time I had no problem with it being administered. They let Mark sip on it to dull the pain. At some point he passed out, probably more from the trauma than the moonshine.

"Agent Miller," Charlie finally said. "You can't do us no good here. We appreciate the way you helped Mark, but y'all even now. We don't need you around here no more. I don't mean nothin' by it but that's just the way it's got to be. Now why don't you go and take care of your bidness?"

I was sad to hear what Charlie had to say, but he was right. I could only do harm by lingering around the house with my car in the front yard.

Mark spoke up again. His lips and mouth were swelling more now and he was harder to understand.

"Mr. Miller, there is something else you need to know," he said.

"What is it Mark?"

Mark Anthony asked Charlie and his wife to leave the room for a moment. They did so without asking questions. Then Mark said, "You did everything you could for me, and more than just about any man, black or white, has ever done for me. I want you to know that I will never forget that. But you have to watch yourself at the point of your pride. You are not God's avenging angel, you're just a man. There's an evil about in this world and sometimes it gets the better of us. No one man can stop it. You'll die trying."

I paused for a moment as the words of Rose, Mayhayley Lancaster, and Roxanne echoed along with Mark's. Then, without another word, I turned and walked into the darkness.

CHAPTER 56
ALERT THE MEDIA

I had spent more time tending to Mark Anthony than I realized. It was 3:00 AM when I started trying to raise dispatch so that they could get me through to Sheriff Lamar Potts. I told them I had critically important information for the sheriff and to wake him if need be. Eventually dispatch called me back.

"Calling Agent Miller, come in Agent Miller."

"This is Miller, go ahead dispatch."

"Agent Miller, Sheriff Potts is unavailable at this time. Over. If it is urgent that you talk to him, he has driven out to the old Ivy Plantation in Meriwether County, over."

"Understood dispatch. Over and out."

There was no doubt in my mind now. Hitchcock had beaten the information out of Mark Anthony. Then he had gone to Potts and taken credit for finding the site where Turner's body was burned. No sooner had I finished my conversation with dispatch than I began to see lights off in the distance, lots of lights. I was only a quarter mile from the old Ivy Plantation and the spot where Doc had let me out of the car just over a week ago today. I believed now that the button, the hair, the broken twigs and the tobacco can *had* all been a long a line from some point along the road to the abandoned well.

Mayhayley Lancaster had been hinting at a well when she talked to me on the road that night. She had mentioned walls and water closing in on someone. Mark Anthony had said Wallace moved the body after Lancaster told him it would be found in the well so I suspected Wallace was the one that had told her it was in a well in the first place.

There had been no signs of a fire there when Doc and I explored the still site. That only left a window of a few nights where the body could have been moved and the fire set before Potts arrested Wallace.

The distant lights got brighter until I rounded a sweeping curve and saw people and cars everywhere along the shoulder. There were squad cars and civilian cars. With a crowd like this at this time of night, I knew that Turner's remains had been found. My heart sank at the thought. There was a five hundred dollar reward for information leading to the location of Turner's body. I knew Mark Anthony would never see a dime of it.

I got out of the car and walked up to the first group of people I saw. There was a woman standing there with a couple of guys who had cards labeled "Press" stuck in their hat bands. The group was standing bathed in the headlights of a green Oldsmobile. The woman dressed for trekking through the woods, wore dungarees and army boots as she took notes in a notebook she had flipped open as she listened to a guy in the center of the circle. I drew closer.

"L.Z. will be out here after while. But it was an honor, I'll tell you a dadgummed honor to get to work alongside the man for a bit. I'm tellin you, that man could track a danged kitty cat down an asphalt highway. I never saw nothin like it. He tracked right to that site back there.

There's been a huge fire back there in the woods alongside, what we call around here, Potato Creek. I was there when L.Z. called out to Sheriff Potts. By then he had made his way down there too, and L. Z. calls out, he says, 'Hey Lamar, you better get over here. I found something.' It wasn't but just a few minutes later, they run us amateurs off. Told us to wait by the road. But Potts and his brother and a few other lawmen are still down there. I tell you, they've done found that boy. I didn't see it with my own eyes but I just know they have."

The woman spoke next, "Well, sir we appreciate you telling us what you saw," she said.

"When will my name be in the papers?" he asked.

"This will probably run tomorrow in the evening paper," she said smiling.

The man grinned from ear to ear and then walked off, probably to find some other reporters to listen to him. I didn't recognize him.

The woman looked around and saw me standing there. I saw her eyes go from my face, to my badge, to my pistol. She smiled at me and started to walk over.

"Officer, I'm Celestine Sibley of the Atlanta Journal and Constitution. Would you mind if I asked you a few questions?"

"Yes I would mind," I said. "I'm not interested in talking to the papers. I'm here to do my job."

She frowned for a second but quickly recovered. Celestine Sibley was known all over the South. She'd been covering the Wallace case ever since Turner was killed. I had seen her articles. She was a talented writer and a veteran reporter. She had likely been rebuffed before tonight by rougher lawmen than me.

"What is your role in the case," she asked, undeterred.

"I've got a better question. How did you find out about these goings on way out here. It's four thirty in the morning. You come all the way down here from Atlanta for this?"

"No, for your information the paper got me, and my photographer over there, rooms in the Warm Springs Hotel for a few days so we could cover this story."

"Okay, so how did you get from the Warm Springs Hotel to a fresh crime scene?"

"I thought I was going to ask you the questions. But if you must know, Agent Hitchcock called me a little over an hour ago, told us to get dressed and meet a state trooper car in Durand. The trooper led us here. Agent Hitchcock is with the Georgia Department..."

"I know Hitchcock quite well, we answer to the same boss."

"Well he has been very helpful in getting me information about this case out to the public. He's quite a bit more cooperative than you, if you don't mind me saying."

"Oh, I'm sure L.Z. is a wealth of information," I said sarcastically. With that I brushed past her, trotted down the embankment and stepped into the woods. I heard her call after me.

"Wait a minute, you never told me about your role in the case. You never even told me your name."

CHAPTER 57
LAST WORD ON THE MATTER

I didn't have to walk far before I picked up a beaten down trail where investigators had been walking back and forth to the still site. I didn't get all the way there before I met Sheriff Potts and Hitchcock coming up the trail towards me.

"Well, you two make quite a team I understand," I said, my eyes never leaving Hitchcock's face. He showed no reaction to me whatsoever.

"Miller," Potts said. "We have Corpus Delicti." There was excitement in his voice. "I think we've got enough here."

Potts held out a match box for a second and then put it carefully in his shirt pocket.

"You have Wilson Turner in that matchbox do you?" I was still mostly watching Hitchcock.

"I think we've got enough," Potts said. "Wallace burned the body. Hitchcock here found bone fragments and ash in a little bend of Potato Creek yonder. It was trapped in a bend there right along the bank."

"Gosh L. Z.," I said. "That's quite a piece of work. How did you ever manage to find it?" I made sure my sarcasm came through loud and clear.

Hitchcock squinted at me. He was likely in a hurry to get out of here. He had interviews he wanted to do. "Well, I just did what I always do Miller. I followed the sign, a track here, a broken twig there. Next thing you know, I found a patch of charred tree trunks, knowed then what Wallace had tried to pull off."

"Well that is quite a story, L. Z.," I said. "And you did all of that in the pitch dark and still had time to call in the press. You don't mess around do you?"

Potts interrupted. "Miller, whatever burr you've got under your saddle will have to wait. We've got to get this evidence to the crime lab up in Atlanta. You're welcome to stay and look for more evidence if you want. We could use the manpower."

There was no use in me pursuing this further. It was done. Hitchcock always did know how to work the papers to his advantage, and he was going to be the hero in all this. Maybe someday they would make a movie about his legendary tracking job. I thought for a second about hitting him. But I knew the bigger I made this, the more danger I put Mark Anthony and his family in. And Mark had been right. I couldn't protect him. Not from this. Too many people had too much at stake now. Too many would be trying to protect their reputations.

Hitchcock "the hero" would call Mark a liar and say that Mark was just trying to get the reward money. Then when the story was out of the papers he would go find Mark Anthony again. This time, maybe Mark wouldn't survive. So I stepped aside and let the two of them pass.

I had no intention of searching the burn site for long, but I did want to have a look around, so I took a step that way. Before I could get far however, I heard L.Z. call out to me.

"Don't worry, Miller," he said. "You just keep busting lady moonshiners with little ol' hundred gallon stills. That's enough for you for now. One day you'll learn how this business gets done."

My jaw clenched and I balled up my fists. He was baiting me. I took a deep breath and didn't turn around. "You're right L. Z. one day maybe I'll learn to play the game the way you do. And when I do, some people around here are going to pay a hefty price."

Hitchcock laughed a dry, sardonic laugh. Then I walked away.

CHAPTER 58
HIGH FINANCE

After looking around the charred site of the burn on Wallace's place that night and finding nothing, my role in the investigation of Wilson Turner's death ended. I didn't go back to that site again for a few days. Instead, I focused on my other cases and aiding Earl Lucas and the federal boys as much as I could in our ongoing conspiracy case against Wallace. The case we were building was solid, but I knew that despite all our hard work, if Wallace was convicted of murder, the special prosecutor wouldn't pursue the conspiracy case to trial. Resources were too precious to bring lesser charges against a man already convicted of a capital offense.

A full week had passed since I had even been over towards Stovall. But I had kept myself good and busy and had a pretty productive week. I had made a decent bust a few days before back over in Upson County, where I confiscated five thousand dollars' worth of moonshine out of a man's barn. I was also on the trail of a shot house somebody was running on the other side of Talbotton, but I still had a ways to go on that case.

On the Friday evening before the Wallace trial was to begin on Monday, I was at home with my family. After we had supper and the dishes were done, Judy sat beside Granny playing with paper dolls and talking a blue streak.

Rose and I were sitting in the living room. I was reading a little booklet by a great mathematician who lived back in the 1600's named Blaise Pascal. It was one of the many classic books that Papa used to read to us when we were children most of which I had held onto. The booklet, called Pensees, was about his faith, not about mathematics. As I read, Rose and Granny were knitting and listening to the radio.

I hesitated a minute, thinking of the eight years I spent in a one room schoolhouse. Thanks to a dedicated young schoolmarm, I was good with figures. I always had been.

That young woman was part genius and part saint. She could teach a group of six year olds to write their letters on one side of the room while teaching me and a bunch of barefoot, overall clad, wild-boys and shy girls to do long division on the other. Though she was only about twenty eight years old herself, everybody tended to their lessons, and there was no foolishness allowed. I didn't feel bad over my limited education because I dare say we learned more in that little schoolhouse in eight years than lots of kids learn in twelve or more.

I went back to reading and after a half hour or so, Rose came into the kitchen and began to serve slices from a pecan pie she made for dessert.

"It does my heart good for us all to be together like this," she said as she practically floated back and forth from the pie on the counter to the table.

She sat a slice of pie in front of each of us and then kissed me on the cheek. These were the kind of moments Rose cherished. I was happy that she was happy but it didn't last.

"I spoke with Mr. Woodall today down at the post office. Did you know Edgar McGee is taking retirement down at the bank? Mr. Woodall is going to be looking for a new teller. Cullen you could do that job as easy as pie." She laughed at her bad pun.

I stiffened, though I tried not to show it. One day during our engagement, I had walked Rose to the store. Once inside we split up while collecting things for Granny's shopping list. Somewhere during that time, Rose ran into Mr. Woodall, who was President of Woodland Bank. I walked up near them on the next aisle. They didn't know I was there, but

I heard them talking. Mr. Woodall had said, "Cullen's a good man, Rose, but he will never give you the life you want. You think about that."

Rose hadn't said anything since that day, but Woodall had been right. I signed up for the Revenue Department because it let me be in the woods where I wanted to be. It gave me a chance to fight the wolves of this world. It gave me a chance to make up for that moment as a small, sickly boy that I'll always regret. But even as I sat here I knew my wife and daughters were just getting by in a drafty old house.

In the winter our bed sheets felt practically wet from the cold. The entire house was only heated by a couple of fireplaces. I was barely making enough from the State of Georgia to pay my bills. I certainly couldn't afford to fix this place up. Lately, I had been spending money we didn't have doctoring on my cattle. I had barely been able to keep up with the pink eye that had eventually affected the whole herd. I had been forced to sell the whole bunch of them at a loss. Financially, things were not good for us.

I was trying to think of something encouraging to say to Rose when a loud knock came at the front door. Everyone in the room except little Judy looked at one another with concern. I locked eyes with Rose and nodded toward the back bedroom. Without another word she went and got Granny who scooped up Judy. I reached into the laundry room and retrieved the nightstick from my gun belt. I heard the tumbler turn on the bedroom door as Rose locked them all in.

I opened the back door, locked it behind me and walked around the back of the house toward the front door. I heard another loud rap at the front as I walked. When I rounded the corner, I breathed a sigh of relief. There was a group of businessmen standing on my front porch. From the way they were dressed they certainly weren't looking for trouble. I could see in an instant that these men didn't have the edge that me and the men I normally dealt with possessed. This was proven when I was able to walk right up behind them without a single one of them noticing.

"Something I can do for you gentlemen?" I called out, making no attempt to hide my nightstick. All four of them jumped noticeably. The porch light was already on, and as they turned, I realized I recognized a couple of them.

"Why Agent Miller," the spokesman smiled. "You gave me a fright," he chuckled. "Agent Miller, I am Brooks Brown, Chairman of the Meriwether County Commissioners." He held out his hand and I shook it. Then handshakes were exchanged all around. Some of the men's hands were softer than Rose's.

"Agent Miller, we know you are involved in this investigation of the whole mess over at Coweta County," he continued. "And we know that you are aware that, unfortunately, our county Sheriff has been implicated in the case."

"I am," I said.

"Well, perhaps you hadn't heard, but tragically, when Sheriff Collier found out about his pending arrest, he simply passed away. It seems he had a massive coronary."

I was taken aback. "No, I hadn't heard that, but Hardy is related to my wife. I knew he had a history of heart problems." I didn't offer condolences, but instead listened for what was next.

"Well…uh Agent Miller, we have been asked to represent the commissioners tonight to inform you…well…to ask you as it were…if you would do us the honor of accepting the job of Sheriff of Meriwether County. You see, we are two years out from our next election and it is our duty to appoint a Sheriff in the meantime. I can assure you that you would have unanimous support of the commissioners in the next election.

We have admired your work with the State for some time, and your work on this Wallace affair, we hear, has been stellar. I feel we could offer you better compensation than what you are currently receiving, and the county is willing to include, to alleviate your expenses, a house that is currently owned by the county. We would cover any moving expenses you would incur of course, but umm, we *would* require that you be a resident of our county."

I stood there silent for a few seconds. I have to admit I was honored and my gut instinct was to take the job on the spot, but that would have been rash. "Gentlemen, I am honored that you would think of me. Please allow me some time to pray about it and discuss it with my family. May I give you an answer in two weeks?"

"The deputies can cover for that long, so two weeks would be fine," Mr. Brown said.

We talked a bit more, then we all shook hands again and the men left. I walked back around to the back door, and as I reached for the knob, the door opened in front of me. Rose was standing there, a look of concern on her face.

"Sheriff, Cullen?" she said inquisitively. "Sheriff of Meriwether County? With all the mess that goes on over there? Do me and the girls not have enough to fear as it is?"

She didn't wait for an answer. Instead she turned, left the door standing open, and went back inside.

I pulled the door closed and sat down on the top step looking out into the yard. My bird dog Joe walked up and shoved his snout under my left hand so I would pet him.

"Glad you're not mad at me yet, boy," I said. "About eight more weeks and we can go bird hunting again, forget all this mess for a few hours." As I petted him and rubbed his floppy ears, I thought about things. I wondered what would kill me first, being shot by some moonshiner or being locked up all day in a stuffy old bank.

CHAPTER 59
TWO COURT DATES

The following week I was back in court for the arraignment of Daniel Godfrey. The case was held in the Upson County Courthouse in the court of Judge McClellan. I had heard that McClellan was a tough judge, but I had never been in his courtroom before. I was sitting in the gallery behind the district attorney. The main charge was simply evading the liquor tax. There was no charge for threatening an officer, which was a bitter disappointment to me. But prior to the Judge coming into the courtroom, the DA had told me that Godfrey never actually threatened me with his pistol and so he didn't think he could make that charge stick. I guess the DA figured Godfrey planned to shoot mice with that hog-leg he packed to my house that night.

After thirty minutes of lawyering, I thought the trial date and bail would be set without me getting an opportunity to testify. But the Judge kept looking over at me.

"The Court would like to hear from Agent Miller," he said staring over half glasses while holding the case file in one hand.

"Your Honor," Godfrey's lawyer began.

"I don't need to hear from you Counsel," Judge McClellan said. Godfrey's lawyer sat down. Then the bailiff stood up to walk over to me.

"Sit down! Don't swear him in you durned fool," the Judge scolded the bailiff. "We are not at trial yet. I just want to talk to the man." The Judge eyed the bailiff all the way back across the room.

"Agent Miller, is it the understanding of this court that you personally witnessed the defendant in the act of making liquor at the still that was on his property?"

"Yes, I did your honor. In fact, I saw him supervising others in the act of making moonshine as well."

"And this was prior to your raid of the still, is that so Agent?"

"Yes, your honor. One night prior to the raid, I saw Mr. Godfrey involved in such activity."

I could feel Daniel Godfrey's eyes on me, glaring at me. Then he decided he had something to say, "Miller, you have messed with…"

"SHUT UP!" McClellan pounded his gavel down. "Order in this court, damn you! The Court has not asked to hear from the defendant at this time!" Now it was the Judge who glared at Godfrey. He stared a hole through him for what seemed a minute or so, but it probably wasn't that long.

"The Court has heard enough. The defendant is ordered to be held in the Thomaston Jail without bond until trial."

The defense attorney leapt to his feet. "Your Honor this is highly irregular! The punishment is not proportional to the charge. Let my client have time to go home prior to trial and get his affairs in order!"

"Your client is a threat both to flee, and to endanger the safety of officers of the law!"

"Objection, your Honor! No such evidence has been introduced to demonstrate that my client is any threat to anyone."

"The Court has ears, counsel. Perhaps you should educate your client on keeping his mouth shut in his future criminal proceedings." The judge banged the gavel down hard. "Court is adjourned."

I turned to face Godfrey as he was handcuffed and led out of the back of the courtroom. I wanted to give him every opportunity to finish what he started to say. But he had nothing more. Instead, he held my gaze only briefly and then dropped his eyes to the floor. I watched him go out the back door where a police cruiser would be waiting for him.

• • •

A few weeks later, on an unseasonably hot September day, the murder trial of John Wallace began. It would prove to be one of the most infamous in the history of the state, rivaling the trial of Leo Frank for the murder of little Mary Phagan at the Atlanta Pencil Factory. That trial happened back in 1915. Before the trial could be completed, Mr. Frank, a Jew, was drug from his cell by a mob in the middle of the night and hung from a tree. He was later believed to be innocent.

Reporters, along with seemingly every other person in the South who could make their way there, clogged the little town of Newnan and the Coweta Courthouse. I was subpoenaed to testify for the prosecution almost two months to the day after Turner was assaulted at Sunset Truck Stop.

The streets were so crowded I had to park nearly five blocks away. When I got to the courthouse, people were picnicking on the lawn. Little boys were running up and down the courthouse steps hawking to the crowd. The boys were working together. One would arrive very early, and get a seat in the gallery of the courtroom. Then one of his buddies would come outside and offer to sell the seat to anyone that wanted in. They appeared to have discovered a pretty lucrative enterprise for themselves.

I reported to the court clerk and was escorted to the witness room. There were too many people crowding the courthouse for the ceiling fans to move much air, and I came out of my suit jacket and draped it over my arm. A bailiff opened the door to the witness room and waved me inside. There were benches, like church pews, facing each other around the perimeter of the room. I walked in just in time to see Steve Smith leaving. They were taking him in to testify now. We greeted one another briefly and I found a seat.

At first, the room was mostly empty. I was there, along with some two-bit crook from up in Carroll County. He claimed that he had been a cell mate of Turner's on the night that Turner had been transferred from Carroll County jail to Greenville, where I had seen Turner's name in the log book. He said Turner didn't want to leave Carroll County and that he had said as much to anyone who would listen that night. This man claimed Turner had told him that if he got moved to Greenville jail, that he was a dead man. The man claimed Turner had kept repeating, "They'll kill me" over and over. I didn't want to hear anymore and told the con to stop talking. Thankfully a bailiff came and got him soon and I had a few minutes in the room to myself.

Lately I had devoted all my efforts to working with the federal boys, and with Earl Lucas in particular, to build a conspiracy case against Wallace for the manufacture of moonshine. A whole army of state and federal agents had descended on the Chesapeake Lumber Company and it had taken us a full three days to dismantle and destroy the still there. The owner of the lumber mill had sworn he had no idea what was going on in the back of his own building. He said that Wallace had come to him and asked to rent the back of the lumber mill. Wallace had paid him well and he had not inquired as to what Wallace was doing with the space.

I was sitting there thinking of all this, when Bobby Rodgers was led into the witness room wearing handcuffs. A state trooper I didn't know was escorting him, and he took the cuffs off after Bobby sat down beside me.

"I'll be right outside," the trooper warned. Then he stepped out and closed the door.

"How ya holdin up, Rodgers?" I asked.

Rodgers knew me not only from our prior business when I made sure he did a short bit of time for moonshining but also from my nosing around Stovall and Durand for four or not of five years busting up stills. I had questioned Rodgers a time or two back when I rang Turner up in '43.

Shortly after Potts found the burn site and Turner's remains, someone started talking. Bobby Rodgers, along with Albert Washington had been implicated in helping Wallace move Turner's body from the well to the

Potato Creek bonfire. Though they both had claimed that Wallace forced them to help, which I am certain was true, they had both been arrested as accessories after the fact. I suspected Rodgers was here to satisfy an obligation he had in a plea bargain.

"It's tough, to tell you the truth Agent Miller. It's mighty tough."

"I hear you're being held up at Heard County for your own protection. Is that right?"

"Yessuh. They tell me if I testify against Mr. Wallace, they gonna let me go. Won't be no charge brought against me. Bein' let go after testifyin' against him might be worse than jail."

"You'll have to watch your back that for sure, Bobby. But you might be surprised. With Wallace in jail and him out of commission, all his so-called buddies may go to ground. Anyway, they've got you as an accessory after the fact, so I would say you had better cooperate with them."

"Thats why I'm here," he said. "I guess Mr. Wallace gonna be sittin there looking right at me won't he?"

"Yeah," I said. "He probably will."

"You gonna testify against him too?" Rodgers asked.

"Yeah," I said. "The lawyers tell me Wallace is going to try to blame me for Turner being dead. He's gonna say that if I had run Turner out of the state like he asked me to, none of this would have happened. So I guess he and I will be looking at one another too."

Bobby Rodgers didn't say anything, but I noticed that he kept worrying over the knuckle of his left thumb. He kept rubbing it with his right thumb.

"Say, Rodgers," I said. "I want you to know, I was there one night back in May at Turner's still. I was hiding behind the mash barrels watching y'all do a run. After Turner spoiled the whole batch I thought he was going to shoot you. But I wasn't going to let him do that. After he sent you boys away, I came out and questioned him. This was before I'd found the big still at the lumber company, so I tried to get him to tell me about it. If Turner would have cooperated with me that night, John Wallace would already be doing time in the state penn, and Wilson Turner would still be alive."

Rodgers didn't say anything to that. What could he say? Instead, he shook his head gently for a long while, and I saw tears well up in his eyes. He continued rubbing his thumb knuckle.

"Did you hurt your hand, Bobby?" I asked.

"No sir," he said. "I just can't get that stain off there." He held his hand up close to my face. "You see that bloodstain? That's Mr. Turner's blood. It got on my hand that night Mr. Wallace made us grab him up out of that well, and I can't get it off. I must have washed my hands fifty times a day in my jail cell and I can't get that stain off."

I looked closely at Bobby's thumb. There was no stain. I found myself heartsick for the damage that had been done somewhere deep in the mind of this man. He went on, the tears filling his eyes more by the minute.

"He had us drag that boy up out of that well with a grappling hook, Mr. Miller. Had us stompin' around that swamp throwing that hook with a rope tied to it into one well after another. He couldn't remember which well he had put Mr. Turner in. We finally found the right one and we snagged him. It's a awful, awful thing to see, Mr. Miller. I wish I hadn't never seen it. He was white as a ghost when we pulled him up out of there, Mr. Miller. White as a ghost. He almost didn't look real. We had to touch him. Mr. Wallace said so, and you know he was packin' that big pearl handled pistol. I didn't want to do it but I was too scared to say no. I had to touch him to wrap him up in a big burlap sheet Mr. Wallace had. That's when the blood got on me. I can't get that off to save my life."

Bobby choked up for a second. I didn't know what to say. I didn't know how to respond to a story so horrible, and I wondered how Bobby would get over it.

"The Lord knows who is to blame for what you went through Bobby. The Lord knows Wallace would have killed you if you'd said no. I'm not saying that makes it alright…but he knows."

Bobby Rodgers looked up at me, his eyes clouded with tears, and I thought I saw him nod slightly.

CHAPTER 60

THE ORACLE

I had been stuck in the witness room for three and a half hours. Bobby had been led away into the courtroom a good two hours prior. Others had trickled in and out. Suddenly the door practically burst open, and there stood all five feet ten inches of Miss Mahayley Lancaster. She stood in the door for an extra few seconds. It was apparent that she wanted to make an entrance. Gone was her flour sack skirt. Instead, she wore a red silk dress decorated with a black dragon. The dragon's head was on her right shoulder and it wrapped all around the dress to end at the hem. She had replaced her brogans with some black high-topped shoes. Instead of her Douglas MacArthur hat, she wore a Shriners fez with a gold tassel hanging down from the little button on top. She'd removed her eye patch and had her glass eye in place.

She sat on the bench directly across from me and clutched a little silk drawstring purse closely to her midsection, as if I was going to try to reach out and snatch it.

"Miss Mahalya, nice to see you again," I said.

"I told you didn't I?" she asked. "I told you they put him on a mule and I told you that they had hid him in a well before that."

"Yes, Miss Mahayley, I guess you kind of did," I said. "Now how on earth did you know all that?"

"I am the Oracle of the Ages. The wise forseeth and hideth himself," she said. I had no idea what she meant by that so I just nodded and looked out the courthouse window.

"I got a read on you Miller. I know some about you."

"Yeah, I know. You kind of gave me a run down that night on the road when we met. But don't you have to read my palm or something first?" I joked. After I said that, there was something different about her. Even the sound of her voice changed. It was as if before she had been playing a part. Suddenly she wasn't playing it anymore.

"Don't be like that, Agent Miller. Don't mock me," she said.

I felt a twinge of regret.

"The read I've got on you is that you're a good man and a good lawman. You try and do right by people."

I sat there a minute. I hadn't expected her to say that.

"Well thank you Miss…"

"You ever hear tell of Diogenes, Mr. Miller?"

"Yes Ma'am. My Papa used to read mythology to us."

She went on as if I hadn't answered.

"He used to walk around in ancient Greece carrying a lantern in the middle of the day. He always said he was searching everywhere for a truly honest man, a man of virtue. They were hard to come by back then Agent Miller, and they are surely hard to come by now. You expect there to be more of them amongst those that wear a badge but there's not. That's why the life you've chosen will be hard on you."

Though they shouldn't have, Miss Mahayley's words hit me the wrong way. I was just about tired of hearing from everybody that I was in the wrong line of work.

"Who is this that darkeneth counsel by words without knowledge," I mumbled under my breath. I didn't think I said it loud enough for her to hear me, but she did.

"That's from the book of Job, chapter thirty five and about verse two, I believe," she said. I was stunned because she was right. That was when I decided to ask the question.

"Miss Mahayley, I want to ask you something. Early that morning when we met along the road, you said something about a dark tunnel and water and all of that. Were you talking about Wilson Turner's body being in that well?"

For the first time since I'd known her she looked uncomfortable. She shifted her weight from one foot to the other. "I don't rightly know. I was telling you what I saw that's all. I felt like you needed to hear it. Weren't you looking for him the night before?"

"Yes, yes I was. Miss Mahayley, shoot straight with me. Weren't you really just telling me what John Wallace told you?"

Her voice changed again. It seemed she went back into character. "You think John Wallace told me about you, too, Miller? Was I wrong in what I said about you that night? The Oracle sees and it is foretold," she said.

Though I didn't want to admit it, Miss Lancaster had seemed to understand something about me and that bothered me a little. So I only shook my head and we didn't talk anymore for a time. Then a bailiff stuck his head in the door. "Agent Miller, you should be called in about five minutes. We are coming out of a short recess and you are supposed to be up next."

I nodded at him and began to gather my jacket and my Stetson. I looked up and Miss Lancaster was staring a hole through me. She squinted and kind of chuckled. I didn't know if she was still sizing me up or if she felt sorry for me for having to face the defense attorney. She leaned forward and lowered her voice.

"Did you know I was a lawyer once, Mr. Miller?"

"No Ma'am, I surely didn't know that."

"I was. I passed the bar. In fact, I was a part of the defense team for none other than Leo Frank. They lynched him but the man was innocent. It was a tragedy, truly a tragedy what they done to that innocent man. Now Mr. Miller, what do lawyers and law men do? We observe people, don't we? We watch them and listen to them with a much keener eye and ear than most. We pick up on little things and we remember them. We observe our surroundings."

The bailiff came in the door again. "Agent Miller, time for you to take the stand," he said.

I nodded at Miss Lancaster and started for the door not really sure of her point, but before I could leave she reached up and grasped my arm.

"Do you have any idea how many folks that come to me for a reading either make liquor or are kin to somebody that does? With all the stills you've busted in this part of Georgia, do you really think that night on the road was the first time I had heard of you Agent Miller?" she said, using her serious voice again. "I observe, I listen, and I draw conclusions. I am quite good at it, so I am right often. You're a man of faith. I believe too. Just maybe I believe a little different from you. God shows things to his people. Sometimes we hear his voice. Sometimes he uses visions, sometimes he uses another of his children to tell you something you need to hear. This time, maybe he used us both."

CHAPTER 61

THE SUNSET

After only four and a half days of trial, and only twenty minutes of jury deliberation, John Wallace was convicted of the first degree murder of Wilson Turner. Soon afterward, he was sentenced to be executed in the electric chair down at the state penitentiary. I had helped to place him there.

During the trial, I testified about how I tried to turn Turner into an informant, my midnight meeting with Wallace, and how I had seen Wallace and Sivell a little over an hour before they caught up to Turner at the Sunset Truck Stop. I also acknowledged that I was assisting in an ongoing conspiracy case against Wallace.

As I had expected, the special agent shut my conspiracy case down just a few days after the murder conviction, but at least the huge still had been destroyed. With Wallace out of the liquor business, and the Godfrey brothers in jail, moonshining in my region had taken quite a setback. That had been my motive for being involved in both cases in the first place.

Days turned into weeks. My farm sold, and though I had made a little money on the deal, I was still heartbroken over it. One of the Meriwether deputies was serving as Sheriff temporarily and I still got regular calls from the county commissioners. Lots of folks in Meriwether thought I would make a fine Sheriff. But I couldn't bring myself to commit to it unless Rose changed her mind. I would need her support in order to do the job properly. So, I just kept telling them I needed more time to think it over. Meanwhile my chief in Atlanta was still trying to talk me into staying with the revenue department.

I awoke with a start early one crisp October morning and it occurred to me that today was the day that they would lead John Wallace to the electric chair. I had been invited to witness the execution but had declined. Instead, I thought about taking a little ride around a couple of counties and tying up some loose ends. For now I only thought about it. First, I wanted to set some things right with some folks.

The evening before, Rose, Judy and I had harvested quite a bit of vegetables from my garden. In my trunk I had two half bushel baskets. The baskets each contained a fine mess of fall turnips, greens, some nice heads of cabbage and enough carrots to eat on for a couple of meals. I also had a pretty good batch of scuppernongs, one of the oldest varieties of cultivated grape, in a little paper sack stuffed into each basket. My vines were still producing though it was getting late in the year.

I had been delivering baskets similar to these, depending on what was in season in my garden, once a week for several weeks now. A couple of times I had taken over a mess of quail I'd shot or a good stringer of fish I'd caught when I'd had some to spare.

My practice was to go early and just leave whatever I had brought on the front porch. It was not my intention for the families to know where the food had come from. That just seemed like the right way to do it.

My first stop was Delbert Mangum's house. I opened my trunk but before I took the basket out I walked around to the passenger side and took out two of my carvings, one for each Mangum child. I had started these on the evening after I'd doused Delbert under his well pump. This set of carvings was based on characters from a book that Judy loved us to read to her called Uncle Remus.

I chose a Brer Bear and a Brer Rabbit and laid them on top of the vegetables.

It was a silly thing I was doing I suppose, a grown man carving and polishing on such things. I had hoped to bring them later in the year and let them be a little token that Santa Claus would leave for the children, but Judy had been playing with them and was growing attached. She had her dolls. These were for children who didn't have a toy to play with.

I laid those two figures right on the top there, on top of the turnip greens. Then I was silly again and moved Brer Rabbit and laid him on top the carrots. I walked the basket over and sat it quietly on the porch. It couldn't have been any later than seven o'clock in the morning, and I didn't want to wake the children. I turned back toward my car.

I looked up to see Delbert Mangum standing beside my car, his hand resting on the front fender. I could tell in an instant that he had no intention of giving me any trouble. Delbert was all cleaned up, more so than I had ever seen him. His overalls were clean, his work boots were tied and his hair was combed back with hair tonic. For the first time since I'd known him, he was clean shaven.

His appearance surprised me to the point that I just stopped and stared at him. I couldn't decide what to say. Then Delbert spoke up.

"I'm sober," he said and I saw his chest swell a bit at that. "I ain't touched a drop in pert nigh six weeks now."

"That's fine Delbert," I said. "That's really fine. I know that hasn't been no easy thing. That's mighty commendable."

I felt awkward. I feared Delbert would resent my bringing the food and the toys, but then he spoke softly again.

"The children…umm…they was uhh…"

Delbert Mangum wiped his hand lightly across my fender and stared deeply into the paint as if he might find the words he wanted written there. He tried again.

"When the children didn't have nothing…and I was drinkin…God, I was drinkin mighty heavy…" Delbert grimaced as he spoke. "You uhh… you done for em better than I…"

Delbert's chin began to quiver, his shoulders began to shake, and I saw tear drops fall onto my fender. Suddenly he looked up and his cloudy grey eyes were brimming over with tears. Finally he choked out two more words. "Thank you," he said.

I stepped up, put my arm around him and gave his shoulders a squeeze. I was nearly choked up myself. I slapped him on the back, got into the Ford, and drove away.

• • •

My next stop was the house of Punkin Woodley's mother. There would be no sneaking up and leaving food here either because both children were on the front porch eating their breakfast. They each had some oatmeal on their plates. I was thankful that instead of being scared of me, when they saw me get out, they both gave me a big smile. I had a toy apiece for these children as well, but this time I didn't put the carvings on the basket. Since my cover was already blown, I wanted the fun of seeing their faces when they got them. "Say, would you two believe I brought two little friends with me? In this pocket I've got Brer Fox and in this pocket I've got Brer Rabbit. They cause too much trouble to ride with me anymore. I thought maybe I would give them to you and see if you could make 'em behave."

When the boy took Brer Rabbit, I saw that he still wore a gauze bandage on each palm, but his hands were healing well. Both children beamed up at me before sitting each toy beside their breakfast plates.

I caught myself smiling as well as I retrieved the basket of vegetables from my car and sat it down on the porch. As I took a few steps toward my car to leave. I heard the shuffling of feet inside the house. Then the screen door slammed against the doorjamb.

I turned to see a very old black woman, she had to have been in her nineties, staring almost through me. Her elderly eyes were nearly as white as her hair and it was apparent that she had cataracts. She pointed an arthritic finger at me.

"Greetings valiant warrior, the Lord is with thee," she said. She spoke with authority. I knew that the verse was from Judges 6 when the Angel of the Lord found Gideon. I didn't know what to say and wasn't sure why she had said it to me. But she wasn't finished.

"You done right by dees babies," she jerked her head toward the children. "The Lord seen what you done. He said in his Word, '"He who is steadfast in righteousness will attain ta life. And he who pursues evil will bring about his own death.' You hear me now. You keep goin like you goin in dis life. Maybe nobody knows what you is but da Lord knows. Now go on and walk steadfast like you been doin."

I stood there sort of transfixed, speechless. I felt as if I had been to a tent revival and heard a powerful preacher. The woman stared intently at me for a long moment then, taking up the basket, she went back in the house, letting the screen door slap closed behind her.

• • •

I had one more parcel to deliver. I'd had a bumper corn crop and ended up with way more seed than I could ever use, so I took a bushel basket up to Manchester Feed and Seed to sell to them. Every little dollar helped a man with a family to feed.

I had decided not to make the other stop, not to worry about the loose ends that were gnawing at me, but as I exited the feed and seed I nearly ran full into my friend, Mark Anthony. Charlie was one step behind him, supporting his elbow as Mark struggled on crutches.

I hadn't seen either of them since the night Turner's remains had been found. It still would not have been safe for them to be seen talking to me.

I was taken aback. Mark Anthony looked much improved since the night he'd been so brutally beaten, but he still had gauze around his head. There was still some puffiness and swelling in his cheekbone and he was putting no weight on his left ankle. He winced a bit with each movement on the crutches.

I didn't think really, I just reacted out of a feeling of warmth and friendship. I admired how courageous Mark had been and I just flat out liked him. I reached to put my hand on his shoulder. I never hugged other men. I didn't do much hugging of anybody outside of Rose and

Judy, but I think I was going to put my arm around Mark and give him a gentle hug. Charlie must have sensed it and quickly stepped between us.

Charlie's face said so much. It was as if I could see in his eyes that he appreciated the sentiment, but he wasn't going to allow me to touch Mark. He especially wasn't going to have that happen out here on one of the main streets in Manchester.

The whole interaction probably only took twenty seconds. Not a word was spoken. I don't think anyone walking by on the sidewalk even paid a bit of attention to the three of us. Mark had stopped and was looking me straight in the eye. He was clearly cautious, but I thought I saw regret and maybe a bit of sadness in his expression. I'd gotten the message clearly.

I stepped back, from them touched the brim of my Stetson in a small salute and crossed the street to my car. I accepted as I drove away that I might never get to talk with Mark Anthony again.

• • •

My encounter with Mark and Charlie motivated me to change my mind once more. I was going to look into those loose ends after all. I drove over to Steve Smith's Sunset Truck Stop, and saw what I was hoping to see. Lamar Potts' patrol car and L.Z. Hitchcock's white Dodge sedan were both parked outside. I thought about not doing it. I thought about letting it go. But then, after initially driving past, I jerked the Ford around in a U turn and pulled into the parking lot.

I walked in but didn't remove my Stetson. I didn't plan to stay long. As I suspected, Potts and Hitchcock were eating breakfast together at a table for two by the window.

"Agent Miller," Smith called out from behind the counter. "Nice to see you in here. Say, anything you want is on the house," he said smiling.

"Thank you Steve," I said as I walked over and pulled a chair from another table over to sit alongside Hitchcock. "I surely wouldn't say no to a cup of black coffee."

"Miller," Potts nodded.

Hitchcock stopped eating and stared a minute before speaking up.

"I hear they want to make you Sheriff of Meriwether," Hitchcock said. "Guess you could serve till the first election. Once anybody worth a damn runs against you I'd say you'll be lookin' for work."

Steve Smith brought my coffee over. I took a sip, then another. I leaned my forearms on the table and turned on Hitchcock. "You in here buying everybody pancakes L. Z.? Guess you can buy a lot of breakfasts with that five hundred dollars reward money." He didn't like it and I was glad. I held his stare until he finally looked down at his plate and forked a slice of ham. In all honesty I didn't even know what had happened to the reward money. I was just pushing buttons to see what would happen.

I turned back to Potts. "Lamar, my Chief up at the Capitol got word that my name came up in a letter Wallace wrote to the Governor a while back trying to get a pardon. Seems he feels like the whole thing with Turner was my fault. If only I had run Turner off at his say so, Wallace wouldn't of had to go to the trouble of killing him." I drank some more coffee.

"I've had occasion to visit with John a time or two since the conviction," Potts said. "I wouldn't let it worry you, Miller. John's mind works a little different on these matters."

"Oh it's not worrying me, Lamar. I'm just making conversation," I said as I downed the rest of my coffee.

"Well, you fellas have a nice day," I said. "I've got a little work to get done yet this morning." I stood up and returned the chair to the other table. I acted as if I was going to walk toward the door, then stopped and came back.

"Say fellas, I was kind of wonderin'. When I was building that conspiracy case on Wallace, I was able to find out that he was shipping white liquor all the way to Chicago, Illinois. Can y'all believe that?" I didn't give either of them a chance to answer.

"And I am talking about a whole lot of liquor, thousands of gallons in fact. I got bored the other day and I got my atlas out and drew me a line from Stovall all the way up to Chicago. And would you believe that route would take a man straight through the heart of Coweta County?"

I placed my palms on the table and leaned down in between the two of them. "Now L. Z., that's your territory, and Lamar, that route would take them right by your danged office window. And I just can't help but wonder how they hauled all that moonshine past you two crack lawmen and neither one of you ever noticed it?"

Potts stood up rapidly, shoving his chair into the one behind him with a crash. I stood full-up as he came around the corner of the table to meet me. He realized that the entire diner had fallen silent and all eyes were on us. He lowered his voice to just above a whisper.

"What are you trying to say Miller?" Potts said. "Do you think I am going to let you come into my county and hurl accusations against me? Son, have you ever heard of trains? You were in on the bust back in the old days when Wallace and his Uncle were moving liquor on train cars!"

Potts was right about that and of course I did remember. But I had also busted Dantonio hauling Wallace liquor in a Chrysler Imperial just a few months ago. He hadn't been driving a train and he had been here enough times to know he could find a card game at Godfrey's store. What's more, somebody at a high level in the state capitol had shut down my case against that store there. I ignored Potts' answer and continued pressing him.

"Why didn't you send more men to look for the well after I told you what I found in those woods that day, Lamar?" Then only a few days after that, how is it that Hitchcock here ended up in that sector all alone and finding where the fire had burned all by himself? I'm not making any accusations Lamar, I'm just thinking out loud, that's all."

Hitchcock stood up now too. His red gingham napkin was still stuffed down into his collar.

"I got no cause to accuse you of anything Lamar, and I don't mean to do that," I said. "It's just stuck in my craw that you seem to have befriended this fella," I nodded toward L.Z. "If you're as good a lawman as everyone says you are, seems you'd be a better judge of character."

Hitchcock glared at me.

"Miller, I can pick my friends and officers I like to work with just fine. Now, maybe you better get back across that county line out there before you regret it," Potts said.

I stood there for a moment longer. Then, turning back to Hitchcock I said, "L.Z. maybe I'll see you at a raid sometime before I change jobs, at least I hope to." Then I tipped my hat. I walked to the door and pulled it open. Then, stopped once more. "Tell ya what L. Z., if I accept the Sheriff's job come on by the swearing in ceremony," I said. "I would love to have you over in Meriwether County the day I get my badge."

With that I walked out the door, got into my car, and drove back across the county line.

CHAPTER 62
I FIND MY PLACE

At precisely the time that John Wallace was being led from his cell to the electric chair, I was sitting on a stump at the edge of Potato Creek, just downstream from the charred trees where Wallace reportedly incinerated the body of Wilson Turner. The spot was very near the bend where L. Z. Hitchcock testified that he found two small pieces of bone and some ash at the water's edge. The jury believed the bones were all that remained of that young man. A forensics expert had testified that they were human remains. He never stated they were Turner's. I don't know if he was ever asked that specific question under oath.

One winter I remember Papa shot a small doe and skinned it out. He filleted the meat off the bone and threw the bones onto a bonfire he had started for a cleared field. I went back and looked in the ashes later because I was curious. The large leg bones of the deer were still there. They were charred and brittle but they were mostly intact and lying atop the ash heap. So how was it that deer bones, much smaller than a man's, survived that huge fire but all that was left of Turner fit into a matchbox? I had questions about this case that I would likely never know the answers to.

As I sat there, turning my Stetson around and around in my hand, I had no doubt that John Wallace had murdered Wilson Turner. I had seen Wallace's eyes that night in my car when he threatened to "get rid of" Wilson. I had heard the dead calm in his voice when he told me that he had gone down to his pond with his pistol in his pocket to kill Turner, and that only the presence of Turner's little boy had stopped him.

Not only that, but I also knew something that few, if any on the jury did. Wilson Turner wasn't the first man Wallace had killed. Mark Anthony had confirmed that for me.

Many in the community still saw Wallace as a philanthropist and a charitable man. In some ways that was true. He had helped lots of people through the years. He had given to his church, even donating pews. The problem was, I never took all of that seriously. In my estimation, his philanthropy was all a cover, a means to his own ends. In the same way the Godfrey's weren't "just getting by." They would get out of jail and still be rich men off savings from all the liquor they had sold. I wondered how many alcoholics they had helped create.

I thought back over all that had occurred since the spring and about my career in general. Sure, I had taken a lot of moonshine out of circulation in the last ten years. I had quite a string of convictions. But was anything really changing?

The Godfrey brothers were put away and wouldn't be a threat for a long time. Unfortunately, others in Upson County had stepped in to take their place. There were still shot houses and prostitution houses sprouting up on highway 19 in that same county. Had I done any good at all? Was my son, Buddy, right? Was I spitting into the wind and risking my neck for no reason?

I had no idea where Roxy Coleman was. The "For Sale" sign at her grandmother's house was gone. Someone would be moving in soon. I was sad for Roxanne. Was the world a better place because Miss Coleman had been forced out west somewhere and had to sell her family home? Meanwhile, I was convinced that someone at a very high level had interest in the poker parlor and store that Daniel Godfrey had owned. None of that had been looked into as of yet. I was also certain that that same someone had stopped further inquiries into the store. But all that was another investigation for another time, and maybe for another lawman.

I thought about guys like Hitchcock, who were supposed to wear the white hats. I thought once more about Wilson Turner. He certainly was far from innocent. He was a hot-head to be sure. He was foolhardy and a petty criminal to boot. Yet the macabre and brutal end of his life had been a horrible injustice and the death of John Wallace in a few more moments would not bring him back.

Meanwhile newspapers all over the nation and even around the world were fascinated with the whole wretched mess Wallace had created. Mahayley Lancaster was becoming a celebrity, having made the cover of Detective Magazine along with magazines around the globe. The fascination with Wallace and the desire to delve deep into his personality was baffling. There was no mystery to me.

Wallace, Turner, and even Hitchcock all had something in common. They all had allowed their sin nature to rule them. Mr. Pascal, the mathematician whose book I had just finished had stated it very well. This genius had figured it out nearly three hundred years ago. The Bible had informed Mr. Pascal of the truth of it, and he had put it into a few powerful words. I had memorized a bit of what he wrote:

What a chimera then is man! What a novelty! What a monster, what a chaos, what a contradiction, what a prodigy! Judge of all things, feeble earthworm, repository of truth, a sink of uncertainty and error, the glory and shame of the universe.

Like the Bible, Mr. Pascal was saying that each of us is capable of great love and kindness, yet at the same time, we are capable of heinous evil. In the end, we are all, each one of us on both sides of the law, just men. Some would admit to their baser instincts and run to God for help in conquering them. Others would deny that those instincts existed, and in one form or another, succumb to them. It had forever been so.

What I had to do was to never let myself forget that, but by the grace of God, my own life could have taken that turn. The moment I began to believe that there was an inherent goodness in me, that there was merit in me that made me one of the "good guys," I would be in trouble. The truth was, I had been ready to shoot Daniel Godfrey outside my house and murder Punkin Woodley, yet his own grandmother had called me righteous. All that had happened to me during the summer of 1946 made me see clearly that any goodness in me was only from God and shared with me by His grace.

I had seen too much over the years, skirted too closely to the valley of the shadow of death, to assume that I was good. It was God who spoke to me that day at White Sulfur Springs and stopped me from pulling that trigger. I'd come to face the reality that, left to my own, I would have gone through with it.

As I sat there, thinking about Wallace and what he was about to go through, I found no joy or satisfaction in it. His punishment may have been just, but in this case and others like it, justice was unsatisfying,

In my mind, I went back over warnings and cautions from Roxanne Coleman, Mayhayley Lancaster, Mark Anthony and of course Rose. Maybe they were right and I was just naïve to think I could change anything. Maybe in this sinful old world, I *was* kidding myself. I would never defeat all the wolves and I would never protect all the lambs. Suddenly I spoke aloud to the Lord. "Why don't I just get out of this? Why don't I go talk to Mr. Woodall and get a job in the bank."

I sat there for a long while, twirling my hat in my hands, my forearms resting on my knees. Suddenly, bark began to rain down on me from a tree just above my head. I looked up and a little raccoon, so small that he had to have just been born that spring, was scurrying down the trunk. He seemed not to mind that I had been sitting there praying out loud. It occurred to me that he was the same size as the one me and the little girl had played with all those years ago. All that was missing was the string around his neck.

This little fella seemed thoroughly mesmerized by something in the creek. He kept stopping on his way down the tree trunk and staring into the water. I looked to see what had his attention. That's when I saw the golden clumps. There, floating in the creek, drifting in the slow current, were fifteen or maybe twenty gold colored clumps. I stood up and walked over to the water's edge. That movement was more than the little coon could stand and he hurried back up the tree, dove into a hollow place high in the trunk, then turned and peeked out at me.

I stood with my boot just at the edge of the water, grasped a nearby sapling, and leaned out. I let a couple of the clumps drift into my cupped palm. I was pretty sure what they were but tasting them confirmed it. They were clumps of mash and they tasted scorched.

Late fall is not moonshine season for most because it has to be above fifty degrees for mash to work. The only way to ferment mash in the winter was to keep it warm around the clock. Someone, somewhere up Potato Creek had been attempting to do just that. Likely they had let their fire get too hot and the mash had boiled over and into the creek.

I brushed my hands on my pant legs, stepped back up on the bank, and pushed my Stetson down firmly on my head, pulling the brim down low on my brow. I drew my Smith and checked the cylinder. Then I looked up the creek. Somewhere out there, somebody was getting ready to make a run of moonshine. When they did, somebody else was going to buy it. Somewhere a child's daddy was going to get drunk and not come home, or he was going to spend the grocery money on liquor. I would think about being a banker some other time. For now, I holstered my pistol and moved silently up the creek bank in search of the still. It couldn't be any other way. After all, I was the just the right man to shut it down.

THE END

Made in the USA
Columbia, SC
30 March 2025